Readers love
Knight of Ocean Avenue
by TARA LAIN

"This book turned out to be so much more than I expected and I really connected with the storyline and the characters. I read this from start to finish without putting it down…"
—Prism Book Alliance

"I loved this book. Not only was it well written with amazing characters, it was also extremely interesting and totally inspiring."

—The Blogger Girls

Knight
of Ocean
Avenue
TARA LAIN

"This is such a wonderfully endearing story with characters I couldn't help but love."
—Rainbow Book Reviews

"*Knight of Ocean Avenue* by Tara Lain was simply a joy to read. This series started so good I can't wait for the next one…"
—Scattered Thoughts and Rogue Words

By TARA LAIN

LOVE IN LAGUNA
Knight of Ocean Avenue
Knave of Broken Hearts

LONG PASS CHRONICLES
Outing the Quarterback
Canning the Center

TALES OF THE HARKER PACK
The Pack or the Panther
Wolf in Gucci Loafers
Winter's Wolf
The Pack or the Panther & Wolf in Gucci Loafers (Series Anthology)

Published by DREAMSPINNER PRESS
http://www.dreamspinnerpress.com

Knave
of Broken
Hearts

TARA LAIN

Published by
DREAMSPINNER PRESS

5032 Capital Circle SW, Suite 2, PMB# 279, Tallahassee, FL 32305-7886 USA
http://www.dreamspinnerpress.com/

Knave of Broken Hearts

Cover Art

ISBN: 978-1-63216-961-7
Digital ISBN: 978-1-63216-962-4
Library of Congress Control Number: 2015906566
First Edition August 2015

Printed in the United States of America
(∞)
This paper meets the requirements of

To Jean, who unflaggingly encourages me
and shows how great a sister-in-law can be.

CHAPTER ONE

THE SHRIEK of the alarm shocked Jim's heart into his throat. He slammed his hand onto the computer keyboard and dragged the edge of his sock across his rock-hard dick. Glancing back at the bed, he watched Peggy pull the covers over her ears. At least she was facing the wall. Shit, he wanted to come so bad. He looked longingly at the drawing of those doe eyes and the beautiful full lips wrapped around the guy's erect cock on his computer screen.

"Jimmy, who turned that alarm on?"

"Sorry." He clicked off the video, closed his laptop, and jumped toward the shrieking alarm. *Oh, big mistake.* He flopped back into the chair and caught his head in his hand to try and stop the spinning. That got rid of his hard-on fast.

"You nuts or what?" Her voice sounded muffled.

"Gotta go to work." At his smack on the snooze button, the alarm finally gave up, and he sighed in relief.

"No way." Voice clear now. "I owe you a blow job, and I'm gonna deliver."

"Can't, baby." *Not the right lips.*

"But, Jimmy, that thing of yours wouldn't even wiggle for me last night."

He leaned over and patted her bare shoulder, then sat up very slowly. "I was drinking Jack, right?"

"Yeah."

"Jack and dick don't mix for me."

"Man, you're not kidding. You wouldn't twitch."

Rub it in. "It's not you, it's me." Never had there been a truer statement.

The alarm started round two, and he staggered to where the damned clock stood bravely. He slammed a hand down on the button. "Come on, get up. We both have to go to work."

She rolled over. "Hell, I can cancel my appointments. Those women don't need another haircut."

"Okay, stay there, but I have to go."

"What you doing on the computer?"

"Just had to check something for work." He staggered bare-assed toward the bathroom.

She finally sat up. "You don't usually give a shit about work."

"Yeah, well, this is Billy's last day as a construction supervisor before the wedding tomorrow. After that he's only going to do construction for his own company. I want him to hire me for jobs."

"You know he will."

He stepped into the bathroom and closed the door. *No, I don't know that.* Billy had mentioned a tenant improvement job coming up for Ballew Construction, but he hadn't hired Jim yet. Couldn't blame him. Billy needed the best guys on his jobs, and everybody knew Jim Carney might know his way around an electrical circuit, but he was bullshit in the reliability department. Usually he didn't care, but Billy mattered.

Fifteen minutes later he'd cleaned up enough to get dirty again and stood in his kitchenette. Peggy came walking out of his bathroom looking pretty—and pretty hungover. He handed her a cup of lukewarm, day-old coffee. She took it and looked inside. "How come there are three rings in this cup?"

"Three days, three rings."

She handed it back. "Shit, Jimmy, a girl could catch Ebola in this place."

He set the cup in the sink and herded her toward the door. Suddenly she stopped and looked up into his eyes. "Who's Hero?"

"What?" *What the fuck?*

"When I was sucking you last night, you called me Hero."

He tried to wipe the frown off his face. "Don't know. I guess I thought you were being heroic or something. Superhero of blow jobs, you know?"

"I figured it was the girl you really wanted to have sucking you instead of me. Maybe she could have got you off." She crossed her arms.

"Don't know a girl named Hero."

"Really?"

2

"Yeah." At least that was true.

"You ought to watch what you say, baby."

"Yeah."

"You could give a girl a complex." She kissed his cheek. "Want me to try again tonight?"

"No. I've got some stuff to do for the wedding, but I'll pick you up tomorrow at four, okay?"

She danced a couple of steps. "You and me sashaying at a fag wedding. Jesus, that'll be different."

He frowned. "It's not a fag wedding. Billy's my friend."

"Never said he wasn't. Some of my best friends are fags." She leaned over and gave him a quick kiss. "See you tomorrow."

AFTER SPENDING eight hours finishing their project, Jim sat at the Bay Bar with his final paycheck in his pocket and watched Billy walk out the door with a spring in his step. Billy's last day working for someone else. The day before his wedding. *Jesus, what would that be like, to have that kind of new life ahead of you?*

He turned back to Charlie and Raoul. Charlie sipped a beer. "So when do we start the TI project for Billy?"

Raoul smiled. "Monday sharp, man. That'll be great, working for Billy direct. No more big boss queering the works." He snorted. "I guess Billy does his own queering, but it'll be great working for him." He looked at Jim. "You doing electrical or carpentry?"

Jesus, don't look sad. "Not working this one, I guess. Billy hasn't said anything."

Charlie put a hand on his arm. "You know he will. Billy'd never leave you out."

Why did everybody say that? "Don't know. The job starts Monday."

"Don't worry." Charlie raised his glass of beer in the air. "To Billy."

Jim hoisted his Jack. "To Billy. He's so happy, maybe there's a chance for the rest of us." He laughed.

Charlie looked at him sideways. "You not happy, Jim?"

Raoul blew a razzberry. "Hound dog Jim Carney. What you got to not be happy about?"

He waved a hand. "Nah, man. I'm fine. Just love that Billy's on cloud nine, you know?"

Raoul took a sip of beer. "Yeah, because he's gonna marry a guy, man. I love Billy and I even love Shaz, but, man, that still freaks me out. The day he said 'I'm gay' to the whole crew, I about fell off the fucking ladder."

Charlie nodded. "It's shit strange to think we didn't even know our friend at all after three years." He peeled his label from the bottle. "Does that make you feel weird?"

Jim nodded. "I guess."

"Me too. Jesus, that's, like, fundamental, you know? And I mean, Billy's really a guy. You know, like a dude."

"The dudest." He tried to smile. "He said he didn't know he was gay—until he met Shaz."

"Just goes to show."

"What?"

"I guess all gay guys aren't girlie. I mean, like, anybody could be one."

Raoul shook his head wildly. "No way, man."

"Way. Billy fooled you. You never knew."

"Yeah, but mostly I know. Mostly."

Breathe. Jim slugged back the rest of the Jack.

"Jim." Charlie glanced at him.

"Yeah."

"Ever wonder what else we don't know about each other?"

Jim raised his finger at the waiter. *One more.*

Two hours of booze later, Jim navigated the road slowly. Yeah, he shouldn't be driving, but if he could make it one more block, he was home free. His phone rang, and he pawed the seat beside him until he hit the answer button. "Yeah."

"Hey, Jim, it's Billy. Sorry to bother you."

He smiled. "Thash okay. We were just talking about you."

"You all right?"

He shook his head. *Focus, dammit.* "Yeah. No problem. Just headed home."

"Something exciting happened."

"You mean besides getting married?"

Billy laughed. "Yeah. Well, not married yet, but that's why I called. Shaz just surprised me with tickets to Tahiti for our honeymoon."

Jim shook his head. "Man, Billy, thash's—uh, that's great. Billy Ballew in the South Pacific."

"Yeah. Hard to imagine. But that's the thing. You know how I just got this tenant improvement job on that building in Irvine?"

Jim nodded, then realized Billy couldn't see it. "Yeah, you're starting next week, right?" He wanted to scream *And you haven't hired me.*

"Yes, two days after the wedding, but—"

His fuzzy brain finally put it together. "But that's when you'll be schwimming with the southern fishes."

"Yes, I'd like to be, but only if you'll be my construction supervisor and take over the job while I'm gone."

What? "Me?" His heart leaped into his throat, and the car swerved. *Get a grip.*

"Yeah, you're the only one with knowledge of all the trades, and the crew already knows you. There's nobody else I can trust with this."

"You trust *me*?"

"Yes. I trust you. This is our first big job as a company, and I need somebody good." He said it firmly. Probably trying to convince himself too. "If you won't do it, I'll tell Shaz we have to postpone the trip until the job's over."

"You can't do that, man."

"Then say you'll do it."

Red dots swam in front of his eyes with every heartbeat. *Billy trusts me.*

"I have to put you on the company insurance, so you'll have to get a physical."

Insurance? Doctors? "I don't know, man."

"Come on, Jim. You're healthy as a horse."

"Don't like doctors."

"Okay, no worries. See you at the wedding."

"Wait. What are you gonna do?"

"Not a problem to postpone. Probably better anyway. The building owner is kind of erratic. She may freak if I say I'm going away."

No, no. Wait. Billy just gave him a chance. A chance at—what? Something better. "I can do it. I mean, I think I can."

"I don't want to make you do shit you don't want to do, Jim."

"No. I can do it." He sucked in air.

"I know you can."

"Jesus, Billy, it's your company. Your baby. You really trusht me to do this?"

"I do, Jim."

The question was, did he trust himself?

Fifteen minutes later Jim staggered into his apartment, shoved his car magazines off the ratty green couch, and collapsed onto it. Billy trusted him. He gave him a job. No, *the* job. The one he'd wanted for years. *Jesus.* He couldn't fuck it up.

Billy had always been his friend. Three months before, he'd become his idol. How many balls did it take to come out to a bunch of guys on a construction crew? More balls than Jim had, that was for damned sure.

Jim rolled on his side and tucked his legs up to try to get the sour gurgle out of his stomach. Billy. Big, handsome, sloppy. People would believe Jim was gay before they thought that about Billy. And Billy smoked dick. Tough to believe.

Did he like to ass fuck?

God, no, don't think about that. He pressed his hands against his temples. Billy probably had a schlong to match his size. How could any guy take that in the ass? *I'll bet a lot of guys like extra large. Their assholes stretch to take them in.*

Stop it, dammit.

He sat up fast and nearly puked. *Think about something else.* Grabbing the remote control, he flipped on the football game and stared at it. How many of them were gay?

He stabbed at the remote. *Find something else.*

Like some cosmic horror show, the channel switched to a program he must have DVRed sometime of a Japanese pop star singing to a group of screaming teenyboppers. Didn't remember recording it. *Look at that face.* The long black hair, doe eyes, full lips. *That'd be my style, if I were gay.*

He reached down and adjusted his semihard dick. Peggy had swallowed his cock halfway to Japan last night, but he couldn't come. *What's wrong with me?* He stared at the beautiful man singing on the screen, and his heart beat in his ears. He rolled on his side and grabbed his balls through his jeans. *Don't want Peggy.* His fist squeezed on its own.

In one move he swung his feet to the floor and ran toward the bedroom. Still bending when he got to the bed, he knelt on the ratty carpet, reached under, and pulled out the metal storage box he'd kept there since he moved in. He twisted the combination on the lock, missed the numbers twice, and finally managed to open the lid. He grabbed the magazine on top and flipped to the carefully marked page. Kneeling up, he scooted down his jeans and briefs together and started cranking his dick before his eyes even settled on the illustrations. He didn't need them. Hell, he knew every frame and cell by heart. The big blond guy sucking the juice out of the beautiful Asian with his floppy black hair, wide almond eyes, and gorgeous pouty lips. The look on the hero's face said *rapture.*

Music pounded from the TV in the living room, and Jim flipped the page and watched that perfect guy take a big cock up the ass. Better than any online yaoi site. Better than porn.

He pumped himself harder.

These drawings taught him everything he knew. Everything he wanted. How many times had he come down a hot throat while he stared at these pictures? Spunk bubbled in his balls as he gazed at that spot where the big guy's cock disappeared into that perfect hole.

Two more jerks. His heart beat so hard it hurt. Cum shot from his dick, and tears spilled from his eyes.

He collapsed on the floor and stared at the dust bunnies. Slowly his breath and heartbeat calmed down. *I have to quit this.* He should walk this damned box down and throw it in the trash. He'd just never found anything to take its place. Anyone. When he met the right girl, he'd toss the box. That was a promise. He was hound dog Jim Carney, and he had hot-and-cold running women.

He sat up slowly.

Funny how Peggy didn't think about the fact that Hiro could also be a boy's name.

"YOU OKAY, Jim?"

Jim pried his eyes from the dance floor and looked up at Peggy. "Yeah, sure. Sorry."

"You should drink some Jack. You'd feel better."

He shook his head.

She peered in his glass and sniffed. "You're seriously drinking ginger ale?"

"Settles the stomach."

She laughed. "Okay, baby. Whatever you say."

"I tossed out all my liquor."

She crossed her arms. "You must have been drunk when you did it."

"There is that." He grinned.

"You want to dance?" She smiled and did a little twirl, her pert butt waggling.

Jim glanced at the dancers again and swallowed. "Uh, not right now, okay? I'm not much on the dance floor."

She crossed her arms again, and her cleavage popped. "You said your mom made you go to dance classes."

"She did, and I skipped out and went to a friend's garage to work on cars. Never learned." He shrugged. "Sorry."

She stuck out her lip. "You're not much fun tonight."

"Later, okay?" When the damned band wasn't playing something that ought to be served with syrup and most of the couples on the dance floor weren't made up of two fucking dudes.

He turned away and sipped his ginger ale.

She sighed. "Okay. I'm going to the ladies' room."

He nodded. She walked away, her curvy figure held tight with pissed-offness. Jim's eyes slid back to the dance floor. Two guys, both with full beards and tats on their necks above their black bow ties, pressed together like they'd been wrapped with chains. Jim could actually see their erections rubbing in the openings of their tux jackets. He swallowed hard.

What the hell did you think was going to happen at a gay wedding reception, asshole? Did you think the guys were going to slosh back beers and talk about the Dodgers? Jesus. He slammed his glass on the table harder than he intended.

Of course, he and Billy had sloshed a lot of beers and talked baseball plenty of times, but right now Billy looked right at home at the center of the mass of dancers. All six feet five inches of the big guy radiated joy as he held the slim body of his brand-new husband against his chest and danced like Arthur Murray could take lessons from them.

What does it feel like, dancing with a guy? A shiver ran up Jim's back. He chugged another mouthful of gingery not-so-goodness.

Raoul flopped his compact body into the chair next to him. "Hey, man, you okay?"

"Yeah. Why does everybody keep asking me that?"

"I don't know, man. You look weird or something." Raoul grinned. "I mean, aside from seeing you in a monkey suit."

"I'm fine." Jim stared at his hands.

"It bothering you, all these guys, you know, dancing and shit?"

"No, hell. I think it's great about Billy and Shaz."

Raoul lowered his voice. "Yeah, but that's different than all their pals. There's a lot of gay in this room, my friend."

Jim glanced around. A spectacular-looking group, which made sense since Shaz was this big stylist and the room teemed with movie stars and rich people.

He glanced at Raoul. "It's okay with me. It's only one night."

The music changed to an up-tempo piece. A couple of people shouted and someone started clapping. A circle formed on the dance floor. Jim grinned. Billy and Shaz had to be in the center of the circle. He'd heard the two could clear a dance floor or try out for a reality show, they were so good. He jerked his head at Raoul. "Let's go watch."

He got up from the table and edged toward the ring of clapping, whistling spectators. Slipping sideways, he squeezed between people and maneuvered to the front of the pack, then turned toward the dance floor. *Holy blessed shit.*

Chapter Two

Jim's eyes bugged. He stepped back and bumped the person behind him hard.

"Watch it, buddy." The man rubbed his arm.

"Sorry. Stumbled."

His eyes crawled back to the dancers like he'd been hypnotized. Two men danced all right, but they weren't Shaz and Billy. Those two stood on the edge of the circle clapping with everyone else because the sight warranted a lot of applause. The shorter guy of the pair might be a professional dancer. He'd drop into splits and pull himself up by the strength in his thighs. He was flashy and spectacular, but who the hell was looking at him? Jim wasn't.

He felt woozy, like someone slipped him something in his ginger ale. It had to be a joke. Like he'd created a being from his visions and dreams.

The dancer stood tall and lean but with really broad shoulders, forming that V they talked about as perfect for men. His black tux fit like he'd been born in it—exactly tailored to his body and probably made of fucking silk. Or maybe the way he moved just made it look like silk.

Chinese? Japanese? The guy's inky black hair hugged his scalp on the sides with a long shock that fell over his forehead and flopped as he moved. His eyes were wide and almond-shaped above a slightly aquiline nose and a mouth that would have made Angelina jealous. How did a guy get lips like that? They only existed in comic books.

Jim breathed deep. Had to make his heart stop hammering or he'd pass out. Who was this guy? The dude moved like he was having sex in a vertical position, and Jim knew just what that sex looked like because he'd seen it a thousand times. He could picture the guy's ass, bare and hard, being penetrated by a long cock. *Oh shit.* Jim sucked in breaths and his heart beat double fast.

10

"Hey, baby."

Jim jumped and crossed his hands in front of his crotch.

Peggy's arm slid around his waist. She laughed. "Sorry. Didn't mean to scare you." She gave him a kiss on the cheek, then followed his line of sight to the dance floor. "Jesus, who's that?"

"Don't know." His mouth felt dry.

"He looks like a manga illustration come to life, but taller."

He swallowed hard.

The music changed again to something slow. She grabbed his hand. "Come on, let's dance."

He stumbled again but followed and let her drag him into her arms. He started his boring dance—rock to the right, step, rock to the left, step.

She giggled against his neck as she snuggled close. "Oooh, is that a banana in your pocket, you horny devil?"

He forced a smile. "No, my hammer."

"Sounds good to me."

A solid bump against his back made him turn to find Billy and Shaz grinning at him. Billy punched his shoulder. "Finally got you on the dance floor."

"Yep, I'm a regular Gene Kelly."

The gorgeous Asian guy danced by in the arms of an older dude with silver hair and probably a lot of silver in his bank account, from the looks of him. Jim forced his eyes not to follow, but the guy's beautiful ass still moved through his field of vision. Peggy bobbed her head meaningfully. "Who's your dance competition?"

Shaz glanced. "Oh, that's Ken, a guest of one of my clients. He's in medicine or something. Gorgeous, isn't he?"

"He looks like a manga doll."

Shaz grinned. "Yaoi."

Jim sucked in breath and got a look from Shaz. "You're familiar with yaoi?"

"Everyone knows what yaoi is."

"Not in my experience."

Jim shrugged. "I read about it somewhere."

Billy put a hand on Jim's shoulder. "We should touch base before Shaz and I go running out of here."

Shaz took Peggy's arm. "Come on. Let's leave these two to talk. Want some champagne?"

"Always."

Billy stared after Shaz and Peggy. "She seems like a nice girl."

"Yeah."

"I haven't seen her before. You been dating long?"

"A couple of months."

"Serious?" He looked at Jim sideways.

Jim shrugged. "You know me. Not such a serious guy."

"You're plenty serious. Just not about women."

Jim's head snapped up.

Billy raised a hand. "Sorry. That came out wrong. I mean, you have as much trouble settling down as I used to."

Jim stared at his shoes. Billy had been engaged to three women before he met and married—the right guy. "I just like playing the field."

"Yeah, I was always crap at that." Billy curved his sweet smile. "Let's go out in the hall so we don't bother the party animals."

Jim followed Billy through one of the side entrances of the ballroom into a relatively quiet hall and grabbed a seat on a bench beside Billy. Jim smiled. "I haven't really gotten to say congratulations. You two are gonna be good together for life. It's inspiring."

"Thanks, man." He ducked his head. "I can't tell you how much your support means to me."

"Being your supervisor is a real opportunity for me."

Billy glanced sideways at him. "I actually meant the way you took the fact that I'm gay."

Jim smiled at his friend. "I liked you before I knew. Why would I feel different after?"

"A lot of people do—feel different, I mean. You influenced all the other guys on the crew." He smiled. "Only a few of them hate me."

Jim shrugged. "There's a dumbass in every stable."

"Yeah." Billy fished in his inside pocket and pulled out a piece of paper. "Here's the address of the doctor you need to see for the physical. It's in the same building we're doing the renos on, so it's convenient."

He took the paper, glanced at it, and tucked it in his pocket. "Thanks. For the chance."

Billy patted Jim's arm. "I'd never leave the job in somebody else's hands. You're making this honeymoon possible, and I really appreciate it."

Jim shook his head. That was a lie, but he liked that Billy said it.

"I e-mailed you all the contact information for the building owners. The woman is a real pro. She approved all the plans for the tenant improvements, so everything should be clear sailing. She'll probably come in to check on progress, but that's all. If you have any trouble, call or text me. I'll be a long way away but only three hours earlier, so you should be able to get me."

"I'll try hard not to bother you. Hell, a guy only gets one honeymoon."

Billy laughed. "Until the second one. You know Shaz. He's already planning where we'll go next. But the business is my top priority right after my husband, so if you have any questions or worries at all, be sure to let me know, okay? If this goes well, we could get a lot more work from this client, plus we'll have a good reference for other TI jobs."

Jim smiled. He liked that word *we*. "Since I don't have a husband, it's my top priority, boss."

Billy laughed and stretched. "Back to the dancing."

Jim stood beside Billy. *Sound casual.* "That was some pair performing on the dance floor."

Billy chuckled. "Hell, yeah. Amazing dancers. And I don't often see men prettier than Shaz, but Ken's gorgeous, and don't tell my husband I said so."

Jim laughed, but his heart did that racing thing as they walked back into the heat, noise, and happiness of the ballroom.

Billy looked at him. "I guess it's about time for me and Shaz to make our getaway." He leaned over and gave Jim a kind of awkward hug. "Thanks again for taking on the job."

"My pleasure." He sure as hell hoped that was the truth.

Billy turned and walked toward the dancers, where Shaz was boogying with two or three partners, both male and female. *What a handful that guy must be.* Billy rushed forward like he was heading for the gates of paradise with a bevy of vestal virgins waiting inside. Or maybe that was just Jim's imagination.

Jim crossed the room to his table, where Raoul and his wife, Mercedes, and Charlie and his current girl, Angela, sat talking. No Peggy. He surveyed the dance floor and sure enough, she'd hooked up with some guy and was dancing her feet off. The woman loved to dance, and he was crap at it. Couldn't fault her. He should have learned, even if it was tough admitting his mother had been right about anything. Besides, the little guy with the big muscles she was dancing with was probably gay. Jim flopped into his chair.

Raoul sipped his beer. "Say good-bye to Billy, man?"

"Yeah."

"So are you on the new job?" He grinned.

Jim smiled back. "Yeah, I'm the supervisor."

Charlie leaned over. "See, I told you. Congrats, man."

Jim ducked his head. "Thanks. I've got some extra guys for demo. We gotta keep the noise and dust down, since people will be working in the building. We'll start at 6:30 to get a jump on the day. We may have to pull some night hours later in the job."

Angela shook her head. "Enough business talk, you two. I see Charlie little enough as it is."

Jim took a pull on his flat ginger ale. The musicians paused, chatted among themselves, and then started a really sappy love song. The lead singer said into the microphone, "This is Chase and Billy's last dance before the honeymoon, ladies and gentlemen, so line up for a short spin with them."

Angela stood. "Come on, Merce, let's go show those boys how it's done."

The two women joined Peggy, who'd already hopped into the line. A few men also queued up.

Jim jiggled his ice. "I'm going to get some ginger ale. Want anything?"

Raoul raised an eyebrow but didn't comment on the lack of alcohol. He nodded. "Yeah, bring me a beer."

"Charlie?"

"Yeah, sure."

The line for the bars had shortened as people gathered to dance with the grooms, so Jim made it to the bartender pretty quick. He popped a couple of bucks into the tip jar and carried one soda bottle and two beers toward the table. Somebody catcalled, and he glanced up in time to see Shaz spin and dip some blond guy. He laughed along with most of the spectators.

Jim took one more step. His foot caught on the edge of the wood dance floor, the slippery shoe slid, and—*whoa!* He stumbled forward, his arms flailing. Beer sloshed in a big gold arc. *Shit, the tux!* He raised the bottles high in front of him to keep the beer away, slid into a half circle, and timbered toward the floor face-first. "Damn!"

Strong hands grabbed him from behind and he twirled into a tight, warm embrace, his feet tangling but his body upright. "Got you."

"What? Jesus!" He tried to twist his feet back and lurched again, but the hands held. Finally Jim planted himself steadily and looked up into eyes so shiny black they practically reflected his face. Wide and almond-shaped. Yaoi man. *Hellfire.* About 100 percent more beautiful up close than from a distance. Skin like beige marble, hair like midnight. Eyes straight from his fantasy.

The guy smiled. "How fortuitous. I was just coming to ask you to dance."

"What?"

Dimples popped out in places where lean hollows had been. "I'd love to dance with you." Shit if he didn't just start dancing, holding Jim's hands, which in turn held the bottles. Dance or fall? That was his position, so he moved his feet. *Jesus.* He couldn't resist without spilling the beer down the guy's expensively dressed back, but every movement rubbed him in places that really needed rubbing and were getting a very embarrassing reaction.

Wake up. "Uh, sorry. I'm, uh, I mean, I don't normally dance with guys."

Gorgeous smiled again, and it made Jim want to smile back. "You're doing fine."

Sweet Jesus, the guy smelled like something spicy. Grapefruit and cinnamon. Real subtle but sneaky. It kind of tiptoed in Jim's nose and attacked—lower. "What?"

"The dancing. You're doing fine." He spun, holding Jim in his arms gracefully, and for a weird second Jim felt almost graceful too.

That didn't happen often. Between the smell and feel, Jim's head spun and his heart hammered. His eyes closed on their own. He was floating like some gently moving leaf. Could move this way forever.

The silky voice whispered, "Want to deliver the beer to your friends and be hands free?"

Friends. He dragged his eyes from the man and looked toward the table. Charlie and Raoul stared, full-on, no smiles, amazement written all over their faces. Behind them in line, the women stared too, but they were laughing. Except for Peggy. She looked half pissed. Hell, it was okay for her to dance with gay guys, but not him? *What the hell am I thinking?* He stopped moving and tried to take a step back out of this person's arms. Every inch away felt cold.

Mr. Beautiful cocked his head and dimpled again. "Oh dear, he's come to his senses. Why do all the gorgeous ones have to be straight?"

Gorgeous? "Man, you've got some seriously bad taste."

His face sobered just a little. "Quite the contrary. I'm known for my exceptional discernment."

What the hell could he say to that? "Thanks for catching me."

"Any time, dear. Any time." Yaoi man turned and walked like some jungle cat back onto the dance floor, grabbing a handsome guy from the line as he went. By the time Jim's heart started beating again, the guy was dancing and laughing with someone else.

Charlie and Raoul both rushed up. Charlie waved a hand toward the beautiful one. "What was that all about?"

Jim frowned. "The guy caught me when I nearly fell flat on my face." He shoved the beer bottles at Charlie. "Here, take these."

Raoul grabbed one of the beers. "Looked more like a tango to me, man."

"Cut me a break. The guy was just joking around."

Peggy's voice came from behind him. "Oh, I don't know. That dude is prettier than me."

Jim turned and slipped his arm around her. *Don't force me to agree.*

Charlie stared out at the dance floor, where pretty-face rested his head against a handsome blond's shoulder. "Looks like you don't have to worry, Peg. That dude's got a guy for every night."

True, and Jim fucking wished he didn't feel jealous.

CHAPTER THREE

THE PRETTY blond guy—*what was his name again?*—nuzzled Ken's neck. "Aw, come on, baby. I live close by. We can have a quick drink, a good time, and you'll go home tomorrow with a smile on your face." He kept nibbling as he pulled on Ken's arm to get him away from his car and across the parking lot.

Ken pressed his fingertips against the man's forehead and pushed. *Nibbling? Seriously?* "Sorry, dear, but I have to be at work early tomorrow."

"That's okay. I'll nudge you."

"No. You'll hop in your lovely car and take your cute butt home while I do the same."

The guy's hand wound its way down Ken's back and grabbed a handful of ass. "And it's such a gorgeous butt. I want some. Please."

"Ken. Hey, where are you going?" The voice rang out across the parking lot, and three couples waiting on the valet looked up with interest.

Well, hell. Gene stood on the porch of the club, waving.

Blondie looked over. "Who's that?"

Ken sighed loudly. "The man who brought me."

"But you have your car."

"Yes, I drove. I arranged for a friend to take Gene home. So be a dear and run off before he thinks I'm ditching him for you."

"But you want to, don't you?"

Enough of this shit. "As I said, I have to work." He pulled his arm away.

"Jiiiim, come on, my hound dog, take me home and fuck me."

The slightly slurred woman's voice stopped Ken, and he looked over his shoulder. The woman with the spectacular bottom he'd seen inside moved across the parking lot toward a beat-up truck, hanging on the neck of the guy Ken had tried to dance with. The big, beautiful, sexy, mouth-watering guy who'd branded Ken with a hot erection before suddenly becoming the straightest human on earth and about dying of embarrassment. What had she called him? Jim? So this woman was Jim's type. Funny. She seemed a little obvious. The type of woman a man chose to prove his balls. But something about this man named Jim wasn't obvious at all.

Someone grabbed Ken's arm from behind. "Ken, you're not leaving?"

Ken turned to stare at his handsome, pain-in-the-ass date. "Sorry, dear. I have to be at work early. I asked Alvin and Marshall to take you home."

Gene crossed his arms tightly over his well-dressed chest. "Are they supposed to suck me off as a consolation prize?"

Blondie stepped up and stuck his shoulder between Ken and Gene. "If anyone's sucking around here, it's going to be me."

"Like hell." Gene pushed his hand against the blond's shoulder, and the man staggered back. Gene looked seriously pleased with himself.

Ken glanced toward Jim and the woman. Both of them stared at Ken's little ménage.

Blond guy pushed Gene back. *Enough.* Ken stepped away, opened the door of his Lexus, slipped inside, and slammed and locked the door before either of the combatants even realized he was gone.

Outside the car, Gene screeched, "Ken. What the fuck?" He slammed a hand against the door, but Ken just pressed the accelerator and pulled away. As he passed the guy called Jim and his girlfriend, Ken turned his head. The woman stared at the two fighting men with a smile on her face, but Jim looked up, and his eyes met Ken's. He wasn't amused or horrified. How did he look? As if he'd like to punch the fucking lights out of both those guys. If he'd beaten them, would he have wanted Ken as his prize?

He sighed and pulled out into traffic. *Wishful thinking.*

JIM GLANCED over at Peggy as she bounced in the passenger seat and clapped her hands. "Man, wasn't that something? Who ever thought we'd see two gay guys fighting over another one? That was better than late-night wrestling." She laughed. "But I gotta say, that Asian guy was something to fight over. Shit, him being gay is a waste of raw material. He's movie-star handsome."

No. Graphic-novel handsome.

"You coming in, baby?" Peggy gave him that big smile that promised sex with no preamble. *Wish I was tempted.*

"Sorry. Can't. I've got to start that new job for Billy. I've got serious shit to do, and you're too distracting." He leaned over and kissed her to soften the blow.

"Aw, come on. I've got a new bottle of Jack and a hot mattress with clean sheets." She giggled. "Let Charlie and Raoul take the early shift."

How many times had he done just that? "Not tonight."

She stuck out her lip. "Damn. You're no fun."

"I've spent my life being nothing but fun. Time I got serious, you know?"

"But I like your fun self." She threw her arms around his neck and managed to lean far enough across the console to grind her impressive rack against his chest. "Come on, baby. I'm serious— seriously horny."

Why was it when you tried to make a change, everything in your damn life conspired against you? He took hold of her shoulders and pushed her away gently. "You're some Jezebel, baby, but this is important. Get your cute butt home and let me do the same."

"Oh hell, Jimmy. Aren't I important?"

What could he say to that? He just smiled.

She climbed out of his truck, turned back, and crossed her arms. "When you fall off this holier-than-thou shit wagon, don't come crawling to me. The door will be closed." He startled when she slammed the passenger door, then watched her walk into her condo and slam that door too, never looking back once. At least she'd made this breakup easier than most.

He twisted the key in the ignition, and his gut twisted at the same time. He'd just turned down sex *and* Jack so he could get up early and work. That constituted one helluva change of motivation. He'd fallen down a rabbit hole where his best friend turned out to be gay, hot guys danced together, and one of them looked like the incarnation of his childhood dreams.

Something was getting closer. Closing in. Something he didn't want to look at or it'd eat him. He shuddered.

Get your head on straight and stop this shit.

Twenty minutes later at his apartment building, he checked his mailbox and climbed the outside stairs to the second floor. Crap place to live. You couldn't make noise because it bothered the people below you, but nobody seemed to tell the renters above him about that idea. Elephants trained for Cirque du Soleil in that apartment.

He shoved the advertising flyers from his mailbox under his arm and reached for his key. *What the hell?* Ahead, sitting on the outside landing beside his apartment door, a guy lolled against the wall with his head turned away from Jim and both hands clutching his chest.

Jim stopped. He clamped his hand on his phone. *911 time?*

The head turned toward him, showing short dirty-blond hair just a shade lighter than Jim's.

"Ian?" *What the living fuck?*

Wide eyes opened. "Hey, Jim."

"I about called the cops. What are you doing here?"

Jim's younger brother slowly gathered up his skinny body and, still clutching his windbreaker to his chest, got to his feet.

Jim shook his head. "Jeez, man, you're almost as tall as me."

"Yeah. I still haven't stopped growing."

"Last time I saw you, you barely topped Mom."

"Late bloomer."

"How old are you now?"

"I just turned eighteen."

"Sorry. I'm not much for remembering events."

Ian smiled. "That must win the award for understatement."

"So what are you doing here?" He glanced at the kid's clutching hands. "And what's wrong with you? Gunshot wound? Heart attack?"

Ian shook his head and slowly unpeeled the windbreaker, revealing a small, furry, silvery white head. "Cat attack."

"You're sitting outside my apartment at ten at night with your cat?" *Take a breath.*

Ian's green eyes flashed. Looked kind of like Jim's. "He's more your cat. I mean, I found him out by your trashcans. He's a scrawny bugger. I think we need to feed him."

"We? Ian, I'll ask again, what are you doing here?"

"Mom and Dad kicked me out."

Well, hellfire. He shook his head. "Last I knew, you were the honor student superstar who they bragged about all the time. Going to Berkeley for architecture. Dean's list. Valedictorian and shit?"

"Yeah."

"So?"

"I guess they didn't count on me being gay."

Jim's mouth opened, closed, opened again. "What the hell makes you think you're gay?"

Ian's voice rose. "How about my boyfriend's cock in my mouth?"

Shit. He grabbed his brother's shoulder. "You better come in."

"Yeah. Me and your cat."

"Not my cat." He unlocked the door, pushed it open for Ian to walk through, and reached in to flip on the light.

"I see you haven't applied for any HGTV home decorating awards lately."

"If you'd like to leave for more posh environs, be my fucking guest. Besides, you should have seen it yesterday."

The kid shook his head, and even looking at his tense back, Jim suddenly felt sorry for him. Thrown out of his home by people he trusted to love him no matter what. Hell, at least Jim had walked out on his own. Kind of.

Jim pointed at the ratty couch. "Sit. Give me your jacket."

He looked down at the kitten. "I think he likes it in here."

"Yeah, well, what are the chances he's housebroken? You could end up with more than fur in that jacket."

"He pooped while I was waiting for you. Peed too."

"In your jacket?"

"No. On the ground. You got something we can use for a litter box? And what about some food?"

"For you or the cat?"

"Both, I guess."

Jim walked into the tiny kitchenette and found a pizza box he'd stuffed in the trash. He pulled it out. *Could work.* "I got this, but what could we put in it?"

"Shredded paper towels or toilet paper or something?"

Jim narrowed his eyes. "Maybe. That critter's little. Probably's got no idea about doing its thing in one place."

Ian pulled the feline from his jacket and held it up, getting a "mew" for his trouble. "I'm guessing you're smart." He looked over at Jim. "I think he looks like Anderson Cooper, don't you? All silvery white fur."

"If you say so." Jim had a stack of paper napkins he'd gotten from the pizza takeout over the months. He ripped them up and tossed them in the box, then set it in the corner beside the refrigerator.

"I'm gonna call him Anderson." Ian stood, carried the little cat to the box, and plopped the beast in the shredded paper. "And this must be the Anderson pooper." He laughed at his own joke, but it sounded tired.

The kitten immediately started scratching, tossing paper around, then squatted and peed. *Damn. He gets it.* The beast scratched some more, then hopped over the low side of the box and started sniffing his way around the room.

"So your plans are what? To keep this cat and stay here?" Jim crossed his arms.

Ian scrunched up his face all adorable-like. "Yeah, I guess so. I didn't think about it too much. They yelled that they didn't want any fag children in their house, and I walked out and drove here."

Shit. "So you've got a car."

"Yeah. Dad bought me one when I turned sixteen."

"But he makes the payments?"

He nodded slowly. "He did. I've always paid the insurance, but he bought the car."

"You reckon he's going to let you keep it?"

"Jesus, Jim, I don't know."

Jim sat next to him and put a hand on his arm for a second. "You said something about a boyfriend."

Ian wiped his hand over his face. "Yeah. Ricky. I really liked him. His folks gathered him up and sent him to some military school or something."

"When they found out, you mean?"

"When they found me sucking their son's cock. His father decided any kid could be seduced by a good blow job, so they figured if they got him away from temptation like me, he'd be okay. Crap, he'll seduce every guy at his school."

Talk about drowning in déjà vu. "Jesus, kid, I'm sorry." His stomach turned, and he breathed out slowly. "So Berkeley?"

"Gone, I assume. I can't figure they'd let me live on the streets but pay my way to architecture school."

"Yeah." He didn't see his brother much, but he knew that was a big dream.

Ian looked at Jim with shiny eyes. "Can I stay here, Jim? Until I figure out what to do?"

How much of a grown-up was he prepared to be? "I guess so. I don't have much room. There's this closet-sized space they had the gall to call a second bedroom. It's full of crap, but maybe we can clear some room."

"I won't be any trouble."

Right. An eighteen-year-old with a cat. How could that be any trouble? "Come on. I'll show you the space, and then we'll try to find some food. I got a big job tomorrow, so I need to get to bed."

"Shit. Sorry, Jim."

Yeah, sorry. Two hours later they'd managed to find spaces for all the crap Jim had dumped in that extra room—including a lot in the trash cans. Fair trade for the cat. He'd shoved some vegetable soup and turkey slices into Ian and just turkey into Anderson. The kid's long frame barely fit on the secondhand daybed, but his head hit the pillow and his eyes closed at the same time. Anderson made himself at home next to Ian's head. The feline seemed less lost than the kid.

Jim pulled the door most of the way closed and walked to his room. Could you hate your own parents? He sure as fuck came close. Ian was a good kid. Their late-life baby who'd always been their crown prince—as long as he fit all their pictures. Jim had never fit in, so when he walked out the door after—when he left, they were probably relieved. But to throw out Ian? Hell, whoever thought up the idea of unconditional love was smoking something illegal.

He took a quick shower so he didn't have to spend time in the morning, set his alarm for 5:00 a.m.—*Just four hours in the future. Damn!*—put the clock across the room so he wouldn't turn it off, and crawled in bed. He sighed. This morning he had a hangover. Tonight he had a serious job, a kid—and a cat. Jeez, when he was asking the cosmos for more responsibility, he hadn't really meant that kind.

Okay, sleep. Wonder what Billy and Shaz are doing? Well, hell no, he knew what they were doing. It was their honeymoon. *What do gay guys do exactly? Is it like the comic books?*

What had that guy in the parking lot said? He wanted to suck the beautiful guy? Jesus, gay guys probably did a lot of that. They must like it. Probably more than women did. *Bet they're better at it too.* Jim swiped at his face. *Like the lips on that guy at the wedding.* In that lean face, those Angelina lips looked really startling. Did that guy like sucking off another dude like in the yaoi comic? *Stop thinking, idiot, or you'll be up all night jerking off.*

He flipped on his side. *I'll plan the suite remodel. How do I want to organize the guys? That should put me to sleep.* With lips and cats and tenant improvements swimming through his head, he finally dozed off.

Chapter Four

Hoo boy, did he feel crappy. Three days in a row. But this morning it was too little alcohol, not too much. That was a vague improvement.

He dragged himself from the distant alarm clock straight to the bathroom. *Don't sit on the bed or you're toast.*

Teeth brushed, he wiped a damp washcloth over his dick that had still managed to ejaculate all over his sheets despite his best intentions. *Told you not to think about blow jobs.*

He pulled on some clothes and barged out the bedroom door, then stopped himself. *Shh.* He now had a roommate. That felt weird. He tiptoed into the kitchenette, started the coffee, and toasted a piece of bread. *Need to shop today or Ian will starve.*

"Man, you're up early." Ian staggered through the small living room wearing only pajama bottoms and collapsed on the couch in sight of the kitchenette where Jim stood.

"Sorry. Didn't mean to wake you. I thought teenagers could sleep through anything."

He shook his head. "I started waking up back when Mom and Dad took to fighting. Hard to stay asleep."

"Want some toast?"

"Nah. I'm going straight back to bed when you leave."

"Wise choice. Where's Anderson?"

"Uninterested in getting up. Told you he's smart."

Jim smeared peanut butter on the half-cooked toast. "I left before the fighting got too bad. With the folks, I mean."

"Yeah. Before Dad started cheating."

"I guess I really left you alone with those people, didn't I?"

"Yeah. But you were so much older. What'd you have in common with a pipsqueak like me?"

"I was their worst nightmare. I liked to work with my hands and didn't want to go to college." He didn't mention the other shit.

25

"Well, as nightmares go, I got you beat."

"What's so bad about being gay? You're their poster-child son. Smart, ambitious, obedient."

Ian fell back on the cushions, his legs draped over the sofa arm, and flopped an arm over his eyes. "Ass fucking trumps everything."

"Yeah, the old man's probably worried you inherited gay from him."

"I guess."

"So what do you want to do?"

The kid propped himself on his elbows. "I'll get a job, sign up for community college. Hell, I got such good fucking grades, I might qualify for a scholarship. Then maybe I can get loans to go to architecture school."

"Still the dream, huh?"

"Yeah. Building monuments to my ego on the earth." He sat up. "But I think we can use the earth better, you know? Humans don't have to live like some cancer or virus. We can do better. Build better."

"Kid, you're inspiring. I'm almost twenty-seven, and I just got my first supervisor job."

"Hell, Jim, that's great."

He shrugged. "I only got it because my friend Billy wanted to go on his honeymoon. He had to have somebody take over."

"I'm sure he had lots of people to pick from. He chose you for a reason."

"Yeah, I was there." He laughed. "And if I don't get to the job, I'll be an ex-supervisor."

"Want me to go shopping while you're gone?"

"Yeah. That'd be great." He pulled out his wallet and put sixty dollars on the counter. "Don't get healthy."

"Thanks, Jim. I'll pay you back. I promise."

"Hey, it's kind of fun to have some family for a change." That was almost true. He walked over and gave his brother a one-armed hug. "See you tonight." He headed for the truck.

THE EIGHT-STORY black-glass office building gleamed in the sunrise. His baby. Or at least one of the suites would be his. He parked, pulled his tools and the plans from his truck, and rang the night bell. The security guy buzzed him in, and he went straight from the lobby to the office he was set to demo. His first day as a construction supervisor. The facility had three private offices and a large open space where banged-up cubicles had been abandoned. Soon it would be one big open room, ready to be rebuilt.

He checked his wiring plans as the demo guys arrived. He gave them Billy's talk about demolition safety and put them to work. Charlie and Raoul came in on time, looking kind of bleary-eyed, but then, he was sure he did too.

In five hours they'd set up the site, pulled plastic sheeting over the door to the hall so they could pass in and out, and torn into the existing cubicles and walls that needed to be changed for the new tenant. They'd be done fast. Jim looked over the approved plans from Billy's architect. It wasn't a big job. He'd be able to get far along before Billy got back. Make the big guy happy and maybe get some more supervisor jobs. He smiled. *I love the sound of sledgehammers in the morning.* Jim waved at Charlie on the top of his ladder.

"Yeah, boss." Charlie grinned.

That had a good ring. "Come down for a second."

Charlie balanced his bulk on the rungs and made it to the bottom. "What's up?"

"I've gotta go have this physical for insurance. Will you keep a close eye on the demo guys? They seem pretty careful, but you know what Billy always says."

"More guys get hurt in demo than any other time."

"Right. The doc's in this building, so I shouldn't be too long, and I've got my cell if you need me."

"No problem, man. Go do what you need to do."

"Thanks." He waggled the cell phone as a reminder and headed out through the plastic sheeting. He was a little dusty, but that probably wouldn't interfere with his blood pressure.

He took the elevator two floors up and found the suite that said Dr. Haselbaum. He didn't like doctors. He avoided them like unprotected sex, but this was just routine, so no biggie, right? He signed in and took a seat as the receptionist suggested. Just being in a doctor's office made him antsy, so he flipped through a copy of *Men's Health*. *Shit, look at those bodies.* He ran a hand over his own barely realized six-pack. *Bet a lot of guys in this magazine are gay. Good thing I don't have to compete with those hunks for dates.*

A woman and a man also waited, but the door to the inner sanctum opened and the nurse called his name. She smiled as he walked in and led him to an exam room. "Please put this on." She extended a stack of white paper.

"On?"

She unfolded it into something resembling a short paper coat. "Opening in the front, please. I'll step out."

She closed the door behind her. Jim pulled off his dusty jeans and long-sleeved T-shirt, tossed his briefs on top, thought better of it and hid them under the shirt, then pulled on the gown. *Hellfire, not much point in her stepping out. This thing barely covers the necessaries.*

Nurse Ratched bustled back in. "All set?"

For the next half hour, she weighed, measured, listened, tapped, prodded, drew blood, and then hooked him up to some sensors all over his chest. He lay on the exam table and listened to the EKG machine go *bleep* and watched a little slip of paper slide through in seconds. The nurse started removing the sensors.

"Is that all there is to it?"

"Yes, it takes a lot less time than it used to. Excuse me while I give this to the doctor."

The door went *click* as he sat up. Before he could even glance at the credentials on the wall, she came back in, followed by a man with a white coat, thinning hair, and pleasant face. "Hello, I'm Dr. Haselbaum."

Jim nodded.

The nurse gathered up her vials of blood in a plastic dish like an efficient vampire. "We're finished, Doctor."

"Good. Thank you." The doctor stuck the stethoscope in his ears, pushed it against Jim's chest, and listened all over, then stepped to the side and pulled the paper robe farther down Jim's back. The doc tapped a couple of times. "Cough, please."

Jim coughed and the doctor listened; then he stepped back and looked at Jim with a little frown.

Jim tried to smile. "Something wrong?"

"Has anyone ever told you that you have a heart murmur?"

"Uh, no, but I don't see doctors a lot. Is that bad?"

"It's generally benign, but I'd like to have you check it out before we sign off on the insurance papers." He picked up a prescription pad and wrote something. "I'm going to refer you to a specialist. His office is here in the building. Before you leave I'll have someone from my office staff call to see if they can fit you in, since we need to get these papers back quickly."

"Okay, thanks." Jim slipped a hand over his chest.

The doctor smiled. "No reason to worry. Heart murmurs are fairly common and can be caused by a number of conditions, but it's good to keep track of them. You can get dressed. Stop at the desk before you go to check on the referral."

Bam. Just that fast, the doctor was gone. *Hellfire. Drive-by bad news.* Jim dressed and walked out to the front desk. The lady handed him a slip of doctor paper. "Your company insurance will cover this exam, Mr. Carney. Here's the suite number of the cardiologist Dr. Haselbaum wants you to see. I called their office, and they said they can fit you in at 4:00 p.m. today. Does that work for you?"

"Uh, yeah, sure."

"Excellent. No need to confirm. Just go to that suite at three forty-five."

He wandered into the hall with a hand on his chest. Did he feel weak? What about that weird racing he got in his heart? Maybe he shouldn't be swinging a sledgehammer. What if they didn't approve him? That would probably fuck up his job chances. *Hell!*

When he got back to the job site, Raoul was pulling debris into plastic bags. He looked up and frowned. "Hey, man, you okay?"

"Yeah, fine. I just have another doctor I'm supposed to see."

Charlie walked over. "Everything all right?"

Raoul nodded. "Jim's gotta see another doctor."

"Yeah, they say I have a heart murmur."

Raoul smiled. "No worries, man. My wife's sister has one too. She just has to take some kind of medicine before she goes to the dentist or something."

"The doc said it's no biggie." Jim forced a smile.

Charlie nudged him. "Always thought you were healthy as a horse, man."

"Yeah, well, I am. Get back to work."

He tried not to think about it. Worked, ate a hot dog and Coke for lunch, and worked some more. About three thirty, he started gathering up tools. *Go face the music.* "Hey, Charlie, I—"

The plastic covering the construction area pushed aside and a woman burst through. Blonde hair, pretty face, and formal business suit. "Hello. Where's Mr. Ballew, please?"

"He's not here. I'm his construction supervisor." That made his heart pound. "Can I help you?"

She started at his dusty boots and traveled up slowly, frowning like there'd been an election and he'd lost. When she made it to his face, she suddenly smiled. "I'm Constance Murch. I own this building. You're working for me."

Holy hellfire. "I'm so pleased to meet you, uh, ma'am."

"So Mr. Ballew is—" She waved a well-manicured hand.

"On his honeymoon, ma'am." Shit, maybe he shouldn't have said that. "Uh, I expect he let you know about the time off."

"Oh yes, I guess he mentioned being gone. I forgot. What's happening is that I may have a change of plans on this build-out."

"Oh?" He tried not to choke.

"Yes. A different tenant might take this suite, and I'll put the tenant that was to occupy this one on the eighth floor. We would need to alter the plans."

Sweet Jeez. Billy was design/build, and Jim only occupied the build half. "We might need to get new permits." That sounded authoritative. His heart hammered. *Damn, slow down.*

She scowled. "If we can't move fast, I could lose the second tenant. Is Mr. Ballew being gone going to be a problem?"

No way was he losing Billy's big job. "No, ma'am. I'll stop work after we've finished demolition today. You let me know if you're changing tenants and I'll have, uh, my designer here to discuss the improvements."

"Good. Give me your number."

No cards. "Uh, I left my cards at home, but if you've got something to write on and with?"

She produced a pen and a business card from her purse. He jotted his name and cell number on it and handed it back. She nodded. "Thank you.

KNAVE OF BROKEN HEARTS

I'll let you know within twenty-four hours." She handed him another card. "Here's my card." She smiled slowly. "In case you need it."

"Thank you?" His brain whirled. He barely knew the architect Billy worked with, but if Billy trusted him, he must be good.

"Unless you might have a moment to discuss it now? Like over coffee?"

What? He looked at her and smiled automatically. "Oh, actually I have an appointment in a couple of minutes." He glanced at his watch. *Almost late!* "Sorry, I'm supposed to finish my physical for an insurance report. I need to get to the doctor's office."

She raised an eyebrow. "Doesn't that leave me with no one in charge, Mr.—" she glanced at what he'd written. "—Carney?"

"No, ma'am." He waggled his fingers to Charlie, who was obviously listening as hard as he could at the top of the ladder.

Charlie lumbered down.

"Ma'am, this is Charlie MacIntosh, as reliable a foreman as a guy could ever have. He'll be in charge while I'm away for a short time."

Charlie's eyes widened at the word *foreman*; then a slow smile spread across his face. "Yes, ma'am. May I show you the details of the demolition?" He glanced at Jim like *Get out of here* as he led the pretty woman farther into the suite. "We gotta be careful. Demo is the most dangerous time on a job. We take lots of precautions."

"I've been to many demolitions, Mr. MacIntosh."

Charlie smiled. "I'm sure you have, ma'am, being an entrepreneur."

Jeez, the man was a miracle worker. Bonuses for Charlie. Jim glanced at his watch. *Late.* He could lose the appointment. He pushed through the plastic and took off at a trot.

Where is the damned elevator? The indicator looked stuck on nine.

Hell, if he blew this physical, he couldn't work for Billy. He ran down the hall, threw open the hall door, and hit the stairs. Two at a time, he climbed one flight, then had to switch to one stair at a time for the other three. He ran the last flight, pushed open the door, and, gasping for breath, turned left and found the suite number the receptionist had given him. By the time he got inside, he had to stop, lean against the wall, and grab his chest. *Out. Of. Shape.*

"Sir, are you okay?" A nurse standing behind the front desk ran through a door into the reception room. Other people who had been waiting jumped up or leaned forward. He was making a scene, but he couldn't catch his breath. He staggered a couple of steps and flopped into a chair. The nurse grabbed his shoulder. "Sir, put your head down." She didn't wait for him to comply but shoved his face into his lap. A few more inches, he could have sucked his own dick, which he'd probably have to do now since he'd managed to lose his girlfriend. "I'm fine."

"Excuse me?"

"I'm fine. I just ran up the stairs."

The nurse took her hand off his back and let him rise to sitting. Another woman shoved a paper cup of water at him. *Try for nonchalant again.* "Sure know how to get your attention, don't I?" He sucked in some deep breaths. Man, the air felt so sweet.

"Do you have an appointment?" The nurse seemed to want to return to normality.

"As opposed to dropping in for a heart attack?"

She grinned. "Yes, as opposed to that." The nurse was probably in her midtwenties with sleek brown hair pulled back at her neck in a tail, wide blue eyes, and dimples that wouldn't quit. "I'm Jim Carney. You're working me in at four. I was trying not to be late and overdid it."

"Your zeal is commendable. Why don't you come back with me? We need to reward such devotion to punctuality."

Truth was, he still felt light-headed. Trying to recover some particle of macho, he stood, squared his shoulders, and followed her. When they got to an examining room, she stepped aside, let him enter, and closed the door partway. He flashed the lopsided grin. "Do I have to put on a paper dress?"

"No, removing your shirt will do fine. The doctor doesn't find many hearts below the waist."

He laughed—loud. "What's your name?"

"Andrea."

"I would have bet no one could make me laugh right now. Does the doctor know you're so good at your job?"

"Oh yeah. He pays me the big bucks."

He laughed again.

"Are you bragging about your outrageous salary again, Andrea?" The silky voice came from outside the exam room. Jim looked up as the door pushed inward and a man in a white lab coat backed in carrying a chart he was reading.

Andrea smiled. "I have to extol your virtues."

"Ah yes, because certainly no one else will." He turned, extended a narrow, long-fingered hand, and Jim looked up into the face that had launched a thousand wet dreams. *Mr. Beautiful. Yaoi man.* The doctor smiled. "Hello, I'm Ken Tanaka."

CHAPTER FIVE

DID I just make that eep *sound?*

The doctor must have heard it, because he cocked his head. "I know you." A slow smile spread across his face. Damn yeah, he remembered.

"You just kept me from crashing to the ground at the wedding last night. You look pretty different today." As if he wouldn't know those lips anywhere.

"Of course, I remember." He glanced at the nurse. "I'll take it from here, Andrea."

She flashed a grin that might have just been friendly or might have had more significance. "Yes, Doctor." She turned to Jim and touched his arm. "Be sure to tell the doctor about your weakness and shortness of breath after running up the stairs, okay?"

Well, hell, how much undermining could his manhood take?

Dr. Tanaka leaned against the examining table, his long legs in dark trousers crossed at the ankle. "Good to see you again."

"It's a weird coincidence." Cosmic, in fact.

"I suppose. A number of us go to the same club—the man I went to the wedding with, the people who own this building, me." He smiled. "So what happened with your shortness of breath?"

"Your hair's really different." Did he just say that?

Another grin. "Yes, I try for serious and professional in the office. At parties, not so much."

"So you're really a cardiologist?"

"What, you think I play one on TV?"

"I just never saw a cardiologist who, you know, looked like you."

He laughed. "I'd say thank you, but I have no idea if that was a compliment. I also don't know how many cardiologists you've seen."

Jim shrugged. "I hardly even go to a general practitioner, much less a fancy heart doctor." But he certainly knew one extremely well.

Tanaka struck a beauty-queen pose. "Very fancy."

"Yeah, well that's another thing. I guess I never thought about a cardiologist being, you know, gay."

Ken raised an arched black brow. "We're everywhere."

"Nothing on it. I just don't know much about doctors." That he was willing to admit.

"So why don't you take off your shirt and tell me what's going on with you?"

"Oh, okay." He pulled the T-shirt over his head and wrapped his arms around his chest.

"You cold?" Tanaka pulled out another damned stethoscope.

Jim dropped his arms. "Not really."

"You certainly look fit." Tanaka grinned, and Jim felt a warm flush that started somewhere below his belt. A picture of his cardiologist dancing like some sexy snake with the gray-haired man the previous night flashed in his mind.

"Thanks."

The combination of the cool stethoscope and the warm hand gave Jim shivers in very inconvenient places. Thank God, no paper dress or the damned thing would have turned into a flying flag. He folded his hands in his lap as the doc listened all over his chest and back.

Tanaka stood up. "What were the symptoms Andrea was describing?"

"No biggie. I just ran up four flights of stairs at top speed and got light-headed."

"That will certainly do it." Tanaka stepped back and looked at Jim. "You can put your shirt on."

"That's all there is?"

"Actually, I'm going to schedule you for an echocardiogram. I suspect you have mitral valve prolapse."

Jim's heart really leaped. "What's that?"

"It's not much to worry about. It's a leaking in your mitral valve that may cause some regurgitation. It's quite common, and most people have few if any symptoms. It's just good to know about it so we can keep an eye on it."

"Sometimes my heart beats really hard."

Tanaka grinned. "I'm glad to hear that."

Hell, doctors weren't supposed to be so flirty, were they? "It can get a little scary."

"It may be related to the mitral valve or may be another cause. Let's get the echo first and we'll go from there." He ripped a page from his prescription pad. "There's a lab here in the building."

"I think everything is in this building."

"We try."

"Uh, I work construction. It's pretty tough duty. Should I be cutting back?"

"Quite the contrary. Assuming it's mitral valve prolapse, exercise is good for you. And I'm sure your body is used to the rigors of your job. But eating right and getting good sleep is never bad advice."

Jim cracked half a grin. "Sounds like bad advice to me."

Tanaka laughed. "Also relieving stress."

"Yeah, right."

Tanaka cocked his head. "Do you have any unusual stress right now?"

Jim snorted.

"Ah, I see. Getting married, divorced, having a baby?"

"I guess my stress is pretty small potatoes compared to that kind of stuff, but I'm overseeing a job for a friend and I don't want, uh, anything to go wrong. Plus my brother just showed up on my doorstep and needs some looking after. With a cat."

The doc laughed. "That sounds like a fair amount of pressure to me. Do you know how to meditate?'

Jim snorted again.

"I'll ask Andrea to give you a worksheet on the steps. Meditation is hard, but making the effort actually reduces stress."

He shrugged. "I hate to take the instructions when I know I probably won't do anything with it."

"It's okay. Just take a look. It's there in case you need it. My receptionist will make you an appointment for the echocardiogram. Then you'll come see me again."

"Oh, okay." *Don't be so damned happy about that, Carney.*

At the desk, Andrea stood behind the receptionist. She flashed a big smile. "So Doctor's sending you for an echo."

"Yeah." The words pushed out. "Does it hurt?"

"No. It's just an ultrasound. Have you ever had one of those?"

"Uh, I don't think so. Maybe."

"Anyway, they'll just put some cool gel on your chest and press a wand against it. No discomfort at all."

"Thanks."

The receptionist put her hand over the phone. "They can take you tomorrow at 4:30. Does that work for you?"

"Sure. I'm working downstairs so I can just jog—" He looked at Andrea and grinned. "—uh, walk slowly to the lab from there."

The receptionist went back to the phone, confirming his appointment.

Andrea beamed. "Okay. See you later." Her dark hair flipped as she walked back into the inner sanctum of the office. The receptionist handed Jim his appointment card and a sheet of paper with meditation instructions on it. Just what he needed. *Not.*

Out in the hall, he stopped. He had a weird ticker that might or might not be a problem. And he had a doctor who made his heart beat hard. Further down the damned rabbit hole.

This time he took the elevator to the lobby. Quiet had started to settle in on the building. After hours. He pushed through the plastic. Charlie was still there. The other guys had left. Jim slapped Charlie's shoulder. "Hey, thanks, man."

"Took you a while. Everything okay?"

"Yeah. I mean, kind of. I have something called a mitral valve collapse or something. I have to go get an echo thing tomorrow. The doc said it's not much to worry about."

"Shit, man, that's crap."

"No worries. Thanks for taking care of the owner. What else did she say?"

"Not much. Pretty thing. She loosened up a little while we talked. She said she'd let us know if they're changing tenants by tomorrow noon."

"If she does, I gotta get the architect to design and sign off on new plans."

"The guy Billy uses?"

"Yeah. I don't really know him, but he's familiar with the job. I'm not in touch with any other architects. Are you?

Charlie shook his head. "Billy's guy has his number on the plans."

Jim walked to where the suite drawings were spread out on a pile of wood. He found the number and dialed it. Two rings. "Hello, you've reached Brian Oliver, architecture and planning. Our office will be closed for one week with limited e-mail availability. Please leave a message and we'll get back to you on our return." Billy clicked off. "Well, damn. He's gone."

Charlie frowned. "Maybe the owner won't change tenants."

"Right. Maybe." He tried to smooth out the lines that must be popping on his forehead. No use worrying Charlie. "Thanks for being so great. I about busted a gut when you started explaining Billy's philosophy of demolition."

Charlie laughed. "By the way, she sure asked a lot of questions about you."

"Me?"

"Yeah. Like were you married or did you have a girlfriend kind of questions."

"Nah. It was you she was charmed by."

"If you say so."

"Go on home. We'll worry about this tomorrow."

"Want to go for a beer?"

"No. Believe it or not, my kid brother dropped out of the clouds onto my doorstep last night. I need to go home and see how he's doing."

"Man. You weren't expecting him?"

"No. Long story. I'll fill you in tomorrow."

"Okay. Watch out for that ticker."

"Going to."

Charlie waved, and Jim followed him through the plastic into the lobby of the building. *Real quiet now.* Jim sat on one of the guest chairs by the window. It wasn't dark yet since it was rising June, and the early evening light filtered in. Who could he call? He started flipping through his contacts. There had to be an architect in there somewhere. He was not going to bother Billy. Billy trusted him. Hollering for help at the first hurdle was chickenshit.

He made it to the *S's* before slight panic set in. Maybe he could call one of the other contractors he'd worked for and ask for a referral. *Yeah. Tomorrow.* That was starting pretty far back, and he hated for the contractors to think he'd gone into competition with them, but he couldn't think of another option. He ran a hand through his too-long hair.

"It doesn't appear you're working hard at relieving stress, Mr. Carney." The soft voice danced with humor.

Jim didn't even have to look up. His cock did. "Maybe I should try some meditation right here." He closed his eyes. "Ommmm."

Tanaka laughed. It sounded like music. "Point taken. But you seem to be upset about something. I should repeat that the mitral valve prolapse is not a cause for deep concern. Honest."

Jim breathed out slowly and looked at the doctor. He'd taken off his white coat and wore dress slacks, a white shirt, and a sport coat. The hair was still brushed back off his face, not flopping like a silk curtain the way it did at the wedding. "Actually, it's an issue with the job I'm managing. I need an architect who can do some last-minute tenant improvement plans, and the guy my boss uses is on vacation."

"Doesn't he have a backup?"

Jim shook his head. "Probably. But my boss is Billy Ballew. You know, he's on his honeymoon, and I don't want to bother him if I can avoid it. But I guess I may have to."

Tanaka folded his arms and stared at Jim. "I happen to know an architect who might be able to help."

"Seriously? I can't ask you to do that." But man, he sure wanted to.

"Yes, well, he's a, uh, social acquaintance. In fact, he was my date at the wedding last night." He grinned.

"I don't want to put you in an awkward position with your boyfriend." He swallowed hard.

"He's definitely not my boyfriend. In fact, he's a pain in the ass, but he owes me a favor. Want me to call him?"

"I'm not completely sure I'm going to need an architect yet. The building owner said she'd know by noon tomorrow."

"Ah, in time for lunch. So what say I line him up for a 12:30 lunch meeting at my club, and if you don't need him, I cancel at the last minute?"

"I don't want to take your time." That was a lie.

"Nonsense. We have to eat. Besides, I can't leave Shaz's husband in the lurch."

"That would be amazing." *The doc should listen to my heart now.*

39

"I'll call him first and make sure he does what you need done. TIs, right?"

"Yes, and he may need to sign off on Title Twenty-four calcs."

"Twenty-four. I can remember that. Want to give me your phone number so I can let you know if I strike out?"

"Uh, okay."

"And I'll put mine in your phone so you can tell me if I need to cancel."

They swapped phones and started tapping keys. Tanaka's phone was the newest Apple, all shiny and supertech. Jim wanted to hide his old model, but the doc didn't seem to sneer at it. When they exchanged back, Tanaka smiled. "How nice to be in your phone."

Man, did he make that sound dirty.

The doc waved the phone at Jim. "Talk to you tomorrow. Ta." He turned and strolled out of the building like some panther heading out to hunt.

"Man." Just being near that guy made him antsy, but that didn't stop Jim from saying he'd have lunch with him. Oh yeah, and his architect lover who was also gay. Jesus, was everyone he knew gonna turn up gay now? But maybe, just maybe, Tanaka might save his bacon.

He walked back into the suite, locked up, and headed home, trying to keep his thoughts on how he'd change the suite layout if he had to and not on lips that could give lessons in blow jobs just by showing up.

When he stepped into his apartment, he was greeted by smells that only occurred in restaurants and in his dreams. Jim followed his nose to the stove. "What are you making?"

"Pork chops with Italian sauce a la Ian. There are some browned potatoes and spinach."

His mouth actually watered. "Is it illegal to chain your brother to the stove?"

"Only in some states, but it may go to the Supreme Court."

Fifteen minutes later, Ian's claims to chef status were verified. Pork chops juicy and packed with flavor. "This is amazing."

"Glad you like it. I've gotta earn my keep somehow."

"How did your day go?"

"I got a job."

"You're kidding."

"Nope. I'm a busboy at a Mexican restaurant."

"Don't you have to speak Spanish to hold a job like that?"

"I can manage a little since I took Spanish in high school. I think they're pretty amused by me. I'm their token gringo."

"Man, you don't mess around. Can you bring food home?"

"Yep. And I signed up for community college."

"Jesus, Ian, you make me feel like a slacker. No wonder you're Dad's poster boy."

"Was. Was his poster boy." Ian touched Jim's arm. "You're no slacker. Hell, man, you've been fending for yourself since you were sixteen. That's not easy."

Jim shrugged. "I chose it. They would have sent me to college if I'd just toed the line."

"Toed their line."

"Yeah." He took another bite and chewed. "But don't glamorize me, buddy. I've been getting by with the minimum for a lot of years. Sex, drugs, and rock and roll. It's time I grew up."

"How was your day? The new job?"

"Pretty wild. The building owner came in and said she may be changing the tenants and I'll have to find an architect to sign off on new plans. The guy Billy uses is gone." He didn't want to worry Ian with the heart thing.

"What are you going to do?"

"I've got a line on an architect that might be able to help." *Sort of.*

"I'll be glad to look at the plans for you too. Not that I can sign them, but I apprenticed in an architectural firm after school. It was supposed to give me good brownie points for getting into Berkeley." He made a face.

"That would be great. I don't know this guy at all. He's just a friend of, uh, somebody I know. So maybe you can do some of the work, and he can just approve it."

"Sure, I'd love to do that."

Jim grinned. "You're pretty handy to have around."

Ian's eyes got shiny. "Thanks. You don't mind that I'm gay?"

Jim leaned over and slid his arm around Ian's neck. "Hey, you're my brother and I love you. Besides, these days it seems like all my best friends are gay." He gave his brother a quick squeeze. "I'll help you clean up, and then I need to get to bed. I didn't sleep a lot last night."

"No, I got this. You go to bed. I'll turn off the lights."

"I should keep you company."

"Anderson will do that." The kitten lay flat on its back in the middle of the ratty couch, sound asleep.

"Such a sparkling conversationalist."

"He has hidden depths. Seriously, get some rest."

"Okay. I'll take you up on it." He walked into his bedroom and closed the door. No lie. He felt like he could sleep a week. Still. He opened the box under the bed and stared at his favorite magazine again. Every time he saw Ken Tanaka, all he could think of were these drawings. Right on the cover, there he was. The character had short ink-black hair that flopped in front of his face over wide yet still almond eyes that in this case were blue, not brown. Close enough. Of course, this face was pretty boyish. Younger than Ken, but Ken was more beautiful.

Jim traced the lips on the drawing with his forefinger, then flipped through the pages. Oh man. How many times for how many years had he stared at that beautiful ass being fucked by that big cock? He was sick. These drawings ruined his life and the life of his friend. Hadn't he learned his fucking lessons?

Jim's hand slipped into his own lap and squeezed his massive erection.

CHAPTER SIX

KEN BRAKED at the light and reached out to dial the phone, then stopped. Why exactly was he doing this? Gene made him bonkers. When he drove off last night, he'd put a fitting end on his relationship with Gene. Did he really want to start up that whole irritation again for some straight construction worker he barely knew?

His hand danced over his phone. Yes, he actually did. There was a realness about Jim that weirdly appealed—not that he was into seducing straight guys. He pressed the button and spoke into the phone. "Call Gene Willings."

One ring. Two. "Uh, is this Ken?"

He tried to keep the sigh out of his voice. "Yes, darling. How are you?"

"I'm pissed at you. You palmed me off on those two fairies and left me."

"I called to ask you a favor."

"I suppose it was too much to ask that you were calling to apologize, missed me desperately, and couldn't live another minute without me."

"Please, dear."

"Yes, I know to whom I speak. What can I do for you, Ken?"

"I have an acquaintance who may need an architect to do some fast tenant improvement drawings and possibly some, uh, Title Twenty-four calcs, he says. I thought of you."

Gene sighed deeply. "This is a new boyfriend, I assume?"

"Actually, no. He's straight as a plumb line. He just happens to be a friend of a friend of mine, and a patient. Is this in your wheelhouse, darling, or have I called in the wrong favor?" Yes, that was a reminder.

"Favor? Ah, I see. A bit of reckoning, are we? Tit for tat?"

"I have very little interest in tits."

"Ha. Ha. So if I do this, will I no longer owe you for sponsoring me at the club?"

"You can consider all debts paid. And, of course, I assume you will be paid. This isn't pro bono."

"You said fast?"

"My acquaintance won't even know until tomorrow if this is happening, but if it's on, he'll need the drawings right away. I told him we might meet over lunch."

"Are you buying?"

"Of course."

"All right, count me in. How will I know if we're going forward?"

"I'll call you. We'll go to the club."

"At least I'll get a free lunch out of it."

"And my eternal gratitude."

"Yes. That and a hundred dollars will buy me dinner. Talk to you tomorrow." *Click.*

Oh my, he is a pain in the ass.

Ken pulled off the 55, maneuvered the red lights on Baker, and turned into the tract where his parents lived. Their old home in Costa Mesa remained a point of contention between them, but then, points of contention formed the whole foundation of their relationship. He'd tried to move them to an upscale neighborhood. They'd refused to budge from their place with its short walk to the Asian market.

As he pulled to the curb, he saw the strange car that stood in their driveway. Shit. She'd done it again. Who was it this time? One more uncomfortable evening with his mother's latest pick for his wife. One more set of disappointed parents when he respectfully declined to marry their dutiful daughter.

He stared at the red front door. He could just drive away. Live his life. Forget he had a family. His cheeks puffed as he let out a long stream of breath. That was going to happen when sushi flew. He was Japanese. Plus he had a special debt that could never be paid. Filial fucking piety ran in his veins. The beat of his heart said, "Yes, Mother." To everything, that was, except her marriage plans. He'd wrung out the Japanese dictionary to find every variation on the word *douseiaisha* he could find, but whether he tried *gei, homo, barazoku* or even *okama*—which pretty much defined him as a drag queen—she refused to get it.

One more fucking charade. He shoved open the car door and got out before he could change his mind and go drown his sorrows at the club. On the porch he knocked respectfully and waited for someone to answer. So different from his white friends who would have simply pushed open the door and yelled, "Hey Mom, I'm home."

His father did the opening. "Good evening, Kenji."

"Good evening, Father. Who does she have lined up this time?"

His father simply shrugged.

Ken removed his shoes in the small entry. His mother's voice carried from the next room along with a couple of male voices he didn't know, but no other women. Probably some shy, delicate, Japanese flower just imported from the old country.

He took a deep breath and walked into the living room. His mother sat in her favorite high-backed chair—Queen of Fucking Everything—next to the stiff couch where three people were lined up. An older woman in a kimono, a small man with graying hair, and a young guy who anybody with eyes would have to call handsome. Well, at least he was wrong about the matchmaking. *Thank God.*

His mother beamed like a mama lion who'd killed an antelope for her young. "Kenji, may I present Mr. and Mrs. Okuwa and their son, Mikio."

Ken bowed. Both of the parents rose and bowed back. The son got up and stuck out his hand. "Hi, I'm Mickey." He was short like his father, and compact, with nice shoulders and, from what Ken could see, a great ass. He was probably in his early twenties. Maybe his mother wanted Ken to recommend a medical school or something.

Ken smiled. "Ken. Glad to meet you."

His mother waved to the chair that stood conspicuously vacant. He sat. She rose and offered him a tray of beef-and-scallion rolls. He grabbed a small plate from the table and took a roll. "Thank you, Mama."

"I know you never take time to eat. You're too skinny."

Actually, she was right on the money. He'd skipped lunch and was starving. He took a bite and the familiar flavors of miso and sake burst in his mouth.

She turned to Mickey. "You must respect your body, don't you agree, Mikio? Kenji works too hard keeping others healthy and doesn't think enough of his own health."

Mickey grinned. "Oh, I don't know. That body doesn't look unhealthy to me."

Ken glanced up in time to catch the guy's raunchy grin. A fucking flame of knowledge seared Ken's brain. Son of a conniving bitch. Mikio Okuwa was gay. Ken's mother had changed her game. What the hell was he going to do now?

The cook his mom had hired for the evening—definitely trying to impress—called them all to dinner. He sat at the table and tried to smile and be polite but, hell, he felt rocked—and not in a good way. *Come on. You say you want your mother to accept that you're gay. She just did. Be happy.* But why hadn't it crossed his mind that his mother would turn her wedding efforts to male prospects? Because they couldn't produce grandchildren, that's why.

His mother accepted some Kobe beef from the cook. "So, Mikio, what do you do for a living?"

The guy paused in the process of heaping food on his plate. "I'm in law school." He took a bite and chewed, but his eyes took on a gleam. "But what I really love is music. I'm the lead singer in a rock band. We're posting a lot on YouTube. Only a matter of time before something goes viral and we're on our way."

Ken's father said, "Band? This seems like an unreliable way to make a living."

"Yeah, but we're prepared to starve if we have to to make it to the top. I might try for *The Voice*, you know?" He shoveled in a mouthful that seemed determined to independently stave off starvation.

"A television show does not appear to be an effective career strategy."

"You've gotta take what's available in this country, Mr. Tanaka. I'm a great marketer. We're all over social media."

His father frowned more deeply, and his mother leaped in. "Kenji is a cardiologist, did you know? Youngest to graduate from his medical school."

"A broken heart guy, huh?" He grinned.

Mrs. Okuwa said softly, "You must be very proud."

"Yes, I am." His mother looked at his father. "We are."

"And where is your first son?"

For an instant, everyone froze. His mother caught her breath, his father quit moving, and his own fingers tightened on the tea cup.

Mickey looked up from his enjoyment of the beef. "You got a brother, man?"

His mother's head bowed. "Our firstborn son died very young. He had a weak heart and was killed by a doctor during a surgical mishap."

Mrs. Okuwa's face paled a little. "Forgive me. Kenji's name—"

"It is most understandable. You are forgiven."

Mickey waved a fork. "I don't get it."

Ken gazed at him. "Kenji means second son. You don't speak Japanese?"

"As little as possible." He laughed. "Oh, so that's why you became a heart guy, right?"

Ken swallowed more tea.

His mother glanced at Mickey with a little frown. "Kenji was far too young to help his brother. He is a brilliant physician and could have chosen any specialty."

After endless compliments and small talk, the meal that lasted forever finally ended and the Okuwas got up to leave. They all walked to the door. His mother stepped beside him and spoke under her breath. "Walk out with them, Kenji."

Sigh. Ken smiled. "I'll see you to your car."

Out in the cool evening air, he held the car door for Mrs. Okuwa and bowed to Mr. Okuwa. Mickey held back. When his parents had their doors closed, he sidled up to Ken. "Hey, man, time for my good-night kiss?" He winked.

Ken smiled. "I never kiss on a first date."

Mickey lowered his voice. "But I'll bet you fuck on first dates, don't you, gorgeous? Why don't you call me and I'll ream that pretty ass of yours later?"

"I don't bottom for kids." He said it with a smile but let the edge in his voice show.

"I can make it worth your while. Hell, our parents want us to get together. We might as well make the best of it."

"Perhaps." *In another lifetime.*

"Give me your phone."

47

I seem to be doing this a lot today. He handed Mickey his phone and the guy input digits. Funny how the man who had put his number in earlier seemed much more like someone Ken would want to call.

Mickey handed back the phone. "So call me, baby." He opened the back door of his parents' car, gave Ken a long lingering view of his ass in tight slacks, finally closed the door, and they pulled off.

Ken wanted to run. He didn't. With determination he mounted the front steps and entered the house. His mother gave him a huge cat-eating-canary smile.

You can do this. He walked to her chair and bowed. *"Okaa-san,* I am deeply honored and appreciative that you have accepted that I am gay. I know this was a difficult step for you, and it moves my heart that you have shown me such consideration. But I must ask you not to try to pick a partner for me. I'm grown and able to do this for myself."

She shook her head. "It is not your job to find the right man, Kenji. It is mine. You are too busy with man's work. I must find you a suitable partner."

"I must point out to you respectfully that I like men, not boys. This young person you brought here tonight is a boy."

His father cleared his throat loudly at that, but his mother ignored him. "Having a younger partner is appropriate for an established, professional man such as you. This boy has much to learn, and you will teach him. Meanwhile, his youth and vigor will keep you youthful."

"Mother, I'm only twenty-eight."

"Yes, but you have so much responsibility with these sick people, you will be old before your time. You must enjoy this boy's spunk."

He coughed to cover his laugh.

"You must promise me you will give Mikio a chance. His family is old and influential in the community. A match between you would be most honorable."

"Mother, please."

"Promise me."

Oh, what the hell. At least it was a male. "I promise."

It took another half hour to get himself home to his condo in Crystal Cove, and he closed the door behind him like the solid core could shut out his mother's expectations. He stared around the wide living room with its curved tangerine sectional and print chairs. He

48

usually loved coming home. It was one of the few places he ever felt like he could be himself, but tonight not so much. It almost felt too neat. Too perfect.

He shook his head and walked into the gleaming kitchen with its granite counters and stainless appliances. It took two glasses of water to get his throat from feeling stopped up with all the things he'd wanted to say and hadn't. On his third glass, he leaned back against the counter and sipped. What a phony he was. He pretended to be so free, so self-actualized. He couldn't even say no to his mother. Of course, Attila the Hun might have quaked at the prospect of crossing her.

He sighed and walked back into the living room with his water, flopped on the couch, and turned on the sixty-inch TV that established his credentials as a full-on "guy." Now he faced the prospect of calling Mickey Okuwa and making some kind of date. *Giving him a chance.* He made mental quotation marks around the words. The guy was cute as hell, but still Ken didn't look forward to it. *What do you look forward to, old man? Are you getting tired of the scene? Too much sex?* He half smiled. *Nah.*

He flipped through his recorded shows and settled on the new episode of *Project Runway.* Funny. One thing he did look forward to was lunch with Jim Carney and, considering he had to endure Gene Willings to have that lunch, "looking forward to" was saying something big.

He flipped on his side and settled in to watch cat fights and fashion. His anticipation of lunch the next day with a straight, blue-collar worker was not going to get examined.

WHOA. CRAPPY.

Jim sat on the edge of his bed and ran a hand through his sweat-drenched hair. *Drying out, do ya think? Jesus.* Just how much had he been drinking the last few months? One hair from one dog right now would get him feeling right and able to work. He massaged his aching neck.

Not going to happen.

The comic book lying on the floor caught his eye. Of course, it didn't help that he'd wacked off three times to his favorite yaoi comic before he crashed. Probably used up all his energy.

Get up.

Ten minutes of wasting hot water and he felt like he could face a glass of tomato juice—if he had any. Out the window, he could make out the edge of the building next door, so it must be nearing sunrise. *A few more minutes to recover.*

He reached for his faded, dirty jeans and stopped. *Lunch.* That made his heart race, and he fell back on the edge of the bed. *Do not be thinking about your heart or that doctor. Just consider it lunch with some architect who might save your ass. Plus it may not even happen.*

Still, he dragged himself up and got a fresh pair of jeans from the closet and pulled on a clean long-sleeved T-shirt that just happened to be the same color as his green eyes. Quietly, he opened the door into the short hall. Like some kind of symphony, the smell of frying bacon drifted on the air. Obviously bacon went with everything, because his stomach didn't even rebel. It actually growled. In three steps he walked into the living-dining-kitchen room. "Are you seriously cooking bacon at five a.m.?"

Ian, fully dressed in his own jeans and T-shirt, flashed a grin over his shoulder as he flipped bacon in a pan. "Can't think of a better time."

"Jesus, that smells good."

"Come and get it." He transferred some to a plate that he put on the small dinette table. "Want some juice to go with it?"

"Hell, yeah." He sat and picked up a perfect, crisp slice of bacon and took a big bite. *Oh man.* That sharp/sweet, pungent, oily, crunchy experience that every human practically loved from birth. "I'd ask why you aren't sleeping in, except I'd never want to talk you out of making bacon."

"I figured I'd go to work with you in case you need someone to look at that suite layout."

"Hey, thanks, but I'm not sure it's even going to happen."

"Don't worry. I won't get in the way. I have to be at work at noon, so I'll take my own car. Might as well use it while I can." He sounded unconvincingly cheerful.

"Did you get notice that he's going to take the car away?"

Ian shrugged. "Kind of. I talked to Mom. She said he's planning to stop making the payments, so I guess I better drop it off at his place so they don't come repossess it from me."

"The bastard. I'll drive you tonight if you want."

Ian just nodded and breathed.

"How's Mom?"

"She's better than he is, I guess, but she still acts like I brought this on myself by making crappy choices."

"Yeah, sure. It's good ignorance isn't fucking hereditary." The last bite of bacon didn't taste quite as good. "I'll brush my teeth and we'll go to work."

Ian nodded, but a lot of weight seemed to shift around on his skinny shoulders. "I'll clean up."

Jim put a hand on Ian's back, and the boy stopped but didn't turn. Jim stared at those tense shoulders. "You don't have to work hard to impress me. I'm your brother. I love you just because."

Ian's head dropped forward and kind of bobbed. "Thanks, man." The words barely got out.

"Will Anderson be okay alone?"

"Yeah. He's settled in fine. Owns the place."

Jim patted a couple more times, then gave Ian a moment while Jim brushed his teeth. A half hour later, they walked into the building carrying coffee they got at the drive-though. Ian perked up instantly and started examining the plans Jim had from Billy, along with the work that had already been done.

Charlie walked in a few minutes later and Jim introduced Ian, followed shortly after by Raoul.

Jim looked around the wide-open suite. "I let the demo guys go. I figured the three of us can easily finish what's here, and then we'll see if the owner has new instructions. If not, we can start building according to these plans."

Ian nodded. "It's a good, practical layout. Not totally inspired, but workable, I think."

Jim grinned. "I neglected to mention that my brother is the next Frank Lloyd Right-on-the-Money."

Charlie smiled. "So what would you do with this suite, Ian?"

The kid was clearly into it. "It depends on what the client specified, but based on these plans—" He grabbed a piece of extra paper from the stack of plans and sketched. "—I'd open this out so the private offices didn't block all the light from the reception area. Maybe use some glass here."

Jim nodded. "Glass is expensive."

"Yeah, but you'd avoid long institutional-looking hallways this way, so it might be worth it."

Raoul shrugged. "Looks great to me, man. Where'd you learn this shit?"

Finally, Ian looked self-conscious. "I kind of picked it up. Did an apprenticeship in an architectural firm in high school. I read a lot."

Raoul nudged Jim. "Good to see some brains showed up in your family, Carney."

Ian frowned. "Jim's smarter than me. He always had to take care of himself. He's plenty brainy—"

Raoul clapped his shoulder. "Hey, I'm just joking. I know my man here is bright as hell. No offense."

Ian's cheeks turned pink. "Sure. That's good. I figured."

Jim smiled. It was kind that his brother leaped to his defense, but maybe the kid protested too much?

They swung into work, and Ian pitched in. By a little after nine, the trash had been removed and the suite was an empty shell waiting for building to begin. Jim stared at the drawings. Like some cue in a bad movie, the plastic flew back and in swept Constance Murch. She saw Jim and made a beeline. "Oh good, you're here. I need to speak to you right away."

Jim caught his breath. "Yes, ma'am."

She slipped her arm through his, pressing one perky boob against his bicep. "Ma'am? Please, you don't want to make me feel old."

He smiled down at her. "No, ma'—uh, no Mrs. Murch, because that wouldn't be true."

"It's *Ms.* Murch. And you should call me Constance."

"Yes, ma—yes, Constance."

She snuggled her arm more solidly against his body. "So we have moved tenants. The company that was going into this suite has requested the new vacancy on the eighth floor. We have a new tenant for this space."

Small heart attack. Do not show it. "Okay, good. We're ready to do whatever your tenants need."

"Excellent. So come with me to the eighth floor and look at the space so you can determine if the plan for this suite will work there as well."

Would he be able to tell?

She stared past Jim and raised an eyebrow. "Oh, is this a new plan?" She let go of his arm and stepped over to where Ian had left his drawing.

Jim glanced over her back at his brother, who was lurking at the rear of the suite pretending to be working. Ian gave him wide eyes. "That's just a concept one of my, uh, consultants doodled for us. He felt this space could be—" What had Ian said? "—more open, and the light from the windows could penetrate into the interior of the suite." He swallowed hard.

"Very interesting. Quite original. Not just the same old same old. How much more would it cost to build this?"

"Uh, we haven't priced it out, ma—uh, Constance, because it's just a doodle, as I said."

"Do a breakdown and give me a more formal plan. I suspect one or the other of the tenants will buy this—and extend their lease term to do it." She smiled widely. "Very good thinking, Jim." She took hold of his arm again. "So shall we go to the eighth floor?"

"Uh, is there a chance I could get a key and slip in later when I can take my consultant? He'd know better if his idea will work in the space." He held his breath.

Her eyebrows drew together slightly, then smoothed. "All right, it's suite 807. Go as soon as you can. And in exchange, you must agree to have lunch with me to discuss other potential assignments."

This was business, right? Still, did he really want to go to lunch with the building owner? What if he blew it for Billy? Shit, based on the smile he was getting from Constance Murch, if he said no, he'd blow the whole fucking deal anyway. "That sounds wonderful."

"Today?" She wet her lips.

"Uh, I'm meeting with the architect today. About your project, actually."

"Tomorrow, then."

"Okay, tomorrow."

She handed him a key. "Check the suite soon. I'll be back to pick up the key before lunch. I need to let in the new tenant."

"Okay." He felt light-headed.

CHAPTER SEVEN

KEN SAT in the chair beside the planter in the lobby and stared at the plastic sheeting covering the suite where Jim Carney said he was working. He glanced at his watch. How weird was it that he was here early? He of the "keep 'em panting" philosophy. Of course, this was just business. *Umm, what kind of business would that be exactly? What the hell do I care about architecture and tenant improvements?* He breathed. *I'm keeping my patient alive by reducing his stress. There, that's an excellent story.*

The elevator door opened and the man himself stepped off in all his blue-collar glory—tall, though not as tall as Ken, shaggy hair that looked like someone had streaked his light brown with blond, brilliant green eyes that crinkled when he laughed, and hard muscles everywhere from all that delicious hammer swinging. Jim was walking next to a very pretty young guy.

Jim looked over at him and stopped in his tracks. His Adam's apple bounced, and then he painted on a smile and walked toward Ken with the cute guy beside him. "Hey, hi. Hope I'm not late." He stuck out his hand and Ken took it, feeling the calluses all the way down his own arm. Ken eyed the boy. Jim held on a second too long, then pulled his hand back. "Dr. Tanaka, this is my kid brother, Ian."

Brother. Feeling relieved was so damned stupid he wanted to kick his own ass, but he felt the smile spreading. "Hi, Ian. I'm Ken."

Jim nodded. "Uh, yeah, Ken."

Ken really looked at Ian. "I see the family resemblance." His light-haired prettiness strongly resembled Jim, minus a broken nose, work-hardened body, and general air of—what?—ennui, disappointment. No, actually Jim's blanket of world-weariness covered a spring flower of hope. That was one of the things Ken liked about him. One of them. "Can you join us for lunch, Ian?"

The kid shook his head. "Wish I could, but I've got a bunch of Mexican food to clear off plates." He grinned. "It's my job. Take good care of my brother, though."

Jim held up a hand. "I've gotta do a quick check-in with my guys, then I'm all yours." He stopped, blushed, looked at his shoes. "I'll be ready in a second." He turned and ran toward the plastic entrance to the suite.

Ken watched the muscles in Jim's powerful back flex as he moved away. *Damn. Beautiful.*

"You like my brother."

It wasn't a question. "I don't know him at all. We just met yesterday. But yes, he seems like a good guy."

"You know he's straight, right?"

Ken frowned. "I assumed so."

"But maybe you wish he wasn't?"

Ken turned and looked Ian in the eye. "Do you imagine I have to sit around pining over straight men I can't have?"

That obviously threw the cocky kid off a bit. He glanced away and his cheeks turned pink. "No."

"So assume my intentions are honorable. I'm helping your brother find an architect. End of story."

"Okay. I believe you."

If only I did.

"Thanks for helping him out. Maybe I'll see you again."

Ken nodded. "I'll look forward to it." He shook Ian's offered hand, then watched him sprint to the lobby doors and exit into the sunny afternoon.

Voices floated over from the entrance to the suite, and Ken looked up as Jim walked back through the plastic sheeting with an attractive woman clinging to his arm. The building owner, Constance Murch. Jim stopped and smiled down at her while she batted her eyelashes. Ken could hear her say something about "looking forward to tomorrow."

Suddenly his head felt hot and light. He stared at Constance. At reality. Just like Ian said. Had he gotten an impression that Jim Carney was somehow available? Interested? Who the fuck was he kidding? He hadn't been lying when he said all the good men were straight.

Constance touched Jim's cheek proprietarily, then turned on her spike heel and walked to the elevator.

Jim hurried toward Ken with a smile. A smile that lingered from the woman's sensual touch.

JIM GRINNED at Ken. Hard not to smile when you looked at something that beautiful. Weird that he thought of a guy that way, but the resemblance to the yaoi character messed with his head. "Sorry to keep you waiting. I had to return a key to the building owner."

"Yes, she certainly has an air of ownership." Ken raised a brow, and his pretty voice had an edge. Was he upset about waiting?

"Uh, is your architect going to meet us?"

"Yes, more's the pity. But hopefully he'll solve your problem."

"Sorry to put you out."

Tanaka waved a graceful hand. "It's nothing. Let's get going. We're meeting him at my club. It's just down the street." He took off walking across the lobby, then set a fast pace up the sidewalk. Jim had to scamper to keep up. Maybe this really was putting the doctor out. He'd been so insistent last night.

As they got closer, Jim paused and stared at the discreet granite building tucked back in the trees. *Well, damn.* Tanaka must have realized he was alone, because he slowed and looked back. "Something wrong?"

Jim swallowed. "I, uh, didn't know where we were going for lunch."

"It's the Pacific Crest Club."

"I know."

"Is that a problem?"

He didn't want to say it was only a problem if he saw his fucking father. "No. I just know some people who are members here."

Tanaka nodded. "Yes, one of them is me."

Jim looked down at his jeans and T-shirt. "I'm not really dressed for it."

"It's okay. They've gone casual at lunch."

Pacific Crest was never casual enough for him. "Okay." He'd been looking forward to this lunch. Now, not so much.

Walking past the doorman, Tanaka led them through the quiet low-key lobby to the restaurant Jim remembered from Sunday lunches with his family. The restaurant was all dark wood and pictures of yachts and sailing ships and crap. He'd always thought it tried awfully hard to be some kind of old-world club and missed—but his father loved the place. The host in the restaurant smiled and greeted Ken by name, barely frowned at Jim, and walked them back to a table where a man was sitting. Pretty as a picture in a men's fashion magazine, just like in the parking lot at the wedding. Jim controlled his grin at the memory.

The guy stood and stared at Ken. "Damn, even in one day, I forget how beautiful you are."

Ken shook his head. "You should have your memory checked, darling." The two men kissed the air next to each other's cheeks—very European. Ken stepped back. "Gene, this is Jim Carney, the guy I told you about. Jim, Gene Willings."

Gene extended his hand but looked at Jim with slightly narrowed eyes. "So you two are—friends?"

Willings's hand felt like silk next to his rough paw. Jim shook quickly. No use scraping the guy's skin. "Uh, we kind of just met."

Ken sat across from Gene and beside Jim. "I told you, Jim is my patient."

"Seems odd that Ken would go to so much effort for someone he barely knows."

Ken's arched brows drew together. "I'm Mother fucking Teresa." He looked around the intimate room. "How do I get some iced tea?"

"You ought to know, darling. It's your club."

A waiter must have seen the frown and whisked over to fill Ken's glass with tea and ice. Jim's as well. Ken gave him that brilliant smile. He seemed to reserve his annoyance for Gene—and Jim. He sipped. "I'm sure it will be your club soon."

Jim stared around at the crisp white tablecloths and crisp white guests. "This club is pretty conservative."

"Are you surprised they'd accept me as a member?"

He looked at Ken. "No, I'm surprised you'd want to be a member."

Ken held his eyes for a moment, then smiled. "Thank you. Actually, there are a lot of physicians in this club. When I started my practice, becoming a member here was a sure way to get referrals and support. I'll admit it was calculating, but I put on my best suit and my best smile and worked to become one of their token minorities. They had no idea just how much of a minority I am." He laughed. "I'm even on the board. A fox in the hen house." He smiled. "Or more appropriately, the other way around."

Jim had to smile. Wonder if his father knew he had a gay board member?

"I've even sneaked in a few, shall we say, like-minded members." He grinned. "The membership committee is considering Gene right now."

Jim turned to Gene. "So you're an architect."

"Yes. With a license and everything."

Tanaka hadn't lied about the pain in the ass part. "I don't know if you have any desire to help with a tenant improvement project, but I need an architect to draw up some plans—fast." He pulled Ian's sketch out of his pocket. "This is the rough idea of what we want."

Gene looked at the sketch. "This isn't much to go on, and it's not an easy plan to draw."

Hell, this guy was too much trouble. "So you can't do it? No problem." He pulled the drawing back, folded it, and reached for his pocket.

Willings grabbed his hand. "I didn't say that. Actually, it's a clever idea. But I'd have to send someone from my staff to see and measure the space." He sat back. "I don't do the smaller projects personally."

Jim shrugged. "I don't care as long as you sign the drawings. I know how to build it."

"You're pretty sure of yourself."

Far from it, but he'd never tell this asshole. "It's what I do."

Willings stared at him like he was guessing his weight. "All right, I'll do it. I told Ken I would and I will."

"Don't bother if it's too much trouble. I wouldn't want Ken to be obligated to you on my account." He glanced at Ken, who had a slightly raised eyebrow and a half smile.

The waiter took advantage of a slight break in the action to collect their orders. For the next hour, Jim managed a few bites of a Reuben sandwich and wished he could get back to the job site. Ken and Gene alternately snarked at each other and gazed into each other's eyes, which whiplashed Jim between jealousy and embarrassment, both of which were stupid. Jesus, they should fight or fuck and get it over with.

Ken asked for the check, and Jim tried to wrap it up with Willings. "When can you have this guy from your office come to the suites?"

"When do you want him?"

"Later today?"

"I suppose I can arrange that."

"Good. He can meet me in the suite off the lobby that's being renovated. Tell him—"

"Mr. Carney? James? Is that you?"

Jim looked up at an older Hispanic man dressed in the dark pants and white shirt of a waiter. *Son of a bitch.* "Hi, Manuel. How are you?"

"I'm well. I kept staring since you came in and thought it must be you."

Jim ran a hand over the back of his neck. "Yeah, well, I've changed some."

Manuel smiled. "The nose is different, but I'd still know you anywhere."

Jim grinned. "I say it was a bar fight, but I actually took a hammer in the face. It didn't heal well. Manuel, this is Ken and Gene. My friend, Manuel."

Manuel nodded. "Of course, I know Dr. Tanaka and Mr. Willings. I hope your meal was satisfactory."

Ken smiled. "Excellent. Thank you, Manuel."

"Good to see you again, Jim. Don't be so long next time."

Jim shook Manuel's hand. "Great to see you. Say hi to your wife and boys."

"I will, thank you."

As Manuel walked back to his post on the other side of the dining room, Gene said, "So how do you happen to be so palsy-walsy with a waiter from the Pacific Crest club? Is he a neighbor or something?"

Jim leveled his gaze at Gene. The guy's words were benign, but his tone reeked of condescension. *Sick of you, buddy.* "No, he used to wait on us when I'd come here with my father."

"Oh, who's your father?" Ken's voice had a growing sense of realization.

Jim pushed back his chair and stood. "Thanks so much for lunch. I'll look for your guy in about an hour. I need to get back to my work site." He turned and looked at Ken. *What the hell.* "My father's Dr. James Carney, the cardiovascular surgeon." He flicked his eyes to Willings. "You know, the chairman emeritus of the Pacific Crest Club. See you later."

WELL, DAYUM. Ken watched those broad shoulders and tight ass move away from him across the dining room until Jim disappeared.

Gene leaned forward. "No wonder you're doing him a favor."

Ken looked back at Gene. "I didn't know anything about his family until this minute."

"His name *is* Jim Carney."

"I didn't put it together. Would you?"

"No. Who'd have thought Dr. Carney would have this hammer jockey for a son?"

"He's a nice guy."

"Obviously you think so." Gene sat back, and his pretty lips pursed.

"Give it a rest. He's straight, as you can pretty obviously tell."

"I suppose. But a mouth is a mouth in the dark, love."

He wished. Ken finished paying the check, kissed the air next to Gene's smooth cheek, and headed back to the office. Weirdly, Jim Carney being the son of Dr. Carney made him less appealing. There had to be some kind of story there. But being less appealing was good, since the guy was way too attractive. When he'd taken on pissy Gene, Ken thought he'd spew iced tea all over the table. When he'd said, "I know how to build it," Ken had to take a deep breath to control his overactive cock. *What is it about the guy?*

Like some harbinger, his phone buzzed. He looked. *Well, hell.* "*Konnichiwa*, Okaa-san."

"Are you well, my son?"

"Yes, ma'am. I just had lunch and am going back to work."

"I'm pleased to hear you have eaten. Did you eat well?"

No way he'd say that between lusting after Jim and wanting to kill Gene, he'd barely gotten half a salad down. "Yes, I went to my club."

"That is very good. And you have called Mikio for a date?"

Blindsided. "Uh, no. I've been very busy."

"This is important, Kenji. You must do this for me."

For me. There were the magic words that ripped him down to a five-year-old desperate for his mother to love him as much as she loved his brother. "Yes, Mother. I'll call him soon."

"Today."

He sighed quietly. "Today."

"Thank you, my son. You've made me very happy. Have a good day."

"Thank you, Okaa-san." He clicked off the phone. He knew why he liked Jim Carney so much. Shit, the guy had all the guts Ken didn't.

He reached for his cell phone and scrolled until he reached Okuwa. Maybe if he just asked Mickey to lunch, he'd satisfy his promise and get the kid out of his life. Besides, he needed something to help him stop thinking about Jim Carney.

JIM HAD been working for an hour, wiring new electrical in preparation for the redesign, when the plastic pushed away and Gene Willings himself walked into the suite with a cute young guy beside him. Jim pretty much wanted to smack him upside the head after the performance at lunch. *Be nice. He can save your ass.* "Hi. Thanks for coming."

Gene assumed a serious face. "You said it was important so I wanted to check it out." He motioned idly to the guy. "This is Rico. He'll be measuring."

Jim stuck out a hand, and Rico smiled and shook it. The guy had dark brown hair and wide eyes in a really attractive face. Jim pointed to the suite. "We have measurements on this place we can give you." He walked over to the plans Billy had left him. Rico followed him and looked at the drawings. Jim pulled the sketch from his pocket. "The owner wants something more like this approach built in the eighth-floor suite."

Rico nodded. "I like this. It's more original."

"Uh, yeah, a consultant of mine came up with it, but he's not licensed—" Jim glanced at Willings. "—in this state so he can't do the drawings."

"I can use this as a starting place and come up with some plans."

"That would be great. You'll need to measure that space. It's similar to this one, but not identical."

Willings nodded. "Ah well, I'll leave you to it, then."

Jim turned to him. "I really appreciate you helping with this."

He smiled. "You can always feel free to mention my help to your father. I'm trying to get into the Pacific Crest Club."

Knew that was coming. "Sorry. My father and I are estranged. I never see him, and a good word from me would be bad for you."

The smile snapped off Willings's face. "I see."

"If you want to change your mind about helping me out, just say so."

"No. I told Ken I'd help." His eyes narrowed. "And he and I are such good friends, I'd never want to disappoint him."

"I appreciate that."

Willings turned on his heel and left.

"Sorry." Rico smiled up at Jim. Must be tough on Rico working for Willings. The guy pointed at the drawing. "Don't worry, I'll do a good job for you. This approach is really my aesthetic, so I'll enjoy putting my spin on it."

This guy he liked. Jim looked at his watch. "As long as I get some plans fast with an architect's signature on them, I'm good. Come on. I'll show you the suite. I may have to leave you, since I have this medical test I have to take for insurance."

"No problems." Rico grinned a bright, toothy smile complete with dimples. "I won't steal the silverware."

After forty-five minutes, during which he felt like he'd lucked out getting Rico to do his plans, Jim left the guy measuring and hopped the elevator down to the suite number Dr. Tanaka's office had given him. Man, who'd have thought he had something wrong with his heart? His own father hadn't found it. Or maybe he just never told him.

After a short wait, a woman in a lab coat came out. "Hi, I'm Marsha. I'll be doing your exam."

"Okay." She looked like a nice lady. Not too scary.

She led him into a room with a lot of equipment. He pulled off his shirt as requested, and she laid him on the table and hooked him up to some more electrodes. "They already did an EKG on me."

"Yes, we do one to correlate with the echocardiogram. Nothing to worry about.'

He wasn't worried—exactly. "I feel like Frankenman."

"No, you're the monster and I'm Dr. Frankenstein, right?" She smiled. Then, as advertised, she pumped some cold, sticky stuff on his chest and pulled out a lightsaber and started running it around in the gel. *Woosh, woosh, woosh.* The sound of his heart echoed through the room. He chuckled, and she smiled.

A voice came through the partly open door. "It sounds like you're having altogether too much fun in here."

Oh man, he'd know that tenor anywhere. He glanced over at Ken standing by the door to the room, looking very doctory in his white lab coat with his floppy hair tamed back on his head. "Hi, Doc."

"Hey, Jim. I don't mean to intrude, Marsha. Do you mind if I observe?"

She flashed exactly the kind of sappy smile that question was designed to get. "Of course not, Dr. Tanaka. Please do."

With a gentle shove, she pushed Jim onto his left side, which meant he faced Ken directly. The *woosh*ing sound got stronger.

Marsha said, "Don't worry. It's normal for the heart rate to increase in this position." Did that mean on his side or staring at Ken Tanaka? Jesus, why did the man have to look like a fantasy? Those lips couldn't be real. Marsha pressed the wand thing harder against his sternum. He pulled back a little. "Sorry, I know it can be uncomfortable. I need extra pressure to be sure I get accurate results."

Ken stepped closer. "Can I take over for a minute?"

"Of course."

The wand was removed from Jim's chest as Ken stepped out of his field of vision. Then a gloved hand that still managed to be very silky took hold of Jim's shoulder, and the wand was reapplied to the area around his heart. *Thump, woosh, thump, woosh.*

The pressure of the wand was just as hard as the woman had done it, maybe harder, but that gentle hand on his shoulder somehow made it less—and more. *Thump, thump, woosh, woosh.* Ken leaned over and murmured, "You're doing fine." *Fine. Oh yes, fine.*

The wand traveled across his skin, both warm and cool, but Jim's whole brain focused on the hand still holding his shoulder with those long fingers stretched out just an inch from his right nipple. Jesus, was his heart speeding up?

He wasn't sure about his heart, but his cock sure as hell wanted to be examined. He shifted his hips. Ken's hand grasped more firmly. "Just a bit more now."

More? Good Lord, his wood was turning into a log and he didn't have anything to hide it. His kingdom for a paper dress!

The wand traveled over his throat, and the hand slipped lower. *Lower. Just a little more—shit.* He softly gasped as Ken's fingers found his nub. Did Ken notice? Hopefully he didn't hear, what with all the *thump*ing and *woosh*ing.

Why the hell am I reacting to a guy? Pretty sure Dr. Haselbaum could have sucked my dick and I wouldn't have felt horny.

But Ken's fingers didn't slip back. Instead, the wand kept exploring, and the finger of Ken's left hand moved just a little across Jim's most sensitive spot—well, at least the most sensitive on his chest. It moved a little more. Jim held his breath. That finger gently rotated on his hard-as-a-diamond nipple. Round and round, every circle sending shots of electricity to Jim's cock until the thing throbbed like a wild animal. It couldn't be an accident, could it? Was Ken doing this on purpose? Maybe he didn't realize what his hand was up to? Oh God, why did Jim want to flip on his back and guide Ken's hand to his cock? One more circle and he'd come. How the hell was he going to explain that? "Uh, I think—"

"Just a little more."

Oh hell, he knew what kind of more he wanted.

Thump, woosh, thump, thump, thump.

"Doctor, I think we have enough." Marsha sounded neutral. Did she notice? Crap, who wouldn't notice the anaconda trying to escape his jeans?

"Yes." Ken's thumb slid across Jim's nipple one more time, sending Jim's dick into a spasm of need.

The wand came off his chest, the *thump*ing stopped, and all Jim could hear was his own panting.

"You can put your shirt on, Jim. Here's something to wipe off the gel." Marsha handed him a bundle of not very soft paper. Not soft like Ken Tanaka's hand. Jim grabbed the paper and stuck it in front of his crotch as he rolled onto his back and sat up fast before the leaning tower of Carney could take over the room. He heard Ken say, "Thank you for letting me participate. You'll have the results back to me tomorrow?"

"Yes, Doctor."

The door clicked closed.

Gone. The source of his torture just up and left. Jim finished wiping off the gel. It made him think of other sticky substances he could find on his chest. *Jesus, one-track mind.* As he slipped on his shirt, Marsha said, "You're really lucky. The doctor never does the echoes himself."

"Yeah?" Why the fuck did that make him smile?

CHAPTER EIGHT

FIFTEEN MINUTES later Jim walked out of the building to his truck, having been assured by Marsha that she'd have the report to the doctor tomorrow. The doctor. That meant he had to see Ken Tanaka again. How awkward would that be?

He headed down the freeway south toward home. Maybe Ken didn't even know he did it. Maybe his fingers accidentally found the nipples of guys because it just seemed normal or something? *Yeah, right.* Obviously Ken knew what he was doing, and he also knew he had to see Jim the next day, so he must not think it was going to be awkward. But maybe that wasn't the right question. Maybe he should be asking, why had his dick taken off like a skyrocket because some guy flicked his tit? If he hadn't gasped when Ken touched him, would the doc have gone so far? And now that he had done what he did, what did that imply to Ken? Did he think Jim was gay and ready to fuck him? Hell, he needed advice. Fortunately he knew right where to get it.

He pulled into the parking lot of his apartment. How would he go about this? No idea. Hopefully, Ian would give him an opening. When Jim walked into the apartment, Anderson leaped out from under a chair like the mighty half-pound hunter. Jim reached down and picked up the fur ball. Seemed like the critter was staying, so might as well make friends. He held the cat in one hand and scratched under its chin with a finger. "Hey guy, where's your daddy?" Okay, that sounded weird. "Brother?" That made Anderson Jim's sibling. "Where's Ian?" Unfortunately no delicious smells announced Ian's whereabouts.

The door to the tiny second bedroom opened and Ian's wet head popped out. "Hi. I just got home. I smelled too much like tacos to be fit for company, so I took a shower."

"How about we go out to dinner—no tacos. We'll take two cars, and then you can drop your car off at your parents."

Ian stepped out of the room wearing a towel over his ultra-lean body. "They're your parents too."

"Not so you'd notice."

He leaned against the wall. "It's weird. I knew they hated anything gay, but it never crossed my mind they'd throw me out."

"You figured they'd rise to the challenge and support you—like any real parent would, right?"

"Yeah, I guess so."

"They missed a chance to impress the hell out of both of us." He hugged Ian's neck. "Nice to have each other."

"Yeah. I don't know what I'd have done if you didn't let me in."

"A. You're damned resourceful and you would have thought of something. B. No way I'd leave you out in the cold."

Ian gave a slight turn of the lips. "I'm really glad you're my brother."

Well, that made his day. "Likewise."

"How'd the day go? With the architect and all."

"Get dressed and I'll tell you over dinner."

After a mew of protest from Anderson and twenty minutes of dressing, Jim pulled into a glorified coffee shop that he liked because it had good, big burgers at low prices. He searched for a booth in the back and away from the other diners. All the better to talk about sensitive subjects. They ordered and settled back with Cokes. Ken's beautiful face telling him that eating a good diet was sensible floated through his tangled brain. *Fuck that.* He'd shelved drinking. Damned if he'd give up food he liked. *What about your heart?* He sighed.

Ian sipped. "So tell me about the architect."

"He's a royal pain in the ass."

"Oh no. So you're back where you started."

"No. I think the dude wanted to impress Ken Tanaka so bad, he sent somebody from his office to do the drawings, and I think the guy's really good. He loved your sketch."

"Obviously a guy of supreme good taste." Ian grinned. "I think Tanaka has a thing for you."

His heart skipped. "Why do you say that?"

"He looks at you like sushi and yes, the cultural reference is intended." He shrugged. "But he denies it, and I will admit he doesn't look like a guy who needs to chase straight men. I mean, seriously, that dude is gorgeous."

"What do you mean 'denies it'? What the hell did you say?"

"I just kind of asked him if he was interested in you. Said you were straight. He said he knew that and asked if he looked like he had to chase straight guys."

Well, fuck, he felt too many ways about all that to sort through. The fact that disappointed was one of the feelings gave him the willies. He cleared his throat. "So you think he's gorgeous?"

"Don't you?"

"Like you said, I'm straight."

"But you're not blind."

His laugh escaped. "Yeah, I think he's gorgeous." He sipped Coke. Where was that burger? "So how did you know you were gay?"

Ian glanced at Jim, then down at the salt shaker. "I waited for all the feelings and stuff they kept saying I'd have over girls. Never happened. Then one day I realized it had happened, just not for girls."

"How old were you?"

"Going on seventeen. Late bloomer."

"Do, uh, most guys catch on before then?"

"I don't know. I'm only now making a few gay friends. But it seems like it's both earlier and later than me. Some guys don't know until they're, like, forty."

"No shit?"

"Yeah. A lot of guys have had relationships with women. Because they thought they should, right? It never occurred to them that it could be any other way. Then one day they meet a guy and want to fuck him." He looked around and lowered his voice. "It's really tough because they have these whole phony lives to disassemble. Kids and everything." He shook his head. "So I'm an early bloomer by comparison."

"That's really tough." *And really scary.*

The waitress brought the burgers finally, and Jim grabbed a huge bite. "But, mmph—" He shoved lettuce into the corner of his mouth. Who said he never ate vegetables? "Aren't all men kind of attracted to other guys, you know, sometimes? Doesn't make them gay."

Ian frowned. "Don't know about that. I'm not sure most guys really are attracted to dudes. I mean, some of my friends in high school probably never thought another guy was beautiful. They wouldn't even appreciate Ken Tanaka." He laughed. "That takes serious heterosexuality, man."

Shit.

Ian seemed to like this subject. "I mean, do you think Dad ever lusted after a guy? I mean, do you?"

Jim caught his breath. He breathed out but no words followed the air. The question sat there like a turd in the middle of a bowl of cereal.

Ian narrowed his eyes. "Wait, do you?"

"Uh, no, of course not. I mean—"

"Do you think you're gay?"

Jim glanced around frantically. "Shit, no! Why would you say that?"

"You brought it up."

"No. I was just trying to show support for you. That's all."

"Oh, okay. Sorry." He bit his hamburger.

"That's okay." Jim shoved the rest of his burger aside and sipped the last bit of his watery soda. *That sure as fuck did not go well.*

Neither one of them said much while Jim paid the check and they walked out to their respective vehicles. Not awkward, exactly. Or maybe, yeah, awkward. The lightly used Subaru seemed like a great car for Ian. Too bad he was about to graduate to the bus.

Ian took off out of the lot, and Jim followed. His head hurt from Ian's oversharing. Forty-year-old guys who suddenly want to screw dudes. That idea was fucked up. But sweet Jesus, Billy had been twenty-five before he realized he was into guys. Jim ran a hand through his hair. *Why didn't you just tell him about the yaoi? Ask him what he thinks? Because you're scared to know, you giant pussy.*

As they pulled up to the gates of Pelican Hill, Jim shuddered. A drive down memory lane, and not in a good way. He remembered powering out of these gates in the old truck he'd paid for himself, carrying his clothes, toothbrush, and a bucketload of scared in the back. He'd lined up a job as a drywaller, two extra gigs doing painting and assisting an electrician, and a room in a guy's house he could rent. He'd been sixteen but big for his age so he got away with it.

Ian passed through the gate, and Jim rumbled the truck up to the guard. "Good evening, sir. You're following Mr. Carney, correct?"

No, I'm a fucking cat burglar. "Yes."

The guy handed him a yellow card. "Please display this visitor's pass in your front window while you're here."

"Thanks." Because otherwise he might be lynched before sunrise.

He pulled away from the gate and saw Ian waiting ahead of him. Falling in behind, he wound through the wide, quiet streets accented by low lights so they wouldn't interfere with the spectacular view of the entire coastline below. He hadn't thought about this view as a kid. It was the way things were. How times had changed.

Around the next curve, the big Tudor-style mansion came into view. Impressive, pretentious bullshit. Once it had just been home. *Heart beating too fast. Calm down.* Ian navigated the Subaru into the long circular driveway. Jim just pulled to the curb in front. Ian bobbed around in the front seat for a while, then climbed out with a box probably holding all the crap he'd kept in the car. His sweet, pretty face looked so sad, Jim wanted to jump out and hug him. Ian took two steps, stopped, fished in his pocket, and brought out the keys he'd clearly forgotten to leave. He opened the car door again and put them on the dashboard, his shoulders bowed like the keys weighed fifty pounds.

He got partway down the drive toward Jim when the front door of the house opened. *Shit.* Dr. James Carney wasn't a big man. Jim and Ian had inherited their height from their mother, who equaled their father in stature at five ten. But he sure as hell could look formidable. Their father called Ian's name, and the kid stopped but didn't turn around. His father said something else Jim couldn't hear, and Ian cringed. *Fuck that.*

Jim opened the squeaky door of the truck and stepped out. He walked toward his brother, staring at their dad.

James Carney frowned. "I should have known he'd go to you."

Jim cleared the space and took the box from Ian but still looked at his father. "Where the hell did you expect him to go when you threw out your own son, you self-righteous asshole?"

"He's no son of mine."

Ian jerked like he'd been hit, and Jim put an arm around his shoulder. "Even animals don't deny their children."

"Alligators eat their young. Sounds like a good idea to me."

"It would, you fucking reptile."

"You're two of a kind."

"You ought to know. You produced both of us." He turned and guided Ian back to the truck. The kid managed to stay straight-backed and tearless until they'd driven away from the curb and powered down the winding street with zero regard for the speed limit. Then Ian dropped his face in his hands.

Jim gave Ian's knee a squeeze. "Damn that asshole to hell. I'm so sorry this happened to you. But you're smart and talented. You don't need him."

"He—he was always hard on me, but I thought he loved me. How can he say I'm not his son?"

"He's just stuck in his righteousness and can't back down."

Ian nodded and mimicked their father's slightly nasal voice. "'Homosexuals are warping our society. They want special treatment when what they should get is shipped to an island where they can fuck each other and leave the rest of us alone.' He probably wishes I'd go to an island and he wouldn't have to think about me anymore."

"Maybe he'll wake up one day and be sorry he lost both his kids."

"You think so?"

"No, probably not." He gave Ian a one-armed hug across the console. "At least we've got each other, okay?" Jesus, how did he get to be a grown-up so damned fast?

"God, I'm sorry, Jim. Now he hates you too."

"He always hated me. You didn't do anything."

"No, he didn't. He talked about how you made it on your own and that was admirable."

That gave him a weird shiver. "He's perverse. Just trying to make you feel bad."

"I guess. I don't get why he'd say we're two of a kind. All you did was walk out and live your own life. You weren't caught sucking dick."

Jim just kept driving.

COME ON. *Come on.* Jim paced inside the empty, bare suite. Constance Murch would be there any minute for their lunch, and he really wanted to have something to show her. Rico had said he might have roughs. Jim wanted those roughs.

He glanced at his watch. The crew had stayed home since he didn't have an approved plan for them to build to. One precious day wasted. God, he needed to be well underway before Billy got home. If Billy got back from his honeymoon to find the suite not even started, he'd have to think Jim was a fuckup, even if the owner had changed tenants. *Come on.*

The door pushed open, and Rico rushed in carrying a handful of papers.

Jim hurried over to meet him. "Have you got something?"

"Yes. It's rough, but at least you have an approach to show the owner."

Jim opened the folded printouts. Man, it looked authoritative. "This is great. I'll go over it carefully and show it to the client. I really appreciate you making such a huge effort."

"I'll confess to not getting much sleep, but I appreciate the chance. I'm new, and this is the first time Willings has let me do something on my own."

"I know just how that feels."

"I'll get out of here so you can talk to the client, but I would appreciate knowing her reaction."

"You got it. I'll call you."

Rico stuck out his hand. "Thanks."

Jim shook. "No. Thank you."

Rico ran out as fast as he'd come in, and Jim started looking at the plans. He got through the whole set once when the door opened again. "Hello, Jim. Ready for lunch?"

Constance Murch looked different. Not quite so buttoned-down and businesslike, she'd worn a blue dress and higher heels. Her blonde hair hung to her shoulders real smooth. She looked pretty, which was nice, and she'd obviously made an effort, which was scary. "Yes. Thanks." But he'd made an extra effort too, putting on a pair of dark blue khakis and a long-sleeved shirt.

"I thought we'd go to the restaurant here in the building. Their food is good, and I made a reservation."

He smiled. "I'm in your hands."

That got a big grin out of her. "How nice." She nodded at the papers in his hands. "Looks like you have something to show me."

"Yeah. Just rough, but it'll give you an idea of the approach."

"Excellent. I can't wait to see them. Let's go get our table and we can talk." She slipped an arm through his and led the way out the door.

As they walked, her boob pressed against his bicep. It was kind of nice. *See, I really like women.* She didn't let go until they'd walked across the lobby, been shown to a table in the back of the pretty garden restaurant, and were seated. "Do you want iced tea, or shall we have some wine to celebrate our future collaborations?"

What the fuck did that mean? God, wine sounded good, and he didn't even have to pay for it. "Uh, I'm working, so I better stick to tea."

She nodded. "I like a serious man. Good."

Had he passed some sort of test? He glanced at the menu. "I haven't eaten here before. What's good?"

"They have excellent salads."

Yuck.

"And I'm told their burgers are memorable. You impress me as a burger man." She smiled.

He grinned. "Then I impress you correctly." He glanced at the list, and they had every kind of thing you could do to a burger, from avocado to wasabi.

The waiter arrived, and she ordered a salad and he got a burger with cheese plus sweet potato fries, which sounded weird, but Constance assured him were good. When the waiter left, she leaned forward, flashing more than a hint of cleavage. "So show me what you've got."

That could be interpreted a lot of ways. He unfolded the drawings and spread them out on the tablecloth. "Since you liked the consultant's sketch, my architect—" He almost laughed at the possessive. "—kept it in mind while working out these plans. Notice that he's maintained the light and visibility but cut back on some of the expanses of glass, which should keep the costs down." Oh man, he was full of shit, but that's the way he saw it.

She stared at it with a crease between her light eyebrows. "Have you done a cost estimate?"

"No, ma'am. He just finished this rough this morning. But if you like the approach, I'll get right on it." His shirt should be jumping, his heart beat so hard.

73

"You've based both suites on the same concept?"

"We can, or we can simply use the approved plan for the lobby suite and this approach for the eighth floor. It depends on what your tenant wants."

"You like this design better?" Did she like the damned thing? Her deadpan gave nothing away.

He took a breath. "Yes, I do, but it could be a little too, you know, much for some tenants."

She stared at him, the crease still there. He noticed she lined her lips with something darker than her light pink lipstick color. Then her face lit up. "A perfect assessment. I think this approach is brilliant, and since my upstairs tenant is a designer, he'll love it. The new lobby tenant is a physician and quite cheap, I must admit. The existing design will be perfect for him. I think you've created exactly what I need—assuming the price is right for my eighth-floor tenant. Can you cost it out for me tonight?"

Whew. "Yes. With pleasure."

The waiter delivered their food. The warm smell of the burger filled his nose along with the flowery scent of her perfume. It all made him a little light-headed.

She clasped his forearm, and the warmth spread up in waves to his shoulder. "Now let's discuss how we might do things together in the future." Her smile had a lot of layers.

What did she want, exactly? And why should he care? She was a pretty, apparently available, and maybe even rich woman. He was an unattached heterosexual man. He had no problems at all. He smiled back. "I'd like that."

"I've been looking for a good construction company to do work with me."

"TIs?"

"Yes, but also more significant remodels. I'm considering buildings I want to invest in, but I need to know if they can be renovated both attractively and cost-effectively. I was impressed with Mr. Ballew, and I adore the building he remodeled for Chase Phillips, but knowing he has a man like you at the helm—" She tightened her fingers. "—convinces me that we have more to talk about."

Holy jeez, he might have a heart attack right there. If Billy came back and Jim had been able to line up more work—that would be the best. "I'd be very interested in discussing that with you."

"Excellent."

He chewed around his burger. *Think. Don't appear too anxious.* "Let me price out the new concept tonight to be sure we're on the same page. Then I'd be delighted to speak with you further on any additional designs you'd like to pursue." Jesus, he should have recorded that for the Cool Hall of Fame.

"That sounds perfect."

They chatted about her other buildings while they ate. "You've certainly accomplished a lot for a young woman." He smiled.

She looked at him through her lashes. "Thank you for the 'young' part. Sometimes I feel old with all my friends married and having babies."

"You've made good choices. Look what you've accomplished." He meant that. No bullshit.

"Thank you, Jim. My father's a developer. He taught me everything I didn't get in school. I started with one small strip mall and have been growing my investments ever since."

"You're amazing." He meant that too.

"I'm glad you think so."

The waiter came with the bill and he reached for his wallet, although he could barely cover it in cash, and he and Billy had never discussed an expense account. Hell, Billy would hardly have thought Jim would be lunching with the client. She stopped his reach. "No, this is on me. Your firm can pay next time."

His firm. Next time. Jesus, he liked the sound of all of that. "Thanks so much. Do we need to show the existing suite design to your new tenant?"

"I already did. He approved it."

"Then we can get going on the build-out?"

"The sooner the better."

"With your permission, I'll get the crew working this afternoon. I may keep a skeleton crew on a few nights. That will get us caught up."

"Excellent. I like that you're willing to work nights for me." Her eyelashes batted a couple of extra times.

Whoa. Should he flirt back? This was the client, and he was way out of his range of experience. Most of the women he dated were like Peggy. Blue-collar gals whom he met in bars. He swallowed. "Any time."

He got up, helped her out of her chair—which won him another big smile—and they walked toward the front of the restaurant. She took his arm. "Are you going back to the suite? I'll walk with you."

"Sure." The sound of a musical laugh from one of the side booths of the restaurant shimmied up Jim's spine, and his head turned automatically. Against the wall in an intimate booth sat Ken Tanaka across from a really attractive, very young guy. The companion had just thrown back his head and laughed very loudly, and Ken's lilting chuckle joined in. As the guy opened his eyes, he brought both his hands down over Ken's and leaned toward him with a possessive smile.

Jim's heart leaped, hammered, his face went hot, and the rubber sole of his shoe caught against the stone floor and made him stumble.

Constance tightened her grip. "Jim, are you okay?"

"What? Oh yeah."

Ken's eyes rose from the man opposite him and connected with Jim's. Then his gaze traveled to Constance, whose grip on Jim's arm was anything but casual. His gorgeous lips parted slightly. A weird little crease popped in his forehead, then his eyebrow rose and a slow, not happy smile played over his lips. His eyes jerked like he ripped them away, and he started talking to the other guy as if he'd never seen Jim at all.

Constance pulled on his arm, and somehow Jim managed to keep walking.

"What happened?"

"Uh, damned rubber shoes. I just tripped."

"You seemed surprised to see the doctor."

"What?"

"Dr. Tanaka. My tenant."

"Oh yeah. He's signing my insurance forms. He told me I have a heart murmur. It's no big thing, but I was surprised."

"A lot of the people from the building eat here, especially at lunch." Her hands tightened on his arm as they walked out of the restaurant into the bright lobby space. "You're okay, aren't you?"

KNAVE OF BROKEN HEARTS

"Sure. I'm fine." If you didn't count the heart failure he somehow felt like he was having. Weird. He'd seen Tanaka with a bunch of guys, so what the fuck was this reaction about?

"I'd hate to lose you right after I found you." She beamed at him.

Jesus, here was a pretty, smart, accomplished woman practically throwing herself at him, and he was thinking about some guy with yaoi eyes. He should ask Ian about that.

CHAPTER NINE

"DO YOU know that guy?"

Ken looked up from staring at his iced tea. Mickey gazed toward the door, where Ken wished he was also looking. "Excuse me?"

"I asked if you know that guy. The one who about fell on his face when he saw you."

"Yes, he's a patient of mine."

"Man, some hunk. How do you keep your hands off him?"

He just smiled and sipped his tea. The answer to that, of course, was he didn't keep his hands off, and he should be ashamed for violating the patient relationship instead of sitting here pissed that Jim was out with that woman. The building owner. Maybe it was a business lunch, but she was practically plastered to Jim like a barnacle on the hull of a Newport harbor yacht.

"What's his story? Has the guy got heart problems?"

"I can't talk about my patients." He smiled to soften the refusal.

Mickey grinned. "Aw c'mon. Tell me that under that crisp white shirt beats a heart in a muscled chest above a sexy six-pack."

Ken flashed his dimples. "I guess it doesn't hurt to confirm your supposition."

They both laughed, but Ken's stomach tightened.

"I'll bet you'd like to crawl on that table with him and give him a solid poke in his rock-hard ass."

Ken glanced around. "Keep your voice down." Of course the truth was, he'd like to be the pokee. He'd actually dreamed about Jim Carney fucking him—twice.

Mickey shrugged. "I'm impressed you can live through that kind of temptation."

"You did see the woman he was with, right?"

"Hey, straight schmait. Almost any guy would benefit from a gay blow job."

Man, if only that were true.

Mickey pushed his empty plate away. "Say, have we passed the lunch test? Want to move on to a nighttime date?"

Ken sipped the last of his tea to cover the pause. Mickey was a boy, not a man. Still, he was cute as hell, and being able to say he'd taken the guy out twice would sure make his mother happy. It would also add to his credibility when he told her he had zero plans of marrying Mickey Okuwa. He stared toward the door where Jim Carney's ass had vanished. Besides, he didn't have anything else going on hookup-wise right now. "Sure, when did you want to go out?"

"My band's got a concert tonight. Want to come?"

"Where?"

"A small club in Costa Mesa."

"I guess so."

"My friends will be very impressed if I show up with someone as gorgeous as you."

Hell, it was nice to be appreciated. "Yeah. Just tell me the time and place. I'll take my own car."

Mickey's dark eyes twinkled. "Don't trust me?"

"You'll have a lot on your plate with performing. You don't need to worry about driving me."

"Yep. You don't trust me." He laughed.

Ken smiled. That was the fucking truth.

JIM STOOD outside Ken's office and breathed. Why did the doctor have to call him today? Maybe by tomorrow, he'd have recovered from being such an idiot. Why did Tanaka make him react like some teenage girl all the time? *Jesus.*

Come on. Be a grownup. Dr. Heart Throb doesn't know you exist and doesn't care how you feel. You shouldn't care either. Get your prognosis and get back to work.

He pushed open the door. Nobody in the waiting room. It was late. The girl behind the desk—not Andrea—nodded at him. "Please take a seat. The doctor will be right with you."

He sat. The magazines held no appeal, so he flipped through his e-mails on his phone. Oh, one from Constance Murch. *Do you like plays? I happen to have tickets to a musical this Saturday at the Performing Arts Center. Want to go?*

Well, damn. Lunch could be business, but a play on Saturday was sure as hell a date. If she supplied the play tickets, he'd have to supply the dinner. That made it even more a date. Did he want that? To go out with the boss? Man, he was over his head here. What if he said no? Would she cancel Billy's job? Maybe she'd just not give them the new work she'd talked about, and he wanted to give that gift to Billy because he felt Billy had given him a gift. Maybe more than one. His heart hammered against his ribs.

"Jim?"

He looked up at Ken Tanaka standing in the door to the inner office. The doc came to get Jim himself.

"Are you okay? You look upset?"

"Oh no, not exactly."

"Want to come in?"

"Sure."

He stood and walked through the door, inhaling Tanaka's spicy/sweet scent that filled his head like smoke. God, he felt disoriented, like he didn't know which world he lived in—one where he went out on dates with a rich woman, or one in which he gazed into the beautiful eyes of Yaoi Man and got a hard-on. Hell, both of them had to be fantasyland.

Ken motioned him into a private office that wasn't an examining room. "Please, take a seat."

Jim sat in a guest chair in front of Ken's desk, and the doc walked all the way around to sit in his big leather chair. Very professional. Very distant. Very not a good sign. "So I got back the results of your echocardiogram."

"Yeah?" Shit, they should take another test right now. The way his heart hammered in his ears, he'd sure as fuck fail.

"Your mitral valve prolapse is what I would call moderate to severe. It's difficult to tell exactly without doing surgery."

"Surgery?" *Close your mouth, idiot.*

"Yes, that's how a severely, shall we say, floppy valve is corrected." He smiled tightly.

"Floppy?" It came out like a squeak.

"I'm not recommending surgery now. We're going to observe over the next few months. I want you to let me know any problems, arrhythmic heartbeats, racing heart, chest pains, anything irregular that might occur, okay?"

Shit, all of that was so regular for him, and he was so not going to tell Tanaka that. He nodded.

"Don't worry. Mitral valve prolapse is quite common. Most people never have any real difficulty. Just follow my directions. Don't drink excessively, eat healthy food, even organic would be advisable, and avoid stress."

Jim's mouth opened, then closed. He was okay on the drinking thing so far, although this news made him want to down a bottle of Jack. Still, on the other stuff, the doc might as well say fly to the moon and bring back some green cheese. Hell, even being around Tanaka could give him a fucking heart attack. Sitting here thinking he might die any moment, and his cock still wanted to escape his jeans just from looking at the doctor's lips. Maybe that's how he'd go out. Lean over and kiss Ken Tanaka. Bye-bye, Charlie.

"Does that all seem doable?"

Jim nodded. "Does, uh, that mean I don't get the insurance?" Jesus, that would be bad.

"No. As I told you, mitral valve prolapse is common. I've signed the papers and turned them in. You should get the approval with no problem. You're officially no longer a patient."

That felt both good and bad. "Thanks, man."

"My pleasure. As I say, it's not an inherently worrisome diagnosis." Ken sat back in his chair. "So you're hooking up with our sexy landlord, huh?" He smiled, but something seemed phony about it.

"Uh, no. She was just talking to me about how to build out her suites. And she, uh, has some more work for us."

Ken stood and walked toward the door of his office. "I don't know, buddy. I'd look out for her. You could find yourself hooked."

Buddy? Seriously? "I won't worry too much. You told me to avoid stress." He walked over to the door, looked at Ken, then glanced away. "You seem to have a new boyfriend. Cute guy."

He frowned. "My mother fixed us up."

"Seriously?" Jim snorted a laugh.

"You, my friend, are not Japanese, or you'd understand."

"You were born in Japan?" Ken had no accent at all.

"No, I was born in Costa Mesa, but—well, it's complicated. So don't worry about your heart. My office manager is gone, but she'll call you to make an appointment in about two months. Meanwhile, I'm serious about contacting me if anything unusual occurs."

"Anything?"

"With your health, crazy man." He smiled, and this time it reached his eyes.

Two months. He had no excuse to see Ken Tanaka for two months. Hell, that was good news. Maybe he'd get his feet back under him, if he didn't die of a heart attack first.

"Thanks again for helping me with the architect thing."

Ken raised an eyebrow. "Is it working out with Willings?"

"Yeah. He assigned one of the young guys in his office to handle the drawings, and he's great. He's really saved my ass."

"Good. See, I helped relieve your stress." He sounded sad.

"Yeah." He stuck out his hand. Ken took it, and heat traveled up Jim's arm all the way to his heart. "Guess I'll see you in two months."

"Yes."

"Don't marry any guys you don't want to marry." He tried to grin.

Ken didn't grin. "I'll try."

Jim walked out of the office, across the waiting room to the hall, and to the elevator before he really took a breath. That was that with Ken Tanaka. He'd probably see the doc around, but in two months, hell, he'd be a memory. He took a long, slow breath to keep his heart from tripping.

Down in the lobby, he pushed into the suite where Charlie and Raoul were still working. Raoul stared down from a ladder. "Hey, man, you look like you lost a friend or something."

Jim shook his head. Charlie walked up beside him. "You okay?"

"Yeah. I just found out the heart thing is pretty bad, I guess."

"Shit, man."

"Nothing to get worried about, the doc says. Just something to observe."

"Did that fuck up your insurance?"

"No, the doc says I should get it anyway."

82

"Sounds like a good guy."

"Yeah, he is. So I'm gonna keep working for a while. Why don't you guys go home and we'll start again tomorrow at 6:30? We should have drawings for the other suite to take to the city too."

Charlie clapped his shoulder. "You should quit too. Go home and rest the ticker."

"I will. Soon. Thanks, you guys." He walked over and stared down at the plans while Charlie and Raoul gathered their stuff behind him.

"Night, Jim."

"Night." His eyes wouldn't focus. His heart hurt, and mitral valve prolapse didn't figure into it at all.

CHAPTER TEN

KEN STARED out the car window at the seedy-looking little club on the west side of Costa Mesa. He didn't want to go over there. *So what do you want to do, asshole? Sit here and worry about Jim Carney's heart and Jim Carney's love life?* Shit! He stepped out of the car onto the dirt. He'd parked across the street in a pay lot. That might save his car from destruction, but who knew? Maybe the lot owner specialized in stealing Lexus parts.

As he approached, a few kids lined up to go in—some of them clearly experts in driver's license art. Ken had worn his tightest black jeans, a rock band T-shirt, and his hair floppy. He'd even added some eyeliner and black fingernail polish, despite the fact that it was a pain to take off. Still, he felt like these kids' father. Well, maybe older brother. The one telling them to grow up and get a job.

The bouncer at the door was having a loud altercation with two young girls who looked more like they should be viewing Mickey Mouse than Mickey Okuwa. Ken cut in front, nodded at the guy, and walked in. The place smelled bad. Like sweat and old smoke. Not big, it had a bunch of small tables and chairs crowded around a stage and torn linoleum on the floor. Some guys fiddled with electronic gear while the patrons who occupied about half the tables looked bored.

Ken spied a table a ways back from the stage. At least he might have eardrums by tomorrow if he chose wisely. He slipped into a chair and smiled at the waitress who hurried over. She must figure he could pay for a drink. She'd be disappointed. "Ginger ale, please."

"Oh, okay."

He handed her eight dollars. Even after the $5.00 charge for soda, it left her a tip. "Keep the change."

That made her smile.

"Charming the natives already. Mickey warned me." The voice came from over Ken's shoulder. He glanced back at a young guy with a hawkish but still attractive face and a body so skinny he could pose for heroin chic ads.

"So Mickey's been talking, has he?"

"Oh yes." The guy walked in front of Ken. "I'm GG Shinoda. I have a table closer to the band I was holding for you."

"Sorry. Self-preservation. I don't know how bad the acoustics are."

"What acoustics?" He laughed. "Mind if I sit down?"

"No. Please."

GG folded himself into one of the uncomfortable chairs. "A couple other friends of Mickey's are coming too. Can I save space for them?"

"Fine. I'm not sure how long I'll stay."

"Oh, I hope long enough to get to hear Mickey's best tunes."

"You let me know when those are coming, okay?" He grinned.

Two other guys, also in their early twenties, showed up. One was Anglo, with blond hair and pimples. GG identified him as Harry. The other was a burly Asian guy who would have been a contender for sumo competition if he'd been in Japan. Tommy. The chair protested under his bulk. It was a near thing, but the wood and plastic held.

Squawks and squeals came from the sound system, and the audience shrieked and clapped hands over their ears. Some girl shouted, "Come on. Get on with it."

GG managed to stay beside Ken throughout the arrivals, moving a little closer each time.

GG clinked his glass against Ken's. "To good music." He smiled wolfishly. "What you drinking? Whiskey and soda? Want another?"

"No, thanks. I'm fine." No use disillusioning him as to Ken's coolness. A band took the stage and started in on some cover of somebody Ken had never heard of and would have hated if he had. Ken stared around. "Where's Mickey?

"This is an opening act. They'll just do two numbers, then on with the big guns."

Ken chose not to argue as to the size of the weaponry and tried hard not to grimace as the really bad band played.

GG leaned in but still had to raise his voice. "So you're gay."

"Yeah, so?"

"Nothing. Just want to get that out of the way." He sipped his beer. "You bottom or top?"

Ken raised an eyebrow. "Who wants to know?"

"Me. 'Cause I'm a top, baby, and I like to know when I have a welcoming asshole."

"Have you considered the possibility that you're the asshole?"

GG laughed loud enough to be heard over the dreadful music. "You're really cute."

An announcer took over the microphone. "And now, the guys you've been waiting for. Here's Mickey and the Madmen."

Ken glanced at GG, but the guy's eyes were riveted to the stage. Must be a fan of the "big guns."

Mickey and the Madmen began to play. Compared to the opening act, they were Mozart, but that was saying very little. Mickey did have a charisma it was tough to deny. More charisma than voice, actually, but he waggled his tight butt and moaned into the microphone and the girls screamed.

GG leaned in and yelled, "You like them?"

"Yeah. They're great." No use explaining subtleties in this cacophony. Ken looked up at the stage and got a wink from Mickey. He grinned back.

The band segued into a second number that was slow and sexy— read moanier. Mickey practically swallowed the microphone. A glance at GG showed the guy was glassy-eyed and sported an erection the size of Utah in his tight jeans. He must really like Mickey.

Ken picked up his ginger ale and took a swig. A movement made him look to the side to find GG staring at him avidly. *What the fuck?* He turned back to the stage and started to take another drink. *Wait.* His mouth tasted strange. He looked at the glass. Small blue dots bubbled through the liquid, and icy fear shot up his spine.

No fucking way. Carefully he set the glass down. *Did GG do it? He must have.* How fast would it act? Could he get to his car? *Shit!* He plastered on a smile. "Excuse me. Men's room."

GG's eyes widened. "You're not going to leave before Mickey's done?"

"Sorry, man, when you gotta go, you gotta go." He stood as assuredly as he could, but his feet felt cold and black flashes popped in front of his eyes. Not much time. He strode toward the front of the club, saw a sign for restrooms, and lurched toward them. The people in the seats freaked even though nobody looked glued to the music.

"Hey, man, out of the way."

"Sit down."

"Fucking move, asshole."

He banged his back against the men's room door and kind of fell so he wound up in the bathroom and managed to stagger into a stall and flop on a toilet seat. His whole body felt cold. Thank God he hadn't consumed more or he'd be paralyzed by now.

Something big and solid hit the outside of the men's room door. Instinctively, he pulled his feet up onto the seat.

The big guy, Tommy's voice. "Nah, nobody here, man. He must have gone outside. Shit, if that dude drives, he's toast."

GG's voice sounded farther away. "He can't get too far. He's probably out cold on the sidewalk."

"Hell, I hope so. I never saw a prettier guy in my life. I want me some of that."

"Then quit talking and let's go find him."

Ken shivered. The assholes planned to gang bang him. GG, the bastard, thought he'd mixed Rohypnol and alcohol, a combo that could be fatal. Had to get the fuck out of there. He dropped his feet down, tried to stand, collapsed back to the seat, and nearly landed on the floor. *Shit. Try again.* At least the paralysis wasn't getting too much worse.

He moved more slowly and made it to standing. Cracking the door open, he peered out. Nobody, but the music still blared from beyond the door, so most people would wait for the break to pee. Like a prophecy, the music crashed to a conclusion, and the door flew open as guys rushed in to spill their leftover beer into the urinals. Ken slipped out as three people pushed in. He was taller than most of the crowd, so if GG and his accomplices were watching, they'd see him, but hopefully they were searching outside somewhere.

Staying close to the wall for support, Ken slid to the front door of the club. He looked out quickly, then pulled back. Didn't see them. As a bunch of people crowded outside, cigarettes at the ready, Ken oozed behind them and got as far as a couple of cypress trees planted near the front door. His foot caught on a root, he stumbled, and fell face-first into the trunk of one tree just as he heard GG behind him. "I told you to look in that fucking men's room, asshole."

Ken raised his head, but GG and Tommy seemed to have gone back inside. *Weird and dark. No cabs in Costa Mesa. No fucking chance. Can't drive. Need help.* He reached for his cell phone and scrolled.

SWEET JESUS. Jim cruised slowly down the Costa Mesa street, staring out the window. Shit, his heart beat so hard, he felt like he'd pass out. That'd be zero productive.

"Help me," he'd said. The voice barely sounded like Ken. At first Jim had thought it was a joke, but when he realized it was for real, he'd practically wrecked the car screeching out of the parking lot. How could somebody as capable and self-assured as Ken Tanaka need Jim's help? And why did he pick Jim? The doc had to have a million friends and family members. *Focus, idiot. Too many questions.* He'd thought about bringing Ian to help him, but those very unanswered questions made him stop. Maybe Ken was in some kind of trouble he didn't want anyone else to know about. That would explain why he'd called Jim. Hell, Jim wasn't anyone Ken cared about or whose opinion mattered.

Some neon lights spelled out Whiz Banger with the B blinking weirdly so every couple of flashes it read Whiz anger. That was the name Ken had mumbled. A beat-up Honda pulled away from the curb, and Jim slid his beat-up truck in its place. His feet hit the ground as fast as the engine stopped turning over, and Jim trotted toward the club. Ken had said something about outside, but he wasn't waiting. At least not anywhere Jim could see.

Pausing in front of the double doors, Jim peered past the bouncer and the line of post-teenyboppers toward the inside of the club. No Ken. He stepped past the bouncer, and the guy shoved out an arm. Jim stopped and gave a friendly grin. "Just looking for a friend. I'm picking him up. Have you seen a tall Asian guy?"

"About a hundred. And you have to wait your turn like the others."

"I'm not going inside."

"That's what they all say."

"Look, buddy—"

"Jim—unnnh."

Was that his name? The weird moaning sound came from the bushes beside the club entry. "Look out." He charged past the bouncer toward the sound. Squatting, he peered under the low tree trunks and the prickly bushes. *Feet.* Shoes so damned fashionable they could only belong to one guy. "Ken!"

The bouncer called, "What's going on?"

Jim ignored him and slipped around the foliage until he was pressed against the wall of the club, scooted about five feet, then knelt and found Ken's face squashed against the dirt. Not a sight he would have ever thought he'd see. What the hell could have happened to the guy? Why was he even at a dive like this? "Ken, it's Jim. I'm going to get you out of here."

"Jim."

"I'm coming." Jim slid down lower, reached a hand, and took hold of Ken's arm. Hard not to notice the lean muscle through the tight black T-shirt. Jim pulled and Ken seemed to try and help, because he kicked with his fashionable shoes. Between pulling and kicking, Jim managed to get that long, lean body out from under the tree until Ken could rest his head in Jim's lap. He touched the dirt and a scratch on Ken's perfect skin. "Oh man, what happened to you?"

"Roof."

"You fell off the roof?" *Holy shit.*

"Roofies."

"Who the fuck did that?"

The bouncer's voice came from a few feet away. "What the hell is going on?"

"Don't just stand there. Help me get this guy up. He was drugged in your fucking club, and I'll gladly tell the cops that fact right after I call them."

"Okay, okay. Come on." The bouncer sidestepped behind the tree, reached down, and took hold of Ken's arm. "No drugs allowed in this club. He must have brought them in."

Jim struggled to his feet and took Ken's other arm. "Be careful, man. This guy's a big-name doctor. You could be out of business before he's done with you."

"Shit. Get him out of here."

They walked Ken out from the bushes. He looked like he'd been rolling in the dirt, which he actually had, but nothing more. No signs he'd been beaten or raped. "Doc, you okay? Did they hurt you?"

Ken shook his head and mumbled, "Got away. Didn't take much."

They maneuvered Ken out to the sidewalk and he was moving a little easier, like they'd gotten him into a groove and he just kept walking. The bouncer glanced back at the underagers trying to walk into the club. "You got this? I need to get back to the door."

"Yeah, okay."

One step at a time, they hobbled closer to Jim's truck. Thank God he'd gotten a close parking space.

"Hey, you, let go of him. He's with us." The sharp voice came from behind him.

Jim looked over his shoulder. Three guys strode toward him, one the size of a house. Where the fuck was the bouncer when he needed him? But they'd made it just far enough from the entrance to not be visible. "Not a chance, asshole. You the guys who drugged him?"

The three stopped a few feet away. "He's just had a couple too many, but he's our friend's boyfriend, so we need to take him back so they can hook up, got it?"

Were they telling the truth? That would explain why Ken was at this weird club dressed like this. Still—"Your friend should have taken better care of him. He called me to help him, and that's what I'm doing. They can hook up some other time."

The skinny one said, "I don't think so." But the big one stepped forward.

Ken muttered, "Leave Jim alone."

Jim stepped to the side, took Ken's hands, and attached them to a parking sign. "Hold on." He looked up at the big guy. "Kid, you may be bigger, but I've been winning bar fights since I was younger than you." Okay, he made that sound like decades instead of a couple of years. "You sure you want to do this?"

It wasn't the big guy who answered. Skinny dude said, "He belongs to us. We want to take him to our friend. Right, Tommy?"

Jim sucked in a breath and tried to look bigger. "Tough shit."

Tommy looked unsure. *Good sign.* But he still lunged forward and hurled a wild punch in Jim's direction. Jim stepped in, thrust a mild left into the big guy's gut, and watched Tommy's face crumple as he fell back. Tommy hadn't been hit much, obviously. Jim had. Big advantage.

Jim spread his hands. *See, no brass knuckles.* "All I want is to take Ken home. If your friend really has a date with him, he can find him there. Try that again and I'll get serious. You don't want that."

Tommy shook his head like a bobble-head doll as he backed up.

"Okay." Jim stepped back to Ken, who hung from the pole like a spent horse. "Come on, doc." He slipped an arm around his waist and dragged him the few more feet to the truck. It took some maneuvering because Ken's body kept wanting to collapse, but he managed to prop him in the front seat, then hurried around to the driver's side. Skinny guy and Tommy stood and stared. Jim gave them an evil look, and they finally turned and slouched back toward the club.

Inside the truck Ken had fallen over and his head hung at a sharp angle. Looked like a perfect doll with a broken neck. Jim scooted him into as comfortable a position as he could manage. And took a deep breath. Damn, his chest hurt. "Sorry, doc, we gotta get out of here before those assholes come back with reinforcements. Where to?"

No answer. Just shallow breathing.

"Ken, what's your address?"

Nothing.

Well, damn. He started the truck and pulled out of the parking space to let another eager car grab it from behind him. Probably not safe to leave Ken alone anyway. "I'm taking you to my place. I'm sure it'll be a big comedown, but at least you won't die alone."

Ken mumbled something and slid sideways against the door. Man, he was out of it. Jim clicked his cell phone and dialed Ian.

"Hey, bro." He sounded sleepy. Jim had left him crashed on the couch with the TV on.

"Hey. I'm gonna be there in about ten minutes. Will you meet me in the parking lot? I've got one seriously blitzed dude with me, and I need help getting him upstairs."

"Is that where you went? To rescue a drunk?"

"Kind of. Just meet me. I'll tell you later." Not sure what to say, though. Who knew what happened?

Ian was standing in Jim's parking space when he pulled in. He'd put on one of Jim's jackets, and it hung on him like a letterman's sweater on a cheerleader. Jim stopped the car and jumped out. Ian was peering through the window at Ken's head squashed against the glass. When Jim got to the passenger side, Ian greeted him with huge eyes. "Is that who I think it is?"

"Yeah."

"Wow. How the mighty have fallen."

"No. I gathered he got roofied."

"No shit?"

"He was lying under a tree when I got there, and he hasn't talked much since. Some guys were after him, and I'm betting they're the ones responsible, but I had to get the hell out of there." He eased open the door. Instead of falling out, Ken sat up, so that was a good sign. Still looked like somebody punched him out. Jim reached in and pulled Ken toward him. Ken helped, and they managed to get his feet on the ground. Ian took one side and Jim the other, and they started a halting walk toward the stairs to the second floor.

Ian peered at Jim around Ken. "He looks crappy. Want me to call the cops now?"

Jim shook his head. "I don't know what to tell them."

"No. No cops." The mumbled words made them both look at Ken.

"You sure? Somebody ought to get those assholes off the streets."

"Nuh—no cops."

"Okay, whatever you say, doc."

Ian frowned. "Should we take you to the emergency room?" Hell, leave it to his brother to ask the intelligent questions.

"Nuh."

"You sure? You're in pretty bad shape."

"Sleep."

Ian looked at Jim. "I think we should take him to a doctor."

"He is a doctor."

"Shit."

Jim hauled Ken higher. "Get ready for some stairs, doc."

"Whe ah we?"

"We're at my apartment. Mine and Ian's." He smiled at his brother. "I couldn't wake you up enough to find out where you live."

"'Kay. Sleep."

"Big step." Ken raised a leg in the general direction of the first stairs.

It took five minutes, but they half dragged, half encouraged Ken up the stairs and into the apartment. Thank God the doc's eyes were closed so he couldn't see the rattiness of his surroundings. Of course, he had to wake up sometime.

Jim started toward the hall. "Put him in my bed."

Ian shook his head. "Nah. Give him mine. I'll take the couch."

"No. If he wakes up, I'm better able to handle him. I'll stay out here or sleep in the chair just to make sure he doesn't wander away or something."

They got him to Jim's unmade bed and let him crash. For a second he just lay on his back like a corpse; then he curled on his side like some perfect yaoi teddy bear. Ridiculously cute.

Ian stared at him. Hard not to. "How the hell is he dressed? He's wearing eyeliner, for crap's sake."

"Yeah, this is a new look to me."

Ian stared some more. "Shit, that is one gorgeous man."

"Yeah."

"Why do you think he called you? Doesn't he have family?"

"No idea. He definitely has parents. I've heard him talk about his mother. Maybe he's embarrassed about the situation and didn't want anyone he cared about to know."

"Maybe." Ian kept staring. "Bad off as he is, I'm surprised he could think at all."

"Yeah."

"So it seems unlikely he considered calling someone he didn't care about."

Breathe.

Ian seemed to tear his eyes from Ken. "What happened with the architect thing?"

"The guy came through. But you're the real hero. Your design is what had the boss lady panting. The architect just interpreted it. But he did a damned good job. And he's nice. You'd like him."

"I'd love to see the drawings."

"I'll bring a set home tomorrow."

"Cool." He stared some more, and there was lots to stare at. Ken had flipped on his back, long legs spread, one arm above his head. A little of his eyeliner had smeared on his cheek and the scrape from his face-plant shone red against his smooth beige skin. Ian shifted legs. "Want me to take a turn watching him?"

"Nah, I'm good."

"Okay, I'll go to bed. Glad the drawing thing worked out."

"Me too. Thanks for helping me with him."

"Anytime, man. Anytime." Ian shook his head a little like he was trying to clear it and walked out of the bedroom.

Jim let out his breath. *Okay, here I am. Now what?*

CHAPTER ELEVEN

HE CLOSED the door, then opened it a crack. Well, damn, he was not ten and therefore could be in a room without parental supervision. He closed it again and turned toward the guest in his bed. Ken's incredibly fashionable leather-and-canvas shoes mocked Jim's ugly blue bedspread and grayish sheets, so he pulled them off along with his silky socks. *Wow.* Those slim feet were as elegant as the rest of his body. He didn't even have hairy toes. Jim's gaze traveled up. Ken was only about an inch taller than Jim, but a lot of that was legs. Narrow waist. His T-shirt had untucked and a small triangle of skin gleamed above the top of his low-slung jeans, revealing an inch of flat belly. No happy trail. Not that Jim could see, anyway. He swallowed. Ken's wide shoulders strained the fabric of the shirt; his neck looked like a column of beige marble. Only, that scratch and dirt on his cheek didn't fit the perfection. *Fix that.*

Jim walked into the tiny attached bathroom that was one of the only good things about this apartment and wet a washcloth with warm water. Back in the bedroom, he sat on the edge of the bed and leaned over Ken. Very gently, heart beating fast, he wiped the cloth across the scratch and removed the dirt. Maybe he should put something on it.

Moving slowly so he didn't jostle the sleeper, he went back in the bathroom and rummaged through the medicine cabinet. A tube of antibiotic ointment turned up behind the toothpaste. God knows he'd needed it often enough for all the scrapes and cuts he got on the job. Again he returned to Ken, sat softly, squeezed a little ointment on his finger, and gently touched the red cheek. His breath sucked in all by itself. Warm, smooth. This was the first time Jim touched any of Ken's skin other than his hand. So soft. What would it be like to touch other parts—and why the hell did he want to know?

It was the yaoi comic. Ken's resemblance to the book's hero played with Jim's mind.

He popped to his feet, taking less care not to jolt the bed, and walked to the ratty old flowered chair he'd bought at a thrift store. *Just go to sleep and worry about Ken Tanaka in the morning.* Removing the three layers of clothes from the chair, he tossed them in the small closet and sat. This chair was pretty comfortable. He took off his sneaks, loosened his belt, stretched out his legs, and rested his head on the overstuffed back. *Lights.* He hopped up again, turned off the overheads, and left on the low light from the bedside lamp. *One more time.* He sat. *Wait. Better set the alarm.* He grabbed it from beside the bed and ticked off 5:30 a.m. Not too far in the future—again. *Jesus, talk about no sleep.*

Okay, rest. He propped his head and closed his eyes. Breathing. All he could hear were Ken's soft exhales and inhales. His mind followed the sound. In and out. In and out. He scrunched onto his side and rested his head on the arm. In. Out. In. Out. Damn, his neck hurt. He flipped onto his butt and propped his head on his hand. In and out. Hypnotic. In and— His head flopped off his hand and hit the chair arm. Damn.

Enough. He stood and tiptoed to the bed. Ken lay on his side on the far edge of the queen-sized mattress. *I should go sleep on the couch.* But what if Ken woke and was scared or sick? Jim sat carefully on the edge of the bed, lay down, and slowly pulled his legs up until he was stretched flat on his back. Okay, he felt like a board, but at least his neck didn't hurt. He reached out and flipped off the bedside light, then closed his eyes.

OH. OH. Oh man. Talk about wet dreams! Shit. What the fuck?

Jim's eyes flew open and his head popped up. Too dark to see well, but that was one amazing-ass mouth on his cock. *Shit. Holy shit. Not a dream. Living dream.* "Wait. Stop."

The hot hole in the universe swallowed another few inches of his meat, then pulled back. One slippery tongue laved his crown, then bored into his piss slit. *Oh God. Who?* Had to be—didn't care. *Oh man. Jesus. Don't stop. Don't.* His head flopped onto the pillow and thrashed while his hips thrust up and up. Strong hands held him, but that mouth just swallowed him whole, sucking and licking. In his whole life, this was it on blow jobs. Nothing ever came close. *Oh shit. Oh God, do it. Do it.* "Do it! Don't stop. So close."

Lips sucked his cockhead until it had to be twice its normal size. *Gonna explode.* Cum boiled in his balls, the pressure unbearable and unbearably good. "Oh God, I'm going to come. I'm coming. Cominnnng." Spunk shot out of him, but the mouth didn't pull back. It swallowed and swallowed until everything in Jim drained out, his eyes drooped, and he dropped into sleep.

THE SOUND of the alarm beat like a hammer on his brain. *No way. Want to keep sleeping. So good. Such great dreams.* He slammed a hand onto the alarm clock and pressed his ear against the pillow. Back to the blow job of the century.

Wait. Breathing. Not his.

Shit! Ken. He sat straight up and stared into the still-dark room. He was covered. Had he covered himself when he went to sleep? His hand crept under.

Holy God. Naked. No. Not naked. His hand felt lower on his thighs and discovered his boxer briefs, then lower still and found his jeans pooled around his knees. Okay, this was what a lawyer would call incontrovertible evidence. That dream was no dream.

Well, no, actually it was. A dream of the "come true" variety. The best damned blow job of his life. Just thinking about it brought his morning wood to Rockefeller Center Christmas tree status.

Shit. He lowered his head back onto the pillow and felt his dick throb. How did he feel about this turn of events? He'd received real live head from a guy, and he knew it. He could tell himself he thought it was a dream at the time, but that was a lie. He'd known Ken Tanaka was sucking his dick and he hadn't cared. Hell, that had made it better.

What did that say about him?

Sadly, at this moment, it said he'd like the guy to wake up and do it again. That was fucking perverse.

He grasped his erection and squeezed. *Strangle the bloody traitor.* His hand pumped all by itself. *Quit that.* No way was he lying there jerking off next to his heart doctor. He let go and turned his head. A last sliver of moonlight before dawn showed Ken lying on his back, one arm thrown over his head, and long black lashes making dark half-moons against his pale cheeks. His floppy hair half obscured one eye, and his impossibly full lips turned up in a little smile like he was dreaming something good too. Jim's cock bounced. Maybe they'd shared a dream.

Jesus, stop it! He sat up and threw his legs, bound by his jeans, over the side of the bed. As he stood, he pulled them up and fastened the fly enough to keep them from sliding off. *Shower.*

Bumping into the side of the bed, he staggered in the dark and made it to the bathroom where he closed the door softly, flipped the light, then stripped and turned on the water. As he paused to test the temperature, he caught a glimpse of himself in the mirror on the bathroom door. His cock still stood at half-mast. A cock that had been sucked by a dude. Righteously sucked.

Not like it's the first time.

He sighed and stepped under the water. Kind of lukewarm. This building hated giving up its heat. Still, it felt good. With a few swipes, he lathered some soap and wiped it over his pits and chest, then slid down to the bouncing traitor. Hell, it was his. He could do what he wanted with it. Yeah. He soaped. *No need to think.* More soap.

What the hell. He leaned against the yellowish tile wall, stroked his cock, and let the memories come. Him and Hiro huddled together reading the yaoi magazines, laughing at the romance but still getting hard. Hiro, with his shy smile and bright eyes, looking up at him from his knees. "I'll suck you, Jim. Okay? Like in the story?" Yeah, okay. Okay once, twice, twenty times. Every one of those times, Jim told himself he was just making his friend happy. Yeah, as he pumped a gallon of jizz down Hiro's throat. Then one day Hiro was gone because of Jim, and Jim noticed he wasn't okay anymore. Two days later Jim had walked out the door of his house and never looked back. Ten years. Not one blow job from a guy in all that time. Not one blow job worth mentioning either. Until last night. Ten years. Had he been okay since then?

Maybe not.

He rinsed his soapy cock, turned off the water, and stepped out of the shower. What the fuck did he want? Who the fuck was he kidding? What he wanted beamed in his brain and throbbed in his cock. *More.* That's what he wanted. He dried, grabbed his jeans, and pulled them on. He took a deep breath and opened the door to the bedroom.

Ken sat on the edge of the bed, his head flopped in his hand, black hair falling over his forehead. When Jim walked in, Ken looked up, his face a mask of pain and confusion. "What the hell happened to me?"

"Some guy at a club slipped you a roofie."

"Jesus. I vaguely remember going to some half-assed, hole-in-the wall club and meeting up with some guys. But how did I get here?"

Jim stared. Well, hell, had he dreamed the whole thing? "Uh, you called me. Asked me for help."

"I did?"

He let his breath out very slowly. "Yeah. I was pretty surprised too, but I found you on the ground under a tree, so it's a good thing you managed to call."

"Shit, it's like somebody washed and rinsed my brain. I keep reaching for stuff, but nothing. So, what happened to me that I wound up under a tree?"

"I'm not exactly sure, but those guys were pretty intent on getting you back, so I don't think they got to do whatever they had in mind."

It felt like Ken's eyes could see through him. "Three guys? One of them really big?"

"Yeah."

"So how is it that they didn't carry out their nefarious plans?"

Jim shrugged. "They were better at talking than fighting."

"And I called you." It wasn't a question.

Jim nodded.

"I must have more brains than I thought. Thanks for saving me."

Jim managed a half smile. "Any time." *He doesn't remember.*

Ken squinted toward the window, where very soft light had begun to show. "What is it? Morning?"

"Last I checked."

"Shit. I have patients. Do you think I could bother you for one more favor? I wonder what the chances are that my car is still parked in Costa Mesa?"

"You'd have to hurry. I need to be at work soon." *Heart hammering. Not good.*

"Yeah. Okay. Just let me pee and wash my face."

"Sure." With a shrug, Jim tried to loosen his rock-rigid shoulders.

Ken stood, staggered, and fell back on the bed.

Know how that feels. "Need some help?"

"No. I hope to be able to conquer walking at any moment." His head slid into his hands again.

"Here, let me give you a boost." Jim slid an arm under Ken's, wrapped around that slim, muscled back, and lifted. *Don't think about how he feels against your side.*

Ken's head lolled for an instant against Jim's shoulder, then was gone. "God, you're strong."

That was so far from the truth. He balanced Ken on his feet and supported his walk toward the bathroom. Once in the doorframe, Ken's beautiful brown/black eyes gazed at Jim. "Thanks. I'll try to take it from here."

Ken managed the few steps into the tiny bathroom and closed the door.

Jim walked backward and sat hard on the edge of the bed. *Nothing. The guy remembered nothing. Made sense. Wasn't the date rape drug supposed to mess with your memory? It's for the best. What the hell were you planning? An hour of getting your cock sucked? You gotta go to work. Remember priorities, for crap's sake.* He stood and grabbed his boots, sat again and pulled them on to the sound of running water and creaky old pipes. *Is it possible it didn't happen? Could I have made it up?* Didn't matter. The end result was the same. If Tanaka had sucked his cock, he'd forgotten it completely, and now he didn't even look at Jim like maybe he'd like to give him a blow job.

He dropped his head into his hands, kind of like Ken had a few minutes before. Felt like somebody hollowed out his chest, then overfilled it with cement. He sucked in a breath. *Shit!*

What the fuck do I care? I'm straight. In one move he stood, raised a fist, and gave the door a pound. "Hurry up, doc. I gotta get to work."

KEN STARED out the windshield as the guy pulled aside the gate of the car impound lot to let him exit. What a total fuckup he was. Drugged and left in the dirt. At least his car was only towed, not stripped.

The car lot guy waved him through, and he pulled out onto Harbor Boulevard and pointed toward home. He had to take a shower and get the stink of that club off him before he could see a patient. Jim had only given him a minute. He'd barely splashed water on his face. He'd called his office manager and told her to apologize but postpone his first two appointments. Still, he had to hurry.

Accelerating toward the ocean, he cranked up the air conditioner and took deep breaths. Man, he felt bad. Even a little of that drug made him queasy and empty-headed, but those were just the physical effects. What did Jim think of him? *Loser* spelled out in big letters across Ken's forehead. Used and abused. When he woke up in that bed, he'd panicked for a minute. Then Jim Carney walked in, and Ken's whole body lit up like kindling that just got close to a match. That guy did it for him.

The phone buzzed in his pocket and then rang on the car Bluetooth. He glanced at the screen. *Well, shit.* "Tanaka."

"Ken, thank God. What happened to you? I've been so worried. When you left the club, I thought you didn't like our music, but then I tried to call and got no answer."

Ken narrowed his eyes and glanced at the touchscreen like he could see the little shit. "Yeah, right, Mickey. As if you didn't know that your fucking friends tried to drug me."

"Drug? No way, man. They'd never do something like that."

"I heard them making plans to gang bang me, asshole." His memory might be fuzzy, but that detail stood out. "You trying to say you knew nothing about it?"

There was a pause. Mickey's voice sounded deadly serious. "No way, man. You gotta believe me. I never thought anyone I know would do something like that. I'm so sorry. Are you okay? Do you need help? What can I do?"

"Nothing. Just leave me alone."

"I wish you wouldn't ask me to leave… I really like you, man."

Was it possible the guy didn't know what his friends had planned? How could they hope to drug Ken and not let Mickey know? "I've got to get to work."

"No, wait. Don't hang up."

Ken paused with his finger over the End button. "Yeah."

"Will you go out with me Saturday? My treat. Dinner someplace nice, a show. Please, let me prove to you I'm not involved in whatever they tried to do—and I'm so terribly sorry about it."

Ken sighed and didn't even attempt to hide it. He didn't want to go out with Mickey Okuwa. *And who do you want to go out with?* Not gonna happen. Jim Carney might have come to his rescue, but the guy couldn't wait to get him out of his house. Sometimes Jim acted like he was attracted to Ken, but if he was, he sure wasn't admitting it to anyone—like himself. *Get over it, asshole.* Maybe Mickey really was innocent. Hell, he'd had the balls to call. Dinner with Mickey would make his mother happy, and that might keep her off his back for a while. "Okay, text me where to meet you. I'll take my own car."

He hung up and stopped at the light at Pacific Coast Highway, staring at the sun glinting off the waves. How the hell did his sex life get this complicated? Easy answer. Mama-san. Because she'd refused to accept he was gay, he'd settled himself into a pattern of banging every guy he saw and not thinking past it—since clearly he had no future. Now, with his orientation not only accepted but embraced by his dear, meddling mother, he needed to make life decisions. *And what decisions are you making, dear boy?* When the crap hit the fan, he'd called Jim Carney. Big, hunky, blue-collar, straight Jim Carney. His mother's worst nightmare.

He accelerated through the light and turned left into his condo complex. The fact that his mother would hate Jim was probably the very reason Ken liked him. Choose somebody as inappropriate as possible.

Yeah, just keep telling yourself that.

CHAPTER TWELVE

JIM BARGED into the suite, unfolded the plans, and started measuring for framing—all by himself. Okay, so he was an hour earlier than his crew, but what the fuck? He wanted to get a jump on the day. *Yeah, and you didn't want to talk to Ken Tanaka.*

They'd driven to the car lot mostly in silence. Ken asked a couple of questions about Jim's work and Jim tried to answer, but the weirdness of knowing Ken had sucked his cock and didn't remember just kept fogging his brain. Why did he do it if he didn't plan to remember?

Okay Carney, that doesn't make any sense.

Shit, I wish I had a drink.

That makes less sense. Besides, it's better this way. How awkward would it be if he did remember?

Jim was wrestling some two-bys into place for framing and wrestling Ken Tanaka out of his brain when Charlie and Raoul walked in. Raoul ran forward and took the other end of the long piece of lumber. "Hey, man, what you doing, hauling this shit by yourself?"

Jim shrugged. "Just wanted to get a jump on the day."

Charlie laughed. "Who are you and what have you done with our friend Jim?"

"Come on, this is important. We gotta come through for Billy." Jim frowned and set the wood in place.

Charlie kept smiling. "Never said we wouldn't. We just don't see that kind of enthusiasm for work in you all the time."

"Just keep watching."

Two more guys arrived, and Jim left them framing while he went to the city to pull permits for the other suite. By the time he got back, they'd roughed in two private offices and had started on a third. He'd just grabbed a nail gun when the newly installed door to the suite opened and Constance Murch bustled in. "Wow. You've made a lot of progress in a short time. Are you free for lunch? I'd like to discuss the other suite."

Jim glanced around at the crew. Charlie flashed a tiny grin, but most of the guys didn't seem to think anything about the owner taking Jim to lunch.

"Uh, sure." He looked down at his jeans and work boots. At least he'd worn a collared shirt since he'd had to go to the building department.

"Don't worry about it. You're California casual. Come on."

He followed her out to the lobby, where she immediately slipped her arm through his. "Did you get my e-mail?"

"Uh, yes. I just haven't been certain about my schedule. My brother came to live with me recently. He's kind of working through some things." He was babbling. *Great, Carney, blame it on Ian.*

"That must be a lot of responsibility for a young man like you." They walked out of the building, and she guided him down the sidewalk.

"I'm not all that young. Nearly twenty-seven."

"Sounds young to me."

He looked at her pretty face. "You're not older than me."

"Actually, I am."

"Well, you don't look it." Which was pretty much the truth. He glanced up and stopped walking, which halted her in her tracks. "We're not going to Pacific Crest, are we?"

"Yes. Do you know the club?"

"Kind of. But—"

"It's okay. My father's on the board. I want you to meet him."

"Oh man, I don't think that's a good idea today."

"Please, Jim. I own the building you're working on, but my father has much bigger projects, and I think you'd be a great resource for him. I've been telling him about you."

Holy blessed shit. "I don't own the company, Constance."

"Well, obviously you're very important to it or Mr. Ballew would never have left you in charge."

Jesus, he was slipping into some hole and he sure hoped the walls weren't going to collapse on his head. "Okay. If you think it's wise."

They walked into the club with its nautical paintings and blue-and-white furnishings. The maître d' barely looked at Jim's attire, he was so busy smiling at Constance. "Welcome, Ms. Murch. So delighted to see you. Your father is waiting in the dining room."

"Thank you, Frederick." She smiled at Jim. "This way."

Jim didn't want to tell her he could have drawn a map of the club from memory, including the kitchens where he used to love to hang out and get treats when he was a kid. In the big dining room, Constance walked toward the back center booth, usually considered the most desirable place to sit. The fact that Constance's father was in this booth meant *his* father wasn't there—but he didn't say that either.

A white-haired man, medium height and stocky, waved at Constance.

"Hi, Daddy." She walked over and kissed his cheek.

Her father's wide smile dimmed a little when he stared at Jim. Yeah, he probably looked pretty ratty. Hadn't even managed a haircut. His stomach flipped and his heart pounded. Would her father persuade her to take the jobs away from Jim, meaning away from Billy?

"Daddy, this is Jim Carney, who I've been telling you about. Jim, my father, Alex Murch."

Murch's forced smile remained, but his eyes narrowed. "Carney?"

Jim shook the man's firm hand. "Yes, sir."

"No relation to our James Carney here at the club?"

Sigh. "He's my father."

That inspired a real smile. "Well, I'll be damned. Connie, you didn't tell me your friend was Dr. Carney's son."

She looked at Jim with a little frown. "I didn't know it."

What the hell could he say? "Uh, my father and I are not in very close touch, so there was no reason to mention it."

Murch motioned for him to sit and then slid back into his side of the booth. Jim took the inner seat on the other side, and Constance sat beside him. Murch sipped his drink. It looked like Coke. "You're the prodigal son, right? The one who left home early?"

"That would be me."

"He told me you were in construction." Murch laughed. "Of course, he probably thinks that's a bad thing, but since I started as a hammer jockey and made all my early money in construction, I thought it sounded pretty damned great." He smiled, and Jim smiled back.

"Thank you, sir."

"Hey, call me Al."

The waiter came over, and they all ordered. Jim asked for the club's famous hamburger. This meeting was going so well, he might even be able to eat it. "And I think I'll try the sweet potato fries. Constance converted me."

She giggled and the waiter smiled. When he left with the order, Al leaned back in his seat. "So you're working for Constance?"

"Yes, sir. Just some TIs."

"Hey, TIs are important to building owners. We've got to keep the tenants happy without giving away the store."

Constance put her hand on Jim's arm, which got a smile from Murch. "Jim really came through for me, Daddy. I have this tough new tenant who wanted something different, and Jim suggested this unique design—on a moment's notice."

"How long have you had the business, Jim?"

"It's not my company, sir. I work for Ballew Design/Build as a construction supervisor."

Constance tightened her hand. "But Billy went away for two weeks and left Jim in charge, so obviously he has big plans for him." She smiled. "At least, he better if he wants to work for me."

Murch rocked back. "Whoa-ho, woman in charge, Jim. Never underestimate the power of that female beside you. I taught her everything I know."

Constance beamed. "Yes, you did."

"And she's made the best of it. Do you know this woman owns ten properties on her own and she's not even forty yet?"

"Dad-dy! Please."

"I love bragging about my girl. She's a killer in business."

Food came, and eating wasn't quite as easy as he'd hoped. Why did he feel like he was standing on the edge of a whirlpool about to fall in? He took a bite of hamburger and tried to chew.

Murch pointed at Jim with his fork. "So Constance thinks you'd be good at doing some work for me too."

Jim swallowed fast. "I'd be happy to give you a quote on any job."

"Yeah, I'll bet you would." He grinned.

"My boss, Billy Ballew, has great design ideas and is really good at sourcing product, so he can generally save you money."

He bounced the fork again. "But it's you Constance believes in. And your name is Carney."

Jim took a deep breath. "Sir, you can't base anything about my work or our company on my family. I have no connection with my father, and I'm sure he wouldn't ever recommend you deal with me." There. He said it.

"Okay, that's impressive. See that, Constance? He knows I'm connected with his father, but he doesn't try to trade on that. I like you, Carney."

Constance smiled so big, her face about split. "I knew you would, Daddy."

Jim smiled too and took a huge bite of his burger. He wiped Thousand Island dressing from the corner of his mouth.

"I thought you were going to stay away from junk food." The lilting voice had an edge, and Jim's head snapped up so hard, he about broke his neck.

Ken Tanaka stood at the edge of the table with Gene Willings. Shit, was Tanaka his angel of nutrition? The architect smiled snarkily, which made Jim want to smack him, but that feeling warred with so many others—embarrassment, anger, and a batch of other unidentifiable things. "I never said I'd stay away from junk food. You just suggested it."

"I wasn't talking to hear myself pontificate, Jim. You need to watch your diet." He looked up. "Excuse me for interrupting, Alex. Just a recalcitrant patient."

Al raised an eyebrow. "Oh? Jim having some trouble with his heart? Seems too young."

"Yes, he is. And he won't live to get old if he doesn't take some steps."

Constance grabbed his arm. "Jim, that's awful."

Jim gritted his teeth. "It's no big deal."

Ken gazed at him. "Oh? Thanks for letting me know." He looked at Murch. "Excuse me again. Come on, Gene." He walked away with Willings beside him. Jim wanted to run after him to bash his meddling head in—or something.

Constance was in full hysteria. "How can you have heart problems at your age? You look so healthy."

He put a hand over hers. "I just have a weird mitral valve. Lots of people have it. Even Tanaka says it's no big deal."

"He didn't make it sound that way."

"He just wants me to do what he says. A little hamburger never hurt anybody."

Al nodded. "I couldn't agree more. Sounds to me like you need a different doctor." He stared at the door where Ken and Gene had disappeared and spoke under his breath. "Fucking fag."

Jim dragged his eyes from the door and looked at Murch. *What did he say?* Constance was petting Jim's arm and making motherly soothing sounds. His heart beat way too hard, like it wanted to prove Ken right, and all he could think about was running out the door and bashing Gene Willings in the supercilious fucking smile.

"Jim, you're pale. Drink some water." Constance held the water glass to his lips. Shit, he hadn't gotten mothering from the woman who birthed him; why should he take it from someone else?

Murch leaned forward. "I don't know why they ever agreed to let—him on the board. Jesus, that's taking equal rights about a hundred steps too far."

"Daddy, please." Constance just kept up her petting. He couldn't breathe.

"Excuse me. I really appreciate lunch, but my guys will be looking for some direction. I need to get back."

Murch nodded. "Good man. After all, you've got a tough client to please, right?"

"Yes. The toughest." He slapped a smile on his face.

Constance looked back and forth between them like she wasn't really ready to let go. "Of course. Uh, Jim. Did you think about Saturday?"

The play. *Shit.* "Uh, I haven't had a chance to check on my brother yet. I'll do that."

"Good." She curved a sweet smile. "I hope you can come."

"Yes, uh, me too." He glanced at Murch, who was watching them with a half smile. "So I'll let you know."

"Good." She didn't move and he couldn't exactly push her out of the booth, but that was becoming an option. He was sweating, his pulse pounded so fast. "Thank you again, Mr. Murch."

"Al."

"Al. Good to meet you." He looked again at Constance. She finally seemed to realize that she was the obstacle to forward movement and slid out of the booth. "Thanks again." He held out his hand.

She looked at it, then leaned forward and kissed his cheek. "See you later."

"Uh, yes, great. Bye." Like some animal being freed into the wild, he hesitated, then sped across the dining room to the entrance. The same one he'd seen Ken Tanaka leave from.

KEN PUSHED open the door to their building.

Gene ran a couple of steps to catch up. "Hey, slow down. Your patients won't die in five minutes."

Ken frowned and glanced at his watch. He actually had half an hour until his next appointment, but he wanted out of the club and nowhere near Jim Carney. "If I get behind on one appointment, it screws up the whole day."

"Speaking of patients, weren't you kind of hard on Jim Carney?"

"No." He crossed his arms.

Gene shrugged. "You as much as told him he was going to die. And in front of Alex Murch. Jesus, man, that's tough duty."

Ken puffed out his cheeks as he blew. "He will die if he doesn't shape up."

"Seriously? What's he got?"

"Mitral valve prolapse."

Gene's eyes widened. "Wow. I didn't think you'd tell me."

Jesus. "Sorry. I shouldn't have. Forget I said it."

"But you told me he wasn't serious, right? Hell, the guy looks more than healthy. In fact, I'd call him delicious."

Ken stared at the black tile floor of the lobby, then glanced toward the suite where Jim had been working. "Yeah, but his problem is more severe than a lot of people. He'll be fine if he takes precautions."

"Precautions like kale and wheatgrass juice?"

"Maybe not that far, but he needs to eat a reasonable diet, reduce stress, moderate drinking, shit like that."

Gene flipped his hand. "Yes, well, I've got to admit I didn't believe you when you said he was straight until today. That was one happy family scene there at the club. The blue-collar dude and the billionaire's daughter. Who'd have guessed it?"

Ken gritted his teeth. "He works for them."

"That may be true, darling, but clearly he slept his way to the top." He laughed. "So are you taking me to dinner tonight to celebrate my getting into the club?"

Ken pulled his eyes away from the door to the suite. "What? Oh, I suppose so."

"Don't sound so enthusiastic, darling, but do pick me up at eight. See you later." He looked up at a man about to step on the elevator. "Hold it, please." He glanced at Ken. "Coming?"

"A minute."

"See you tonight." Gene jogged into the elevator, and the door closed.

Ken breathed in deeply through his nose. *Slept his way to the top.* Was that true? Had Jim been banging that woman the whole time Ken had known him? God, why should that be hard to believe? Why should he even care? Jim made him crazy. He'd done two wholly unprofessional things, both brought on by that damned blue-collar guy. He sighed. What had Gene called him? That delicious man.

Movement outside the lobby glass made him glance up to see Jim running toward the entrance. He looked really upset. God, Ken wanted to go smooth the wrinkles in Jim's forehead and tell him to reduce stress. Or maybe hit him for being a straight player.

Tanaka, you're cracked.

He raced to the stairway and slipped inside before Jim made it to the front door.

CHAPTER THIRTEEN

JIM STOPPED outside the suite and braced his hands on his knees, breathing like an old racehorse. A couple of men walked in through the lobby doors, their business casual attire mocking Jim's dusty work clothes, and one of them stared at him like he'd done something wrong just by living. Jim slammed against the suite door with his shoulder and pushed inside. Charlie whipped around from where he held a piece of drywall in place, Raoul stared down from his ladder, and to top it off, Ian looked up from where he sat smiling over the plans with Rico. Just when he'd like a few minutes alone, the fucking gang was all here.

Raoul called, "Hey, man, you okay? You look like some ghosts are chasing you."

Ghosts? Yeah, probably his own from what Tanaka said. "I'm fine. Sorry to take so long."

Charlie shook his head. "No worries. We got this. What did the boss lady want?"

Way more than he was prepared to give. "She wanted to introduce me to her father."

Ian looked startled, and Raoul laughed. "Taking you home to papa already?"

"I told you she was interested." Charlie snorted.

"No, not like that, you assholes. He's this big developer, and she thinks we could do some work for him."

"Hey, man, that's big." Raoul sounded impressed. "Billy's gonna be way happy."

Charlie nodded. "You going to call and tell him?"

"Nah. Nothing's for sure. Billy's only got another week. I don't even want him to think about work."

Charlie asked, "Has he called?"

"No. Texted a couple times, and I just replied things were perfectly boring."

"You mean you didn't tell him about the change of plans and the second suite?"

Jim grinned. "Nope. Just hope he'll be happy when he gets back."

Raoul whistled. "Hell, who wouldn't be? You got that woman twisted around your finger, man. You gonna make Billy rich."

Jim swallowed hard. "No guarantees." And what the fuck would he have to do to make that money for Billy? He walked over to Ian. "Surprised to see you. Did you lose your job?"

Ian grinned. "Nope. Got promoted. I start tonight as a waiter, which means I'll get tips."

"Wasn't that a pretty fast promotion?" Jim cocked his head.

"Yeah, I guess. They love me." His dimples sank so deep, you could sharpen pencils in them.

"Congratulations, bro. That's great. And I see you met Rico."

Those dimples kept flashing as Ian looked at Rico. "Yeah. I came to tell you about my promotion, and he came looking for you, and we sort of ran into each other."

Rico seemed pretty happy himself. "I had to meet the genius who came up with the plans for the suite."

Ian practically fluttered his damned lashes. "You made them better."

"No, I just made them cheaper."

Maybe I should dunk them both in cold water. "Cheaper is better when it comes to TIs." Jim wiped his hand over his forehead to try to get the crease out from between his eyebrows. "I better get back to work."

Ian sobered. "Everything okay, Jim?"

"Sure. Sure."

"The owner of the building. She giving you a hard time?"

He lowered his voice. "Not exactly. No. She's real nice."

"So what, exactly?"

Jim's eyes flicked to Rico. *Not the time.* Maybe there never would be a time. "Nothing. Really. I just need to get to work—" He raised his voice. "—before these ugly a-holes start throwing hammers at me."

"Got that right, man." Raoul hammered extra hard to make his point.

Jim smiled. "I'm really happy for you, Ian. You're great at everything."

Ian got up and gave Jim a hug. Rico stood next to him. "But Ian needs to go to Berkeley. He's too talented to be wasted on some second-class school."

Ian's smile drooped a little, and Jim nodded. "Yeah. Well, he'll excel no matter where he goes to school." But shit, how he wished he could make that happen.

Ian left with Rico after him. Jim considered telling Rico to give Gene Willings a smack in his face for him but resisted. Charlie stepped up beside Jim and put a hand on his shoulder. "What's the architect mean about Berkeley?"

"My father was going to send Ian there, but he threw the kid out when he found out he's gay."

"Shit, man, that's evil."

"Yeah."

"He's a great kid. Talented too. But you can't step in and make up for all the crap your father isn't doing. It's not your job."

Jim really looked at Charlie. "Thanks, man. I try to tell myself that, but I still wish I could make it up to him. He doesn't deserve this."

"Yeah, well, I never saw anybody giving you no rose garden either, buddy."

Jim half grinned. "Nope. I'm too ugly."

"That, my man, is the shit's honest truth."

They slapped backs and went to work.

The guys worked until after five, then gathered their tools to leave. Jim met them at the door. "I pulled permits on the upstairs suite today. You two meet me there in the morning. I'll get Jase and Henry in here to finish this place and send you a couple of helpers on demo for the other suite."

Charlie looked up from where he tucked his work boots into his carry bag. "Want to go for a beer?"

"No. I'm going to button up in here. I'll see you tomorrow."

"'Kay. Night."

He watched the two guys leave and soaked in the silence after the door closed. Pressing his back against the wall, he slowly slid to sitting. *Breathe deeply.* In through his nose and out through his mouth like the doc's meditation instructions said. Reduce stress or he could die. That's what Ken had said. Well, not in so many words, but apparently the doc hadn't told him everything, based on today's overreaction.

So now, there he sat between the official rock and hard place. He was stressed about having to reduce stress. Oh yeah, but that was the mere tip of the f-ing iceberg. He really wanted to do a good job for Billy. Every day it became more obvious that the only way to succeed was to romance the boss. That's what she wanted. If he didn't romance the boss, he could do the best job there was and still fail. Fail not just with her, but with her father. Fail at things he hadn't even tried yet.

But even though she was a nice-looking woman and clearly it would make a fuckload of sense to date her, he didn't want to succeed with her in that way. Her blonde hair and cute butt didn't inspire a particle of lust. Just like Helen and Peggy. *God, who the fuck do I lust after?* Sadly, he knew the answer.

He shook his head until it banged against the wall on both sides.

Man, Carney, you've got failure down.

He breathed out slowly, and his eyes drifted closed.

GIGGLES.

Jim's eyes opened. Dark except for the streetlights shining in from outside the office suite. *Damn, fell asleep.*

"Come on, baby." The voice was muffled, but since Jim's ear was pressed against the door, he could make out the words.

"No. Go 'way."

Jim sat straighter. *What the fuck? What time is it?*

Footsteps, rustlings, and a bump against the wall sounded behind him. He grabbed his phone from his pocket to check the time—9:30 p.m. Man, he'd been asleep for a long time.

"Don' wanna."

Shit, that was Ken. The voice had to be right on the other side of the door. Had he been drugged again? Jim popped up and almost fell. *Butt asleep.* He pounded some fresh blood into his muscles, then slowly pushed down the door handle and opened it a crack.

Over by the elevator, Gene Willings stood with his arm around Ken Tanaka. Ken was a lot taller, so the guy had to reach up. *Fucking midget.*

Gene said, "Come on, baby. We have to get out of the lobby before the guard comes."

"Okay." Ken's words slurred. That sounded like booze, not drugs—and Jim oughta know. So old Dr. Eat-and-Drink-the-Right-Shit-or-You'll-Die wasn't practicing what he preached.

The elevator came, and Gene kind of dragged Ken onto it and the door closed.

Well, fuck. Hadn't he heard Ken say no? Was he just being hard to get? Did he really want whatever Mr. Pain in the Ass Architect was dishing out? What if he didn't?

Jim took off to the stairs at a run. At the bottom of the first flight, he stopped. *Why the hell are you rescuing Ken Tanaka again?*

You know why.

Shit.

He ran up another flight.

Okay, slow down or he'll have to take care of you instead of the other way around. He started up the stairs at a moderate jog.

By the fourth floor, he was breathing hard but not about to have a heart attack. Tanaka would be proud—assuming the doc was sober enough to be anything. Jim stuck his head out of the stairwell and sighted down the hall. *Nobody.* He slipped out and trotted to the office. The outer door was on an autocloser, but it hadn't latched. The door rested against the jam. Jim pushed it open. Dark inside, but dim lights shone from somewhere in the back of the suite. He closed the door gently, then tiptoed across the lobby and opened the door to the inner sanctum. Voices. He couldn't make them out too clearly. No screams or bedpans hitting walls.

He should go, but what if the doc really was in trouble again? Hell, he did have the damnedest way of picking up people who wanted to fuck him. Jim stepped softly down the corridor toward the voices.

"Mmmpft. Oh baby, I love this cock. Mmmmn."

"Oh man."

Jim stopped. *Okay, go now.* This was no rape scene. Pretty clear. He pressed against the wall. *Do. Not. Look.*

"Mmmmmft."

"Oh shit."

Okay, he'd managed to give up booze. Maybe he could stop eating burgers. But not looking into that room to see Ken Tanaka's cock? Beyond his strength. Very slowly he moved so he could see around the edge of the door. *Oh yeah.*

Ken lay on an exam table, his jeans pulled down around his knees. Shorty the Architect had moved a chair over so he could get in position, and he bobbed his head over Ken's hips, the long, surprisingly thick cock disappearing into his mouth and then reappearing as his head moved up.

Jim grabbed his chest. God, they had to hear his heart, it beat so hard. His pulse throbbed in his throat and in his stiff-as-a-board cock pressing against his fly. Dear God, it was like his yaoi dream—except for the short prick doing the sucking. Jim pressed a hand against his own cock. He could come just watching.

"Quit. Quit it." Ken's head came up, and Jim dove back against the wall.

"Mmmft."

"Let go. Don't wanna."

A soft pop indicated lips had left cock. "Come on, baby. You know you're enjoying it."

"No. Quit. Don't want you."

"What do you mean you don't want me? Who the fuck do you want?"

"Want Jim. Get Jim."

What? What did he say?

"You said he was straight."

"Is. Want Jim."

Oh my God.

"You fucking player asshole. You haven't changed a bit."

A slap sounded from the room.

Jim's head exploded. He screamed, "Get your hands off him, you fucking midget." He threw open the door, leaped at Gene, and had him down on the floor before he even retrieved his slapping son-of-a-bitch hand. Jim looked up and saw the pink imprint on Ken's cheek. He clenched his fist.

"Wait, Jim. No." Ken sounded almost sober.

"I'll kill the bastard for hitting you."

"No, I deserved it. Let him go."

Jim stared down at Willings, who had one arm raised in defense. Jim snarled, "Get the fuck up and get out of here."

Willings sneered. "How dare you, you Neanderthal?"

"You should be aware, asshole, that I never do anything Ken tells me to, so I may just punch your fucking lights out."

"You wouldn't." He looked scared.

"I will if you aren't out of here in three seconds. One."

Willings leaped to his feet the second Jim let him up and ran to the door. "Don't expect any further help from members of my staff."

Well, there was that. "Send me a fucking bill." He held up two fingers. "Two."

Willings disappeared out the door, and a couple of seconds later, the sound of the office door slamming as hard as the self-closer would allow confirmed his departure. Jim looked at Ken, who hadn't moved if you didn't count the deflation of his cock. *Keep your eyes above the belt.* "You do have a way of getting into these compromising positions."

"And you have a way of showing up to save me."

"Are you hurt?"

"Drunk."

"Thought you didn't drink much. Practice what you preach, doc."

"Don't drink much. Wanted to get drunk."

"So you could stand looking Willings in the face?"

He shook his head slowly.

Jim's eyes traveled back to the long, relaxed cock all on their own. "Maybe we should get you dressed?"

Ken shook his head again and didn't move. His cock twitched. *Did it get a little longer?*

Jim couldn't drag his eyes away. He swallowed hard. "I heard you say you wanted me to suck you instead of the midget. I guess you must be really drunk."

That head shake again. The cock was definitely longer. In fact, rising. "I don't have to be drunk to want that. But know what I want more?"

"W-what?"

"You to fuck me."

117

No saliva. Mouth totally dry. Heart beating so hard he couldn't hear, but he could sure feel his own dick rising to the challenge. "Not— I mean, never fucked a guy."

"Ever had anal sex?"

"Yeah."

"That's all the practice you need. An asshole is an asshole."

Oh sweet Jesus, that was so far from true. If somebody paraded Peggy's ass or Constance's ass in front of him right now, he knew damned well he wouldn't get a cock wiggle. Instead, he stood here hard as a fire pole and hotter than he'd ever remembered feeling in his life. In the world of time, this was what they called a turning point. "I don't—I'm not—"

Ken just lay there with a rapidly filling cock doing all his talking. *Sweet Jesus, is this what you want?* "Okay."

A slow smile spread across Ken's face, and his cock slapped against his abdomen. "Did you just say okay?"

"Yeah. I mean, I'm not—yeah."

That got Ken moving. He sat up, caught himself on the edge of the table when he looked like he might fall back down, and finally made it to an upright position to match his dick. All this unfortunately pointed directly to the fact that the doc was drunk. *Jesus, what in the hell am I thinking?* "Hey, doc, I don't think we'd be doing this if you were sober."

Ken grinned. "You afraid you're taking advantage of a drunken man?"

"Well, yeah, I guess so."

"That's the most siv, uh chivalrous thing anybody ever said to me."

Jim put a hand on Ken's back and pulled him to the edge of the table. "I'm sorry to hear that." Of course, touching that lean hardness didn't help his own full upright position. He sighed. *So much for what you want, buddy.* "Let's get you home and into bed."

CHAPTER FOURTEEN

JIM STEPPED back as Ken slid one leg to the floor, his loose pants tangling around his thighs. "Easy, doc."

Ken gazed up at him from his half-seated/half-leaning position. Those black eyes looked like deep pools—surrounded by a sea of bloodshot red. He grinned and reached out an arm. Jim leaned down to allow Ken to slip his arm around his neck and be lifted to his feet. "Up you go."

As he stood, Ken twisted, reached up with his other hand, and captured Jim's head. In one smooth, undrunken move, he pulled Jim down and captured his mouth with lips so heavenly Jim gasped like he'd been shot from a cannon straight to heaven. That intake of breath succeeded in pulling Ken's tongue deep into his mouth. *Oh sweet baby Jesus.* Soft, hot, silky, wet, and determined to reach Jim's tonsils. The moan he heard maybe came from Ken. Maybe not. But wrapping his arms around Ken's tall frame and slanting his head to get better access to his mouth was all his own idea.

This stacked up as a first among firsts. Yeah, Ken Tanaka had given him the blow job of the century, but Jim had had blow jobs from Hiro. Not as world class. Still memorable. But never in all the years of their friendship had he ever kissed Hiro. Too intimate. Too committed. Did this make him gay? *Do. Not. Care.*

The next moan came from his gut. Ken stood all the way up and somehow managed to kick his jeans off his legs and across the floor, leaving the whole bottom half of him bare-assed and full-cocked. He used the inch or so he had on Jim in height to push him back over the exam table, rutting his hips against Jim's while he plundered his mouth with a fucking tongue. Couldn't get close enough. *Want to burrow inside and live in his body.*

Ken snaked a hand down and, with the dexterity of a man used to examining delicate body parts, managed to unfasten Jim's snap at the waist and pull down his zipper. Heat slipped inside Jim's boxer briefs and warm fingers wrapped his painfully throbbing cock and extracted it from its too-confined space. Ken pulled back from the kiss and gazed into Jim's eyes as he cranked his cock. "Don't want to suck you because I want you to come in my ass."

Wait. Suck. Jim reached down and grabbed Ken's blissfully moving hand. "Hang on. Are you gonna remember this tomorrow? Because if you don't, or pretend you don't, I'm gone. Got it? You'll never get rescued by old Sir Bangalot again."

Some piece clicked into a puzzle in Ken's eyes. "You mean—?"

"Just tell me you're going to remember."

Ken grabbed Jim's chin and kissed him hard. "No matter what happens, I'll never forget."

Considering his own shaky life situation, that was about as good as it got. "Then turn over and show me how to fuck you before I come all over your exam room."

"Man, that is one romantic invitation." A smile spread across Ken's face that made damned suns rise and comets cross skies. "Be right back."

"What?"

Bare behind glistening in the light of only one lamp, Ken trotted out of the room. *What the hell?* A couple of seconds later, he ran back in with a condom and a tube of lube so huge he must use it to examine elephants.

Whoa. That made it real. He was about to fuck a guy. Suddenly his knees felt weak, and he leaned against the exam table. Ken pressed against him. "Scared?"

"Yeah."

"Nothing to worry about. Close your eyes and pretend I'm female."

"That sure as fuck won't do the job."

"No?"

"No."

"You saying you want to fuck me?"

"I wouldn't be doing it otherwise."

Ken leaned in and grabbed their two dicks in one of his hands. "Feel that? How perfect it is? I've wanted to welcome you into my ass since the moment I laid eyes on you in that damned ballroom. I would gladly have pulled you into the men's room and leaned over before I knew your name. That's how hot you make me. All I think about is you. Fucking embarrassing, but there it is. Get that thing in me fast." He yanked their cocks a couple of times for good measure, then scooted to the side and bent over the table, pointing that ass that ought to be declared a weapon of mass destruction right at Jim. "Stick some lube in my ass and some on your cock. Easy."

Couldn't catch his breath. Ken had to be the sexiest human on earth. He'd made him up from comics and dreams. Sleepwalking, Jim grabbed the lube while he stared at that perfect butt. His cock was going in there. Scenes from his comic flashed. His hero leaning over the edge of a couch while the big blond guy reamed him over and over. Jesus, he did make this up.

"Put some in me. Feel how hot it is." Ken reached back and pulled his ass cheeks apart.

Oh crap, gonna faint. A sweet, pink pucker stared at Jim, inviting. Welcoming. Jim squeezed a little lube on his index finger and touched it to the tight hole. "Doesn't it hurt?"

"It burns, but really good. Put it in."

Jim pressed his digit against the pucker and it gave way easily, sucking his finger in. Sweet God, it was hot, just like Ken promised. And smooth. He pushed deeper and explored, feeling little ridges.

"Oh." Ken jumped, and Jim ripped his finger out.

"Did I hurt you?"

"No, dear. Quite the contrary. That's my prostate and it feels fabulous. Now do it with your cock."

Oh Jesus. Don't think. He ripped the condom package and slid on the rubber, then squeezed some lube into his hand and stroked it on his sheathed cock. The dick clearly knew what it wanted because even though there was a high risk he might pass out, his cock strained toward its goal as he slathered it. *Fuck Ken. Fuck Ken.*

Okay. Okay. "You ready?"

"Fuck me!"

"Okay." *Here goes.* He lined up his cockhead with the awaiting hole. "I'm in danger of coming just looking at your ass." Jesus, did he say that out loud?

121

"Make sure you're inside when it happens, darling."

Inside. Oh man, inside Ken Tanaka. He closed his eyes and pushed. Pressure on his cockhead and nothing else. "I thought you said this would be easy."

"Push, dammit."

He pushed harder this time with eyes open, staring at the target. *Look at that.* The head turned kind of white from the pressure while the pucker stretched and got shinier and—*Je-sus!* He popped inside. Shit, he was inside a guy. No, wait. He was inside his dreams. He pushed harder and his cock furrowed through a hot, silky tunnel, closer and closer into the inferno that was Ken Tanaka. Squeezed beyond reckoning, dragged with the most perfect friction, massaged by the twists and turns of that channel. Like heaven. Surely. "Oh my God, I didn't know."

Ken kind of giggled. "You like?"

"Sweet Jesus." He pulled out and pushed in harder. "Oh God."

"Yes, like that. Hard. You can't hurt me. I want all of you."

Jim leaned both arms on the table beside Ken and popped his hips like a jackhammer he'd used many times. *Bam, bam, bam. Feels. So. Good.* His breath came so hard he could hear it over his heart hammering. "Oh God."

"Yes, Jim. Yes. More, please."

More. Ken wanted more. He even said please. Jim buried his lips against Ken's neck and bit as he pounded his hips. Ken wailed and it shivered through Jim's whole body. Never in his life had he felt like this. Like some jacking animal that never wanted to stop. Like if he died of a heart attack right now, he'd die perfectly happy. Lights flashed behind his closed eyes and heat bubbled so hot in his balls, they had to explode. "Have to come." He nibbled against Ken's neck, then sucked harder. "Don't want to. Can I fuck you forever?"

"Yes, please. We'll make medical history. Coitus uninterruptus." Ken laughed and howled at the same time. "Oh God, Jim. I'm there. Coming. Coming."

Jim reached down for Ken's cock in time to catch a handful of spunk shooting out so hard it made his hand tingle. Sweet Jesus, he'd made Ken come.

An arrow of ecstasy shot up his spine as his balls squeezed until they hurt, and jets of pleasure fired into the condom inside that ass that had launched all his wet dreams. "Oh Gooooood." He was coming into Ken Tanaka's body, and that was so perfect it made him shiver as he convulsed through one, two, three shudders of orgasm. How long had it been since he'd really climaxed? Not since—Hiro. Ten years.

His body kept shaking as he collapsed over Ken and tried to catch his breath. A half sigh, half laugh bubbled out of him. "You told me to reduce stress. You could be the death of me."

A smothered giggle escaped from under him. "I also told you exercise was good for you."

"You're all heart. Want to work me up a regular exercise routine, doc?"

For a second all went quiet. Then that soft, satiny voice said, "Yeah. I'd like that." Ken slowly rose up, pushing Jim's slug of a body, and crawled onto the exam table. He lay on his side and patted the space in front of him. Jim raised an eyebrow. "You think I'm gonna fit up there with you?"

"If we get close enough."

That sounded good. He crawled up and, with some careful jigsaw-puzzle fitting, they managed to get their parts side by side. Ken ran a finger down Jim's cheek, which in the midst of a lot of intimacy, felt the most personal of all. "Tell me something. Why did you say I had to remember this?"

"Because you didn't remember giving me a blow job the night you stayed at my place."

Ken nodded. "I see. I thought I dreamed it—because of the drug. But it was a very happy dream for me."

Jim glanced away.

"So you wanted me to remember."

Jim shrugged.

"What does that mean?"

Oh hell. "I guess for a few minutes I felt like I was ready to admit I wanted more, but when you didn't remember, it made it easy to deny the whole thing."

"You wanted to admit you're gay?"

Jim frowned. "I wanted to admit I like you."

"Have you ever been with a guy before?"

"Yeah. A long time ago. But only women since then."

"Which do you like better?"

"You."

Ken laughed. "I'm honored."

The words popped out before he could retrieve them. "No reason. I'm at the back of a very long line."

Ken stilled and then sighed. "Yes. It's complicated."

"Not like my life isn't." Jim pushed up on his forearm, threatening to fall off the table. "This was probably a crap idea."

Ken touched his cheek again. "No. I'm sorry. I'm sorry I forgot I blew you, or at least that I didn't admit remembering, but I'm not sorry I did it. And I'm not sorry about this."

Easy for Ken to say. Am I sorry? "It doesn't change anything."

"No." He looked up through his lashes. "But I wouldn't mind doing it again—sometime."

Jim slid off the table, then hopped up and sat on the edge next to Ken, who was still lying on his side. Must look funny, both of them bare-assed. He glanced at Ken. No. Nothing funny about that much beauty. "I have this secret kink."

"Oh really? I'm very intrigued."

"I love yaoi."

"That's not really so kinky, except maybe that it's primarily drawn for cute girls in pink bows." He laughed.

"I don't love all yaoi. Just a certain series with this hero who looks—like you. When I first saw you, I about passed out." He raised his shoulders and dropped them on a long breath. "So I guess that's why I'm so attracted to you."

"And the guys you were with before?"

"Guy. One. His name was—is Hiro."

"You don't see him anymore?"

"No." The pain flashed through his chest. "I wrecked his life and that was that."

Ken sounded far away. Like the psychiatrist on his couch Jim had refused to see. "How did you do that?"

"My mom found the yaoi novels, and I said they were Hiro's. She called his mom. They sent him back to Japan. End of story."

"Were they Hiro's novels?"

"I told myself I bought them for him, but they were really mine. I was just scared to admit it to my mother."

"You know that now. Did you know it then?"

"Maybe not."

"How old were you?"

"Just turned sixteen."

"What happened?"

"I left home the day after I found out about Hiro. Never went back."

"Jesus, Jim."

He took a deep breath and let it out. "I guess I never learn. Those yaoi novels have been fucking up my life for ten years." He glanced at Ken. "And they're still doing it."

Ken's brows pulled together, and he sat up slowly. "How do you figure that?"

"Life would be one fuck of a lot easier if I wasn't attracted to you."

"Because of the building owner?"

Jim nodded.

"She seems interested in you."

"Asked me out." That sounded a little cockier than he intended.

"Oh? Not a business excuse?" A funny look crossed Ken's face. Could have been jealousy. That would be nice.

"Nope. Full-on date. Go to a play. Get dinner. Doesn't sound businessy to me."

"When?"

"Saturday night."

"You going to say yes?"

"I don't know what to do. This woman means a lot to Billy's business."

"I doubt Billy expects you to sleep your way to the top."

Jim frowned. "That's harsh."

"Sorry. It's what Willings said to me when he saw you with that woman and her father."

Jim hopped off the table and walked to the dark frame of the window. "I'd expect something like that from him. Asshole."

"Still, there's some truth to it."

Jim looked over his shoulder at Ken and tried to see past the breathtaking face to the gay player beyond. *Get serious, Carney. He's amazing, but what can you be to him but another notch on his bedpost?*

Ken cocked his head. "You're thinking pretty hard."

He stared out at the building lights. "Yes, well, the fact is that she's an attractive woman who likes me and happens to have a lot of money and connections that are valuable. Her father even seems to think I'm okay." *Hell, what are you talking yourself into?*

"But you don't like women."

He caught his breath. Didn't he like women? Some invisible scale rocked back and forth in his heart. Shit, maybe Ken Tanaka made women look simple. "I like women okay. She may not be you, but then, you're not her either, are you?"

That got a fast glance and dark scowl from Ken. "I don't have a rich father I can dangle in front of you to forward your career."

"No. And I doubt you'd even introduce me to your father—or your mother, right? Because I'm the wrong kind of guy for them."

His back straightened. "Correct, because you're not a Japanese woman." But he wouldn't meet Jim's eyes.

Jim turned and felt his shoulders sag. "This is stupid. Neither of us can do anything about the—" He made quote marks in the air. "—complications of our lives. I'll never regret fucking you." Jesus, that was so achingly true. "But I guess we ought to leave it at that."

Jim's stomach knotted when Ken nodded slowly. "I see the logic in your argument." He glanced up with bright black eyes. "But I can be talked out of it."

Jim had to smile. Always the player, but oh so gorgeous.

"So in the interests of not running into each other again, I'll make sure I stay away from the club on Saturday night."

"I figure I'll haul Constance to my favorite bar in Laguna after her play. That should emphasize how different we are." He blew his breath out slowly. He might be feeling heterosexual, but the idea still didn't excite him.

"Which is your favorite bar?"

"The Bay. It gets a lot of blue-collar guys like me, but it's a pretty mixed group—like Laguna."

"I live just north of Laguna in Crystal Cove. I'm always looking for great bars."

Jim cocked a smile. Made sense the doc would live someplace ritzy like that. "Bay's probably not your scene."

"Perhaps."

Jim looked down at his bare legs and the tip of his cock hanging below the edge of his shirt. "Guess I better dress."

"You may be even more popular with the boss lady if you take to that attire."

Why was that more sad than funny? He grabbed his boxer briefs from inside his fallen jeans, pulled them on, then dragged the denim up his legs.

Ken spoke from behind him. "Sorry to see that butt go."

Not half as sorry as Jim was. "My kid brother's probably worried. I fell asleep in the suite, or I wouldn't have been here to save your pretty ass."

Ken's hand landed on his shoulder. "Thank you for that, by the way. Thank you for both rescues and for thinking my ass is pretty."

Jim turned to face him, looking up those couple of inches into dark depths he could drown in. "That's not an opinion. It's a universal truth."

Ken pressed his lips against Jim's. Jim's dick gave a little hop, but it wasn't really trying. *Too sad.* "Guess I'll see you around, doc." He stepped back and walked toward the door.

"Take care of your heart."

Jim cast a look over his shoulder. The only chance he had of doing that was to stay away from Ken Tanaka.

CHAPTER FIFTEEN

KEN'S PHONE rang as he walked to the front door of his apartment. Well, damn, he had a pretty good idea what this call was about. "Good evening, Okaa-san. I'm honored by your call."

"I'm pleased to hear that you are going on a date with Mikio Okuwa. You make me very happy, my son."

"I'm happy that you're happy." He locked the door and headed toward the car.

"Please invite Mikio to our home this week so we can get to know him better."

Never a good idea. "I have to tell you, Mother, that I had a very unfortunate experience in Mickey's company. Tonight he's trying to show that he was not responsible for the bad events that took place. But the jury's still out."

"Excuse me?"

"I'm not sure if I believe him."

"Surely he is innocent. He comes from such a good family."

Ken snorted.

"Kenji!"

"Forgive me, I had to sneeze." He opened his garage door and slid into his car.

"May I ask what he did?"

"His friends drugged me."

"Oh no. That's terrible. Sometimes young men get into bad company without realizing it. You are older and need to guide him."

"I said I'd give him another chance and I will."

"Without the jury?"

He laughed. "Yes, ma'am." He started backing out.

"Very good. Have a happy evening, my son. When I see you next, I'll show you the information I've found on surrogate births."

His foot stomped the brake. "Mother, what the hell?"

"Kenji, just because you are gay does not mean you are freed of your responsibilities to your family. We must get you settled so you can produce your first child."

Dear blessed God. "I have to go. I know you don't like me to talk on the phone while driving." Right. One more announcement like that and he'd wreck the car.

"Take care. We'll see you and Mikio later in the week." She hung up.

He stabbed his finger at the End button on his phone. Damned thing should be attached to a noose that his mother was tightening around his neck. He dropped his head onto the steering wheel. He didn't want to go on this date. *And what do you want to do, Dr. Tanaka?* Easy answer. He wanted to curl up on his couch and think about Jim Carney's cock buried deep in his ass. Jim had made him promise not to forget. Not likely he ever could.

A horn sounded behind the car. *Shit, move.* He pressed the accelerator and headed toward the fate he didn't seem to be able to escape.

A half hour later, he sat in a nice seafood restaurant in north Laguna that Mickey had chosen and picked at his food. It was going on ten, later than he usually liked to eat, but Mickey had chosen that too. *Wonder how Jim's date is going?*

Mickey chewed his steak. "I thought you might like this restaurant."

Ken swallowed a mouthful of tilapia. "I do like it, but you didn't have to pick a place you don't enjoy." He gestured toward Mickey's full fork. "I doubt they specialize in beef, being called Pacific Fish."

"Tough to mess up a good steak." He popped the food into his mouth, then looked up with an expression that dripped concern. "I'm glad to see you're feeling well. I have trouble believing that GG and Tommy would do such a thing, but I cut off my friendship with them since you said you're sure they're responsible. What a terrible experience."

"Yeah, it wasn't fun."

"I've read that drug's usually pretty powerful. How in the hell did you get away?"

"I wasn't drinking alcohol, or I probably wouldn't have been able to function. And I recognized the taste right away so I didn't drink much."

"Yeah, you being a doctor and all." He swallowed a mouthful of red wine. "Good thing. I don't guess there's a chance GG didn't do it, is there? Maybe somebody at the bar?"

Ken narrowed his eyes but kept playing with the fish on his plate. "As I told you, your friends came looking for me."

"Could have just been concerned." He waved his fork.

"I heard them. Didn't sound friendly. And the guy who came to pick me up says they wanted to finish what they started."

"Umf." He swallowed. "About that. GG says they were worried about that guy. Thought he looked pretty sketchballs and they were trying to get you away from him, but he got mean. Hit Tommy pretty hard. I'm glad he didn't hurt you."

"He's a friend of mine." He sat back. "Look Mickey, believe who you choose. I wouldn't want to come between you and your friends."

He held up a hand. "No, no. Like I said, I severed all relationships with those assholes. If you say they did it, it's good enough for me. Hell, I've got more reason to be with you than with them."

"Oh, really?"

"I don't know about you—hey, want some dessert?"

"No, thanks. I'll take a cappuccino."

Mickey waved to the waiter and ordered a cappuccino and a spiked coffee for himself. When the waiter left, he looked back at Ken. "Where was I?"

"I don't know about you—"

"What?"

"That's what you were saying."

Mickey grinned. "Man, you do pay attention. That's one thing I really like about you. Not many guys do, you know?"

"Yes, I do know."

"Anyway, what I was going to say is that my family is really all over us getting together. Hell, you'd think we were the fucking crowned heads of Japan or something. Like the future of the realm depends on us being a couple."

Ken blew out his breath.

"You too, huh?" The waiter brought the drinks, and Mickey cradled the warm coffee in his hands. "I mean, I'm no traditionalist, you know, but my folks still pay for law school and my apartment and shit. Until I get the music thing going, you know? So I figure, what the hell. If you can't beat 'em, you know?"

Ken stared into the blackness of the cappuccino. "Yes, I do know."

"So I hear I'm supposed to have dinner at your place this week. I mean, at your parents' place."

"Obviously, my mother's invitations have traveled far and wide."

"Yeah, man. Some of that Mama-san determination. I love my mother, but she makes me glad I don't get a hard-on for females."

Ken laughed.

Mickey joined in. "Imagine facing that kind of manipulation every day?"

Ken finished his coffee.

"Hey, it's too early to give this up. Want to go someplace for some drinks? A few laughs?"

Did he? Everything Mickey said was true. His mother would never let go of this bone. She'd taken the huge step and admitted he was gay. She'd more than met him halfway. Mickey might be better than some men she could choose. At least he was great-looking and had a sexy charisma that made people stare when he walked in a door. "Okay."

"I don't know this neighborhood very well. You got any suggestions?"

Ken gazed out the door. *Oh, you hopeless piece of shit.* "How about the Bay Bar in Laguna Beach?"

"THIS IS such a fun place."

Jim looked over at Constance, who was surveying the crowd at the Bay. If he'd had some idea that bringing her here would point out the vast differences in their daily lives, he had to think again. She'd ordered a beer, said hi to both Charlie and Raoul on sight—even remembering Charlie's name, threw a game of darts against Raoul and won, and now was leaning back in their booth looking as at home as a dog in a burger factory. Jim smiled. "Glad you like it."

"It reminds me of places my dad used to hang out when I was a kid. He'd bring me along sometimes and let me play on the machines."

"Your mom didn't mind?"

She shook her head. "She died when I was little. I barely remember her. My father raised me."

"He never remarried?"

"No. He said he'd had his wife. There wasn't going to be another one."

"Match made in heaven."

She sipped from her beer bottle and gave him a grin. "Sounds like it, doesn't it? Actually, I think he hated being married, and my mother dying was his way out."

Jim snorted a laugh and some beer sucked into his nose. He coughed.

"Ah, you laugh, but it's kind of sad. I guess they had to get married. He was a blue-collar guy and she was a professor's daughter. Different as night and midday, but for one romantic night they hooked up and produced me. Then the fact that he was an unapologetic redneck and she was a tree-hugging bleeding heart made the remaining year of their marriage pure hell. She died suddenly and he got me. I don't think he even minded that I wasn't a boy. He has some serious asshole opinions, but underneath, he's a good man."

That was not the monologue he'd ever expected to hear from Constance Murch. "He must be if you think so."

She smiled over her beer bottle. "Thank you." She sipped. "He likes me to play Daddy's girl, and I don't mind."

"He knows you're as tough as he is."

She gave him a slow sideways glance. "Yes." She set her empty bottle on the table. "You never told me if you liked the play."

"Yeah. It was funny. It took me a few minutes to figure out that the lead character was a dog."

"That's part of the fun."

Something changed in the sounds from the people at the bar. A little gasp here or there, a drop in tone, and some whispers from two women sitting across from their booth. Jim followed their eager glances toward the door of the bar. His heart actually skipped a beat, and he heard his own breath catch. *Son of a bitch.*

Constance must have heard because she looked up. "Well, I'll be damned. Dr. Tanaka is not someone I would have expected to see in the Bay Bar."

He could feel himself frowning. *Quit it.* "Me either."

"You must suspect he's following you after seeing him at the restaurant and then that confrontation at the club the other day. You can't escape your doctor." She smiled. "Well, I'll testify you haven't had anything but ginger ale the whole evening, and you even ate salmon for dinner. Very heart-healthy."

Ken had to have come here on purpose. *Pissed or psyched? Truth?* Somewhere in between, probably leaning toward psyched.

"That's a very attractive young man he's with. I think he was at the restaurant too. Do you suppose he's Ken's boyfriend?"

There was the pissed part. This was the second time he'd seen Ken with that handsome kid. "Don't know."

"But he was with another man when we saw him at the club. I guess you can't blame a lot of men for finding the doctor attractive."

Jim's frown deepened. "You don't seem to share your father's prejudices."

"No." She shook her head. "He grew up with men on construction crews who aren't necessarily the most tolerant, and if they are, they keep it to themselves." She looked at him. "But you should know all about that."

Jim dragged his eyes away from Ken and the cutie. "Yeah. And I was one of them until the day my best friend and boss came out as gay. Changed everything." *Really everything.*

"Your boss? You mean Mr. Ballew?"

"Yep. He's on his honeymoon with his husband, not his wife. He doesn't hide it, so I think it's okay to tell you."

"He defies one or two stereotypes, doesn't he?"

"Yeah." He sighed. "But it's a good reason why your father wouldn't want to use our company for his construction. I was planning to tell you anyway."

"But he'd be dealing with you."

"Still." His gaze crept back to Ken, who was glancing toward him, and their eyes met. Ken tilted his lips upward and raised a glass of something sparkling just slightly toward Jim. Jim took a deep breath.

"My father's seldom been known to cut off his nose to spite his face. I think he'd still want to talk to you."

"It would be up to Billy."

"That must have been a shock, huh? Finding out your friend was gay."

133

"A surprise, yeah. Billy's a pretty macho guy. But really sweet too, and smart as hell."

She smiled softly. "Sounds like you could be describing yourself."

"What? No. I'm not anything like Billy."

Charlie pushed through a crowd of people and stopped in front of their booth. "Hey, boss lady, I reserved the board. You up for another round of darts? Bet I can beat you this time."

"Do you mind, Jim?"

"No problem but I think you're being optimistic, Charlie." Jim slid out to let Constance exit the booth. "I've got to go visit the men's room anyway." He stepped aside for Charlie and Constance, then glanced at Ken sitting down the bar. Women all over the room still stared at him. At the moment the doc appeared deep in conversation with the pretty boy next to him. Even more than he had Gene Willings, Jim wanted to go smack the kid. *I'll bet somebody's mama thinks that guy is just fine.*

He threaded through the crowd to the bathroom. Two men stood at the urinals. He didn't want to pee so much as just be alone, so he grabbed an empty stall. They had the kind that were little rooms with doors all the way to the ceiling. Nice and private. Inside he locked the door, pulled down the lid, and sat on it. He hadn't exactly planned it, but tonight had been a test to prove to himself that Constance wasn't the woman for him. He'd flunked. He liked Constance a lot. She was funny, smart, and kind. Was she a quarter inch of sugar over a foot of solid steel? Probably, but nothing wrong with that. He admired her. She'd done so much in her life, while he'd been hiding out. But did he want to take her to bed? He sighed. That was a cock of a different color.

The restroom got quiet outside his stall. No peeing sounds. *Best get back to the table.* He raised the toilet lid to use the facilities and unzipped. The sounds from the club got louder behind him as the restroom door opened, then softer as it closed.

"Jim."

His hand froze on his cock. "Yeah."

"Let me in."

"Hell no." But his cock decided peeing was a dumb idea and spronged to half-mast.

"Open up."

Jesus. He tucked the half boner into his open fly and unlocked the stall door, then stepped aside to let Ken in and slammed the door. How could a toilet stall be filled with so much beautiful?

Face-to-face against the two walls of the stall, they filled the place.

Jim flashed a hand at Ken. "What the hell are you doing here with your damned boy toy?"

"I know. I'm sorry. But he asked me where I wanted to go, and the words 'Bay Bar' came out of my mouth."

"You don't belong here."

For a second Ken looked hurt. "I thought it was the woman you were trying to prove didn't belong."

Jim crossed his arms on his chest. "Her too."

"You two look pretty homey to me."

"Actually, she fits right in."

The door outside opened, and two men's voices started chattering against the sound of urine hitting the ceramic. Ken extended a hand and put his finger against Jim's lips. Jesus, even his finger smelled good. Fresh and citrusy.

The guys talked on. Ken's finger moved back and forth against his mouth. Jim turned his head to the side, but Ken stayed with him, slipping that finger between his not-quite-resisting lips until he touched his tongue. Jim gasped and Ken took advantage, pressing another finger into his mouth and sliding it against Jim's tongue, then between his teeth and gum.

Jim's half-mast erection sprang to full life and wouldn't be contained by the open fly. *Pop.* Out it came, waving hi to Ken, who chuckled.

One of the voices outside said, "Do you think we ought to change the backsplash before we decide on appliances?"

The two guys had to be gay. Their conversation ranged from the latest musical at the Performing Arts Center to what type of candles to buy for their upcoming party, and they gabbed on and on as Ken stepped forward and took hold of Mr. Happy with a firm hand. He unzipped himself with the other hand and pulled those two long soldiers together into one foxhole where he started stroking, his face a mask of dark intent.

135

Jim started to moan and pulled it back. His lips parted and Ken leaned over and kissed him, not fun and games, but deep, probing, kick-your-socks-off sexy. The hand on his dick felt so good, he wanted to throw his head back and scream, but he kept holding back his cries until he thought his damned chest would explode.

Suddenly Ken dropped to his knees, dragged Jim's cock into his mouth, and started sucking. Sweet holy hell, something was going to explode and soon. Ken's tongue played up one side of Jim's cock and down the other, then circled the head again and again. Back for a long suck. Jim's hips popped, shoving himself more deeply into that hot hole, but it was the only place he wanted to be. "Oh God."

Ken raised a hand as if to stop Jim from talking, but he didn't stop sucking. His head bobbed like a duck at a carnival stand, and every move produced a flash of fire in Jim's cock and balls.

"Oh God, oh."

Outside the door, one of the guys giggled. "Naughty, naughty."

Ken smiled around Jim's cock but didn't even break his stride. His long fingers clutched the base of Jim's shaft and tickled his balls as he guided that cock deep into his throat. When he'd swallowed most of it, he looked up at Jim with those deep black eyes. Never in his life had Jim seen anything so totally lewd as those full lips stretched around his cock. Jesus, he wanted to see it forever. He pushed his hips forward a little more and Ken's mouth stretched. Then he pulled back and the Angelina lips squeezed tighter, like he didn't want to let go.

Fuck it. Jim gritted his teeth, gazed into Ken's eyes, and thrust, thrust, thrust. His vision blurred, red dots fluttered behind his eyelids, and his heart hammered like someone hitting a ball against his chest. He gasped. Again. His eyes closed, and the first shot of cum timed with the first burst of ecstasy, starting in his balls and firing out like rockets into his arms, legs, head, and brain. "Uhhh, uh."

He opened his eyes in time to see Ken's throat working as he swallowed and swallowed. Dear God, not a sight he'd ever forget.

The guys outside both giggled together. "Oooh, that was sexy. I about came in my jeans. Thanks, you guys."

Some more voices moved into the restroom.

Jim looked at Ken as he rose to standing. Jim nodded toward Ken's obvious erection and whispered, "My turn."

Ken leaned in and nuzzled his ear. "No. We both have to get back. But you owe me big time and don't forget it." He grinned as he adjusted himself. "You taste good." He leaned over and kissed Jim hard, sharing the flavor of salt and musk. "See you soon."

He pressed an ear against the door until Jim heard the voices outside fade away. Then Ken opened the door of the stall, slipped out, and closed it again. *Good thing. Not sure I can recover that fast.*

Jim breathed slowly until he softened enough to pee, dressed himself, left the stall, ignored the two guys at the urinals, and washed. Outside, Constance looked up from where she was talking with Charlie. Charlie stared at him with slightly wild eyes and Jim shook his head. "I'm so sorry. I ran into a client, and he wouldn't shut up."

Constance gave him a little cock of the head. "No problem. Charlie's been keeping me company. I know how demanding those clients can be."

It felt good to laugh.

She grinned. "So do you think I can snag you as my escort to an event on Friday?"

Oh shit.

CHAPTER SIXTEEN

HIT BY a baseball bat. That's how he felt, and he knew what he was talking about because he'd actually had that happen in junior high. Weird, spacey, not aware of the pain yet. He slipped the key in the apartment door and opened it. Anderson, who looked like he'd grown by double in a few days, bounded toward the door, then turned his shiny white back, flicked his tail, and stalked away like "Look what you've been missing."

Ian lolled on the ugly couch with the phone pressed to his ear and a stupid smile on his face. He waggled a bare foot as Jim passed by to his bedroom. Kind of envied him that smile. Looked like romance pure and simple. Jim sighed. He could use a healthy dose of pure and simple.

He turned on the shower in the minibath, stripped, and stepped under water that was just lukewarm. Ian must have used a bit. It only took a bit to empty the apartment's allotted amount. After drying off, he pulled on some pajama bottoms and a T-shirt and was just flopping on the bed when the tap came on the door. "Come on in, Ian."

The door opened and Anderson came first, hopping straight onto the bed and settling on Jim's pillow before Ian even made it fully inside. He smiled. "Hey, Jim, how was the date?"

That might have seemed like an easy, polite question, but it was a total minefield. "Fine. I gather you and Rico have struck up a friendship."

His cheeks turned pink. "Yeah. He's a great guy and has been all the places I want to go—like architecture school."

That felt like a blow to the head. Jim stared at his feet. "Doesn't that make him too old for you?"

"Thanks there, Mom." He laughed.

Dammit, Ian needed more of a mom than the one he'd had. "Sorry."

"Actually he's only four years older. He's this prodigy who started college at sixteen and finished architecture school in five years."

"Talented guy."

"I think so too." Sappy smile redux.

Jim crossed his legs and gave his brother's hair a swipe. "Not as talented as you."

"He agrees with you." Ian's giggle reminded Jim of the guys outside the bathroom stall, and his cock gave a little jerk. Ian flopped on his back on the end of the bed, not distressing Anderson at all. "So tell me more about your date."

"I'm gay."

Ian sat straight up like a zombie. "What the fuck? You told me you weren't."

Jim caught his breath and tried to get his brain to catch up with his mouth. "I know. And maybe I'm not, but—shit, I don't know." That moment in the bathroom stall when he'd come into Ken's hot, endless throat—"I just don't like sex with women as much as I like sex with men." How was that for the understatement of the century?

"Hang on. You've had sex with men?" Ian mirrored Jim's position and stared at him like the head of the Inquisition.

"Uh, yeah. Sort of. No, I mean, once, and some other—sort of."

"I think we better talk about this."

"Now who's being the mother?"

Stern gaze. "You need guidance when it comes to this. Talk."

"I had sex with Ken Tanaka."

"Sex sex?"

"Yeah and a couple of blow jobs." Jesus, that did not begin to do justice to the situation.

"When he was here?"

"Uh, not exactly. Since then."

"That may not make you gay."

"What?"

Ian cocked a half smile. "That guy's so gorgeous, he could seduce Pastor Rick."

"I know, and I kind of agree with you. I don't generally get hard-ons for guys, except for Ken."

"It's a 'gay for you' situation, then."

"What's that mean?"

"A straight man who falls for one guy and never gets tempted by any others. Some people believe in it. Mostly in romance novels." He smiled.

Jim stared at the faded bedspread. "Except I can't get it up for women anymore."

"Anymore?"

"I was never Don Juan, okay? But I've had some orgasms with females. Just not lately."

"What about when you were in puberty? I was little, but I remember you hanging out with girls and shit."

Jim sighed. "Yeah."

"Were you attracted to them? I mean, were you trying to get to first base and all that boy/girl drama?"

"No."

"Bad sign. For your future heterosexuality, I mean."

"I was getting sucked off by my tutor."

Ian's eyes widened. "The Japanese kid?"

"Hiro."

"I remember him. He was a really nice guy. Sweet. Smart."

Back to the bedspread. "Yes, well, I treated him like crap. I told myself I was this great friend, letting him suck me because it made him happy." His heart thudded against his chest. "Then he was gone because of me."

Ian frowned. "Something about some pictures, right? I kind of remember that."

"Yeah."

"That happened right before you left." Ian's head turned. Yeah, he got the drift.

The threads on the bedspread are so even. Jim nodded.

"You left because of Hiro? Because you knew you were gay and Mom and Dad wouldn't stand for it?"

"No. I never thought of that. It was probably true, but I wouldn't have admitted it. Shit, I was the tough guy. The athlete. The one who built things and made them work. I couldn't be a fag." He picked at his socks. "No, all I knew was I'd wrecked the life of the nicest person I'd ever known. I couldn't act like everything was normal. I couldn't go be the football hero and pretend I wasn't a piece of shit. So I left."

"That was so brave."

Jim's head snapped up. "What the fuck? You're crazy."

"You refused to live the life they defined for you, so you went out and made your own."

He shook his head. "Thanks, kid, but that's sentimental crap. It might be true if I'd declared myself gay and made a life working honestly with my hands and proving it's cool to be a blue-collar guy. Yeah—no. Hell, look around. I scrape by doing the minimum except when it comes to alcohol and junk food. I'd still be laying every woman I found if I could just get Roger down there to cooperate."

"You were sixteen, Jim. Hell, it takes time to figure shit out."

His lips turned up, but it hurt. "Ten years is no weekend. Plus now that I'm finally admitting what would have been obvious to someone with double cataracts, I'm hung up on the gay player of the century, who I can never have and who bears an uncanny resemblance to a yaoi character I shared with Hiro. Hell, call in the fucking Freudians. I can fail at anything."

Ian gazed at the bedspread with him, then grabbed a handful of cloth in his fist. "So don't fail. Go get him."

"To coin a crappy phrase, it's complicated."

"Most shit worth having is."

"Write that on an inspirational poster." Ian frowned, and Jim touched his arm. "Sorry. Didn't mean to be nasty. But as you may recall, my date wasn't with him. I was out with a perfectly nice woman who happens to own the damned building I'm working on and, if I suddenly up and tell her I'm gay, I could lose Billy's job. On top of that, Ken is Japanese, or at least his mother is, and she wants him to be with somebody who is not me. There's more, but that's the short version."

Ian frowned and nodded, all solution-oriented. "Okay, so it's not clean and clear, but it doesn't sound insurmountable if you both want to be together."

"I don't have any reason to think Ken wants to be with me enough to defy his family. And I can't let Billy down, kid. Making a go of this job is, like, the only chance I have."

Ian sat up. "No way. You're smart and talented."

He shook his head. "Thanks. But not if I fuck this up. I know I can't live through it. I screwed over Hiro. I can't do the same to Billy."

"Jesus, Jim."

"Yeah."

"HEY, MAN, you okay?"

Jim rose from the electrical circuit he was wiring like a zombie attacker. "Why the hell does everyone keep asking me that?"

Raoul held up his hands. "No worries, man. You just look like fifty yards of ugly road."

Get a grip. Jim shrugged. "That's normal."

"No. You usually only look like twenty-five yards of ugly, man."

"Well, you ought to know." He patted Raoul's sleeve. "I'm fine. Just not used to the responsibility, you know?"

"Yeah, man. That makes sense. But you're doing a great job. Hell, that boss lady's gonna give us so much work, Billy will have to deck out his house with solid gold faucets and shit."

Okay, that just slammed the jail cell. "Yeah." He turned back to his wiring.

Condemned to heterosexuality. Sentenced to a life without Ken. Hell, he'd earned it. How hard had he worked his whole life to never have anybody think he was gay? Not consciously maybe, but hindsight wore contact lenses. Become a construction worker. Be a ladies' man. Toss back Jack and yell for football. Macho bullshit he'd chosen. He sighed. Ken had said Jim owed him big time. True. He owed Ken the shitty realization that he'd likely never be happy in his entire life. They weren't kidding when they said ignorance is bliss.

He stood and looked around at the suite. It was going to be great. At least he'd have that. Fuckup Jim Carney did one good job. "You guys going to get some lunch? Maybe you could bring me a—"

The door to the suite opened and Billy stepped in, smiling like a loon. *Holy shit.* "Billy, what are you doing here? Is everything okay?"

The other guys stopped hammering. "Billy!"

"Hey, man."

Jim crossed to Billy and gave him the one-armed guy hug, but he got a full-on embrace that swallowed him up in return. "Everything's fine. Shaz got a bad sunburn, and we both missed being at home. We're going to take the last few days of our honeymoon in Laguna Beach. Hell, we both work all the time, so we don't really get to appreciate where we live."

"That's great, Billy. Did you have fun before the sunburn?"

The other guys had crowded around and gave Billy hugs and pats.

His blue eyes lit up. "It was amazing. Gorgeous beaches, and the fish! Man, they're indescribable. So I'll show you a bunch of pictures as soon as I sort through them and delete about five hundred."

They all laughed.

"Enough about me. Tell me about this." He spun in a circle and pointed at the suite.

Charlie laughed. "Jim's little surprise."

"I'll say. Why are we working up here? The guys in the lobby suite just said you were on the eighth floor."

Jim glanced at his shoes. "She switched tenants on us. Or rather, moved the original downstairs tenant up here and added a new tenant down there."

"So that means we're doing twice the work?"

"Yep." Jim grinned.

"Did Brian do this design? It's great."

Charlie obviously couldn't wait to tell him. "Nope. When Jim found out the whole deal was different, he tried to call your architect, but the guy was gone. That was a bad moment, I wanna tell you."

"Oh right. Brian said he was leaving the same time we were so that he'd be back to work on new projects."

Raoul laughed. "Jim thought he was screwed, man. But he's got this smart brother and he found this architect, and the boss lady loved it, and—"

Billy laughed. "See, I told you I left the right guy in charge."

Man, that made him feel great.

Billy looked around at the crew. "I've got to hear the whole story. Why don't we all go out for beers after work and share adventures? The company will buy."

The suite door opened and Constance walked in. "Mr. Ballew. You're back. Welcome."

Billy smiled. "Hello, Ms. Murch. Thank you."

She walked up and patted Jim's arm. Billy's eyes widened. "I'm sure you can see what an amazing job Jim and his crew have done in your absence."

Can I crawl under a rock?

"Yes, I can. But I never doubted it."

"You left me in very good hands. Has Jim told you about the future work we've discussed?"

Man, she was rubbing it in. Billy looked wide-eyed. "No. I just got here. I imagine he'll surprise me some more any minute."

She smiled at Jim. "I don't want to interrupt your welcome home. I was just checking on Friday."

Jim didn't blush easily, but this was the moment. "Uh, no decision yet."

"Shall I call you later?"

"Yes. That would be fine."

"Good." She stepped back and let go of Jim's arm. "Welcome, again, Mr. Ballew."

"Billy."

"Yes, Billy. And please call me Constance. Maybe you and Jim can have lunch with me soon to discuss the additional projects I have in mind."

"I'd be delighted."

"Yes. We'll talk soon, Jim." She turned and clicked her very fashionable heels out of the suite.

The guys clearly held their collective breath for a full minute; then they erupted in cat calls and whistles. "Somebody's got a girlfriend. Way to go, Hound Dog."

"Pretty sneaky, turning on the charm for the boss there, Carney."

Jim tried to smile and glanced at Billy, who was grinning, but there were a hundred questions in his eyes. "Looks like we have more to talk about after work than fish."

"SO THEY'VE got fish that look like yellow angels and striped fish and bright orange, and—"

Jim tried to look at Billy's pictures of fish, but his eyes kept straying to the shots of Jack Daniels in front of Charlie, Raoul, Harry,

144

and a couple of the other carpenters who'd joined them. Jim swirled his ginger ale. Shit, Billy was back now. He could relax a little. Let the boss take the reins. No reason to be all holier than thou, like Peggy said.

The waiter walked by, and Jim snagged his apron. "Hey, man, I think I will have a beer and a shot."

"Sure. I'll get it right away."

He looked up and found Charlie staring at him. "You sure you wanna do that, buddy? You been doing really good."

Jim frowned. "Hey, why can't I have a drink to celebrate with the rest of you?"

"No reason." Charlie held up a hand. "You know best."

He took a big swallow of ginger ale. He hated this swill. Hell, he could get work for Billy just by being Hound Dog Jim Carney. He didn't have to have any talent or reliability. He could just fuck his way to the top.

The waiter brought the beer first, and Jim took the glass from the man's hand and drank half of it in one swallow. Bitter. Especially after the soda. But it'd taste real sweet after a couple more swallows. He took another drink, not so big this time. Warmth spread through his veins. Nice. Soon females would look real good.

Billy said, "I want to hear about how you got the great design for the upstairs suite."

Jim didn't have to say a word. The guys plunged in and told Billy about Ian and how talented he was and how he came up with this great idea and how Jim found this architect who drew the plans. Yeah, Jim didn't have any of the skill. He just had to go suck off a doctor so he could get a good architect to work for him.

The waiter brought his shot. Jim stared at it as the guys talked and talked. *Come to Daddy, Jackie-poo.* He slid the slim glass closer and stuck his tongue into the amber liquid. *Oh yeah.*

Suddenly a big hand snatched the glass out from under his chin, and Jim watched Billy drink the liquid down. Jim slapped a hand on the table. "Hey, what the hell?"

"Can't have my supervisor hungover tomorrow. I'm still on my honeymoon. I need you clear-headed."

For a second Jim wanted to hit Billy. That was fucked up. He nodded. "Sure. You're right. Sorry."

Billy smiled. "You're doing an amazing job. Thank you."

Jim smiled back. Maybe that made it all worth it.

"I got a text this afternoon from Constance Murch. She wants to have lunch tomorrow to discuss new work."

"That's great. I'm really glad. You'll like her. She's an okay lady."

"She wants to meet with both of us."

His stomach hit his shoes. "Oh."

"You busy at lunch tomorrow?"

He curved his lips up, but they felt real heavy. "I guess I am now."

CHAPTER SEVENTEEN

JIM TWIRLED his iced tea glass and watched Constance and Billy laughing at Billy's story about dropping binoculars in the ocean when he saw a whale. "I was so amazed, I let go of the things and splash, gone to the fishes. My husband tried to pay the boat captain, but I guess it's not that infrequent an occurrence."

She nodded. "They should have supplied a neck cord with those binoculars."

"I guess they figured they were safe with a big guy like me. I'm not usually so clumsy, but the whale won."

She sipped her tea. "I introduced Jim to my father." Billy glanced at Jim real quickly, then back at Constance. Constance grinned at Jim. "He's a very successful developer."

Billy nodded. "Of course, everyone knows Alex Murch."

"I think you'd be a good resource for him." She looked down, then directly at Billy. "He has certain prejudices about homosexuality, however, so I think it's best if Jim does a lot of the interaction. They really hit it off, so that shouldn't be a hardship."

Billy glanced at his tea, at Jim, then back at Constance. "I don't hide who I am, and I wouldn't want to misrepresent me or my firm to anyone."

"I understand and respect that, but there's no reason for my father to know anything about your private life. And if he does, he can make his own decisions. The fact remains that your team does good work, and I personally think some of his suppliers overcharge him. I believe you could save him money."

Billy cocked a grin. "I'd hate to think we're the low-cost leader."

"Not at all, but Jim does excellent cost estimates and, so far, hasn't exceeded them." She gave Jim a big smile.

There it was. He'd wanted to surprise Billy with a boatload of new work and impress him with what a valuable employee he was.

Constance just did the job for him and tied it up with a bow. Why did that bow feel like it was being tightened around his neck? He slugged back a mouthful of tea. *Wish it was scotch.*

By the time they were ready to leave, Billy had agreed to meet with Alex Murch, taking Jim in tow for good heterosexual PR. Man, that was a joke. But at least if Murch liked Billy, Jim could get the fuck out of the loop. Maybe so far out of the loop he could leave town.

Standing outside the restaurant, Constance got that look, and Jim knew what was coming. "Are we on for Friday?"

If he said no, the whole meeting-Daddy thing would likely vanish in the air. "Yes, thank you. I'd love to go. Shall I call you to make dinner plans?"

Her smile was so sweet. *Wasted on an asshole liar like me.* "That would be lovely. So we'll talk soon?"

"Yes."

As they all walked back to the building, Constance chattered about her plans for a new investment and how she'd love to have Jim take a look at it. When they got to the door, she stopped. "Maybe you can look at the new place later this week?"

"Sure. I'd be glad to."

She smiled at Billy. "So glad you're back. I look forward to working with you."

Billy shook her hand. "Me too."

Her whole expression changed. Softened. "Talk soon, Jim. I have to go to an appointment in Santa Ana, so I'll leave you two here."

"Okay. Bye."

For one horrible second, he thought she was going to kiss his cheek, but she walked away.

Billy just stood there looking after her. The silence was so thick you could lose sheep in it.

"Billy, welcome back. How was the trip?" Every nerve in Jim's body fried at the silky voice. Too much. No way he could even look at Ken Tanaka right now.

Billy turned. "Ken, hi." He looked around. "Why are you here?"

"My office is in this building." His eyes shifted. "Hi, Jim. How's it going?"

148

Lifting his eyes from his boots took almost more power than he could manage. "Fine."

A tiny crease cracked the perfection of Ken's forehead for a second, and then he smiled. "I gave Jim a good report for the insurance, but he does need to take care of himself."

Well, fuck. He should just butt out.

Billy looked at Jim. "Wait. I'm behind here. What report? Didn't you go to Dr. Haselbaum?"

Shit on a stick.

Ken crossed his arms. "Haselbaum sent Jim to me when he discovered he has a heart murmur. I'll let him tell you more." He glanced at Jim, then stuck out a hand to Billy. Hard to not envy Billy's getting to touch him. "So, welcome. I'm sure I'll see you and your crew again since Jim seems to be a favorite of the building owner. Take care." He strolled across the plaza toward the parking garage as if he hadn't just land mined Jim's existence.

Billy didn't frown often. *Welcome to the exception.* "We need to talk."

"I should get upstairs and check on the crew."

"They know what they're doing. I want to know what you're doing. Come on." He started walking toward the parking structure. Jim didn't move and after a few steps, Billy turned back.

Jim shook his head. "I've got shit to do."

"Yeah, like tell me what's going on."

"Nothing."

Billy took one step closer. "You're dating the owner of the building, you have a heart murmur, and most of all you're unhappy as hell. What did I miss? Sounds like something to me."

His friend. Jesus, maybe he could talk to him. "Okay. Where to?"

"Want a beer?"

"I thought I needed to have a clear head while you're on your honeymoon." Jim crossed his arms.

"Honeymoon's over, buddy, when you're this miserable. And I mean one beer. Come on."

Twenty silent minutes later, during which Billy called Charlie and told him they wouldn't be back, they walked into the Bay Bar and grabbed a booth. It was only three, so not many people were there yet.

Billy ordered two beers from the bartender, then scooted in across from Jim. "Start talking."

"Where do you want me to start?"

"Tell me about your heart."

"I went to get a physical and found out I have this mitral valve thing."

"How bad is it?"

"Tanaka says it's usually no biggie, but mine's on the medium side. He says I just need to watch it."

"Watch it how?"

Jim sighed. "The usual shit. Eat right and drink less and crap like that."

"How did you end up seeing Tanaka?"

"Haselbaum referred me to him."

"Interesting twist of fate."

"Yeah. He's in the building." That so didn't cover the subject.

The bartender put two beers and two glasses of water on the table. Billy handed him some bills. When he walked away, Billy said, "How about Constance Murch?"

Jim dropped his head. "She walked in the first day on the job and informed us that everything had changed."

"Yeah, and you did a great job of managing all those changes. That's not what I mean."

"She seems to like me."

"Seems to? Hell, she practically married you in the restaurant."

"She asked me out."

"That's the Friday thing she mentioned."

"Yeah. And we already went out once to a play and dinner." The words came out on a long, slow breath.

"You're not happy about these dates?"

"It's weird dating the boss."

"Yeah, it's always a little strange mixing business and personal, but she's pretty and seems nice. If you're worried that I'll object or something, hell, it's your life, and you can't help it if you're irresistible to women." Billy laughed.

Jim looked up.

Billy gazed at him. "You don't want to go out with her, do you?"

He shook his head.

"Is it because of Peggy?"

"No. We broke up at the wedding."

"So Constance just isn't your type?"

Jim looked into Billy's kind eyes. "Yeah. Not my type." He swallowed. "Because she's a woman."

Billy's lips parted, then closed. He tried again. "What do you mean?"

Jim glanced around. Nobody listening except Billy. *Yep, have his attention.* "I'm pretty sure I'm gay."

Billy grinned, cocked his head, then sobered. "You're serious?"

"Yeah."

"Son of a bitch."

"Yeah."

"You say you're pretty sure. So—"

He took a mouthful of beer, then spit it back in the glass. Tasted bad. "I guess I should have had a clue a long time ago because, well, I had some, uh, experiences with a boy who was my friend. But I never thought it meant I was gay. Anyway, it's a long story that I'll tell you sometime, but meanwhile, I kind of have a thing for a guy, and it's made it pretty clear that I'm not into women."

"Ken Tanaka."

Jim looked up at Billy. "How the hell did you guess that?"

Billy's smile was as kind as his eyes. "The way you looked at each other. I remember looking at Shaz that way when I thought I shouldn't have feelings for him. I'm gathering you two aren't together."

"No. He's pretty family-oriented, and I'm not the one to thrill some Japanese mother's heart."

"I know about mothers and family. I honestly thought I'd lose my family if I came out to them. Hardest thing I ever did, but Shaz helped and we survived. Hell, some days I think my mom loves Shaz more than me."

"Yeah, well, you guys were in love. Ken's pretty much a player, you know. He's got a guy for every night of the week. Why would he want to take on his family for me?" He twisted his glass. "I'm better off with women. Like you said, Constance is pretty and nice and she likes me."

"Didn't you just tell me you're gay?"

"Aren't there people who are bisexual?"

"Yes. Are you bi?"

"I don't know."

"Do you think you are? Do you find Constance as attractive as Ken?"

Jim shook his head.

"How about Peggy?"

"No."

Billy sipped his beer.

"It's just that Ken reminds me of this comic book character I used to love as a teenager. Maybe that's why I like him. I mean, the only reason."

"So this comic book character was a guy?"

"Yeah."

Billy took another sip.

"Shit."

"Is it possible you think Constance won't give us more work if you don't go out with her?"

Jim drank some water.

"Jim?"

"I really want to do something for you Billy. Get more work for the company. Help to make you happy."

"Jim—"

The words rushed out. "I've always looked up to you. You're talented and brave and the kind of man I want to be. When you came out, I felt like—confused as shit, but like someone had hit me on the head, in a good way. Like some door opened for me that wasn't there before. I didn't know what it was then, but I guess I do now."

Billy smiled and put a hand on Jim's arm. "I'm honored. I can't even tell you how much your saying that means to me. But if it's even a little true, do you think I'd want you to give me a gift that denies who you are?"

Heat pressed against the back of Jim's eyes. "I guess I didn't think—"

"We're going to get lots of work together being Billy and Jim. You don't have to date the boss for me. I want you to be happy, and now I honestly know what that means. For me it's been about overcoming fear and being willing to be who I am. Maybe that's true for you too."

Jim shook his head. *Could it be true?* "Man."

"I think you should call Constance and explain."

"Shit. Explain what? How?"

Billy laughed. "Don't panic. You don't have to say anything about being gay. Just tell her you have an attachment to another person that has become more serious, and you don't want to give her the wrong impression."

"Oh man, how do you think she'll take that?"

"I think she'll be very disappointed, but not as much as she would be six months from now when she finds out you've been leading her on when you weren't really interested."

"Yeah. I guess you're right." Some mountain started crumbling off his shoulders. "But do you think she'll take away the work?"

"If she does, it wasn't our work."

"Jesus, who are you? St. Francis?"

Billy grinned. "Sorry. Shaz was raised by a preacher. I listen to him and my mom go at it over scripture all the time."

"So they really get along? Shaz and your mom?"

"Yes. Would she rather I was married to a woman and giving her a bunch of grandkids? Sure. But fortunately I've got a sister who's held up her end in the grandchild department, so it takes off some of the pressure."

Jim smiled.

"See, there's even hope for Ken Tanaka."

The last of that mountain flew off his back like sand. Maybe there was a chance. And even if there wasn't, he had a debt to pay.

Chapter Eighteen

KEN CLICKED out of the patient file, leaned back in his desk chair, and closed his eyes. Tired. After having escaped his date Saturday night without having sex—a fact that was almost as hard to explain to himself as it was to Mickey—he'd spent yesterday visiting relatives with his parents and listening to his mother rave about Kenji's new boyfriend and what a fine family he came from. Wednesday, he would have to endure another evening with the Okuwas while his mother planned his life. It made him want to puke, but he knew his duty.

Don't want to do it.

Grow up.

Don't want to.

"Dr. T, you awake?"

He opened his eyes and smiled at Angela. "Just resting my eyes."

"Umm-hmm, just like I did in my math classes." She grinned. "You have early rounds tomorrow."

"I remember."

"You okay?"

He cocked his head. "Just trying to work out some things."

"Your mom fixing you up again?" He'd told her his troubles in a fit of frustration after one of his mother's most disastrous matches.

"Yes, but believe it or not, she's switched to guys."

"You're kidding?"

"No, but I have to hand it to her. Having embraced my gayness, she's draped herself in the full rainbow flag. To hear her talk, you'd think being gay was an ancient Japanese tradition and only the most fortunate families have gay sons. It might be funny if it wasn't so weird."

"At least she's trying."

"In more ways than one."

She snorted. "Are her male choices any better than her female?"

"I guess."

She leaned against the doorjamb. "Like most moms, she wants to see you married off and happy."

"It's a bit more Japanese than that, but I suppose so."

"Maybe if you pick your own guy, she'll quit trying to find him for you."

He stared at her. "I wish it was that simple."

"Simple? That implies you've found the guy." She flashed a big smile.

Well, damn.

"Hey, can I get a definite maybe?"

"You can get a definite 'I don't know.' Now go home and get some rest."

"Same to you."

"Soon. See you tomorrow."

"Okay." She rolled her eyes. "But I think I got a definite maybe. And you know I'll never give up until I know, so you might as well prepare to confess." Laughing, she pushed off from the door and disappeared down the hall.

He blew out a stream of air. Funny. He was pretty sure Angela liked Jim Carney. She sure seemed to be flirting with him. Even funnier was that made Ken jealous. *Wonder what she'd think if she knew what we did in the Bay Bar restroom?* Wonder what Jim's date would think? *Even for you, Tanaka, this is damned complicated.*

Did he really like Jim Carney? It was as if he watched himself doing strange, uncharacteristic shit—like confronting Jim at the club, showing up at the Bay Bar, and even calling Jim to come to his rescue when he was in trouble. No way he'd do that with most men. What was it about this tough guy who wouldn't even admit he was gay?

He sighed, leaned his head against the chair back, and—rested his eyes.

OH YES, heaven. Never wake up. Live in this dream. Ken stretched out his legs and raised his hips into hot, wet delight. "Oh, sweet."

"Umm-hmmm."

"What?" Ken's eyes flew open. "What the hell—?" He looked down at shaggy streaked-blond hair bouncing up and down in his lap. "God, Jim. How the hell did you—?" Flashes of heat burst in his groin, and gasping for air got far more important than talking. *Shit.* "Fuck!"

Jim's fiery mouth popped off his cock. "We can do that too if you want." His tongue laved Ken's slit, and then he swallowed the shaft again.

"Oh man. Oh God, Jim." He couldn't control his thrusts. Had to be strangling Jim, but couldn't help it. He'd lost control before he even woke up.

Jim pulled his mouth off, replaced tongue with a tight, callused hand doing the strokes, and his mouth surrounded Ken's balls. One got licked and sucked, then the other, while his hand never stopped pumping. As Ken watched, Jim opened really wide and got most of one ball in his mouth. "Ummmpft." Oh Jesus, that felt so good. The other got the same treatment. Then pop went the cock back in and sucking commenced with a vengeance. Head bobbing, lips slurping, cum boiling like hot oil in a cauldron.

"Oh shit. Oh shit." Critical point reached, passed. "Oh shiiiiit." Cum burst out in a blood-boiling stream. *Wait. Jim doesn't do this.* "Pull away. Pull—oh God!" Ken's head pounded against the back of the seat as his hips rose, trembled, popped a couple of times as two more shots of cum spurted forth—and Jim just kept sucking. *Sweet heaven. Amazing. Amazing.* His hips crashed back into the chair, and his softening cock slid from heat to coolness. The weight of Jim's head warmed Ken's thighs. *Focus on moving hand.* He curved his fingers in silky hair. *Breathe.*

For a second, he drifted. When Jim shifted positions, Ken took a breath. "Uh, how did you get in here, kind sir?"

His voice was muffled against Ken's thigh. "Andrea let me in. I told her you wanted to discuss my heart problems."

Ken chuckled. "She believed you?"

"Of course. It's the truth."

Yes, it is, isn't it? Ken raised his head. "You swallowed. That was a trial by fire."

Ken could feel Jim's grin move against his jeans. "Better than junk food."

He dropped his head back and settled into quiet. Busy quiet. "Why exactly are you here?"

Jim looked up and grinned. "If you don't know, I did it wrong."

"No, you did it amazingly right. I thought you were a beginner." Ken threaded his fingers through that shaggy hair again.

Jim sighed. "I am, but fifteen years of yaoi taught me some things."

"Hell, if you're any indication, sex counselors should start using yaoi in their sessions."

"I did okay?"

"Best I remember having." Weirdly, that was true.

"I think that qualifies as an expert opinion."

Ken nodded. "Sorry about that." He closed his eyes. "Do you think we have to keep meeting like this, or would it be okay to have dinner and try sex in a bed when both of us are conscious?"

Jim looked up at him. Those deep green eyes stared, and then his cheeks dented with dimples. "I'm willing to give it a try, doc, if you think it won't get you expelled from the Japanese perfect son club."

"Or you from the straight, macho guy's association." He grinned.

Jim sucked in some breath. He might have agreed, but this was no simple step. That was all over his face. Along with drips of cum. Ken smiled. This wasn't easy for him either. "Hey, we met at a friend's wedding. We became friends. We can have a meal out without it being a statement to the world, right?"

"Sure." Jim nodded once. Then a second time with more force. "Why not?"

Yeah. Why the hell not?

KEN SMILED politely. His mother discussed the potential for acquiring good surrogates for birthing Japanese children, and his father pounced all over Mickey for being distracted by rock and roll when he should be focusing on his study of law. Ken ought to be freaking out. Instead, he just felt bored. Something had shifted in his brain—or his heart.

"So when would you like to make the announcement, Kenji?"

He looked up. "Excuse me?"

"When do you and Mickey want to announce your engagement? I've notified the local newspaper that we will send them the details, and we need to arrange for a photo."

"*Excuse* me?" He looked at Mickey, who appeared a little bemused but certainly not horrified. His stomach flipped. "Forgive me, Okaa-san, but I have no intention of announcing my engagement to Mikio at any time. I have no intention of marrying him."

Mrs. Okuwa slapped a hand over her mouth, and Mr. Okuwa frowned. His mother looked shocked too. "Kenji, how can you say this when you know it is all our expectation and desire that this match should be made?"

He tried to keep his voice steady and calm. "But it's not my desire, Mother. I think that's what counts in a marriage."

"No. Being matched by a wise parent has proven for hundreds of years to be the best way to create lasting marriages."

"I'm sorry, Mother. It's not my way." Why did facing her feel like a battle with a thousand dragons?

She frowned. "You will learn to love each other."

"No, we won't. Mickey and I have nothing in common."

His mother turned. "Mikio, do you not find Kenji an admirable and attractive person, suitable to be a husband?"

"Yeah, actually, Mrs. Tanaka, I think he's pretty cool."

She whipped around to Ken. "You see. This is meant to be."

He stood. "It's meant to be only if I say so. This is my life."

"Your brother would have obeyed me."

He stopped along with his heart and breath. The words slipped past his gritted teeth. "My brother is not here."

She gasped, and Mrs. Okuwa joined her. Ken gasped too in his heart. Did he really say that?

He bowed. "I sincerely apologize, Mother. I deeply respect you and the memory of my brother, but I cannot do this. Please excuse me." He walked toward the door.

Mickey's voice followed him. "I'll bet you're hung up on that white guy you kept drooling over at the bar the other night."

His mother caught the scent. "What white man?"

158

Ken paused. "Good night." He strode to the front door, opened it, and took a deep breath of evening air. It stung a little, but it might be his first whiff of freedom.

HUMMING. WHEN was the last time he'd done that?

Jim tucked in the white shirt and pulled a belt through the loops on his best dark jeans.

Ian peeked in his door. "Fancy schmancy."

"Yeah."

"So you're going to do it?"

"Yep. Dinner."

"Big step. Being seen with the doctor. Might ruin your reputation as a confirmed—blue-collar guy." Ian laughed.

"Smartass."

"Did you tell Billy?"

"No, but I will. Hell, he's been so supportive. Between you and him, I might survive this whole deal."

"So what about the woman? How did you tell her?"

Billy glanced at his dark shoes. Not even sneakers.

"You didn't tell her yet?"

"No. I've got to call her. I just chickened out."

"The longer you wait, the harder it'll be on her. It's only two days until your next date."

"I know." *Shit.*

"You're not playing both ends, are you? Keeping her on the hook until you find out how it goes with Ken? Because gay is gay, my friend." He smiled.

Jim perched on the edge of the unmade bed. "No, women don't seem to do it for me anymore, if they ever did." He shrugged. "I'm just worried about how she'll react, and I like working for her. I know that's chickenshit, but those are the facts."

"That's a compliment to her, I guess, but you still need to tell her."

"Yeah." He sighed. "But it's not like any big happy ever after thing's going to happen with Ken. I mean, he's got huge family expectations and boyfriends for every day of the week. He doesn't need me."

Ian crossed his arms. "But it's you he asked out."

"True."

"You can have what you want if you make it a priority."

"Jesus, have you been hanging out with Billy at some self-improvement seminar?"

"I'm serious. If you want him, go get him."

Things came so easy to Ian. "How's it going with you and Rico?"

"Good." Ian practically kicked the floor and said, "Aw shucks." The kid was a goner. "I'm guessing I might not see you until late, so I invited him over. Is that okay?"

"It's your place too. Just don't do anything I wouldn't do." Yes, it felt a little strange to know his kid brother was hooking up, but times change. Hell, that was the truth.

"I expect that gives me a lot of elbow room."

Jim laughed. "I wondered why the apartment looked so clean."

"Hey, you can't give gay men a bad name. This place needs some serious style."

He stood and grabbed his leather jacket from the closet. "It's a deal. We'll work on making this place a tribute to gayness. Gaydom?"

"I'll settle for a new couch. That thing is wanted by the CDC."

"A valuable antique."

"Yeah, from the Pleistocene."

Jim walked out to the living room and patted the ratty green object of his brother's derision that now provided a reclining space for Anderson's grandeur. "I found this thing by the curb in front of some rich family's house. Stuck it in my truck and thought I'd been given a gift."

"Funny to hear you talk about a rich family." Ian's smile looked sad.

"Yeah, I guess it is." *Change the subject.* "So you going to school this evening before Romeo's, I mean Rico's, arrival?"

"No. My class was cancelled for some teacher meeting thing. We're looking forward to a whole evening without his roommates."

"Or yours."

He grinned. "Rico really wants me to apply for scholarships to Berkeley." He shrugged. "But I'm thinking I'm better off staying down here. Maybe try for Cal Poly. It's a great school. If I can keep up my GPA at the community college, maybe I can get scholarships and work to make it happen."

"I'll help as much as I can." Shit, it would take Ian a long time to get through at that pace.

He shook his cute head. "Thanks, but you've got your own future to figure out. So get to work." He gave Jim's shoulder a swipe. "Have a really great date."

That made him smile all the way to his cock. "Thanks."

Outside the apartment, he walked to his parking space. They'd decided he should drive to Ken's apartment and leave the truck there while they took Ken's car to dinner. Nobody was pretending the date wasn't really about getting to fuck in a bed, and that did sound great, but they both had to work in the morning. Wild that he was calmly planning sex with a guy. Admitting his gayness made a lot of pieces fall into place. Jesus, maybe one of those pieces could be happiness.

He pulled out onto the feeder road that would take him toward the PCH, the ocean, and Ken's place. Jim's stomach gave a flutter. Nervous? Probably hungry. He could impress the doc with his good eating habits tonight.

The phone rang in his pocket. Ken? He scooted to his butt cheek and pulled it out, then hit the button. "Hi, cancelling already?"

Silence.

"Hello?"

"Jim?"

That fluttering stomach turned to a block of ice. "Yes." In ten years, his father had never called him.

"I need to talk to you."

"I don't think we have anything to talk about."

"We do. It involves your brother."

Shit. "When?"

His father's cool voice changed just a little, like maybe he smiled. "Now would be good."

"I'm busy."

"It won't take long and it's important."

"Why can't we talk over the phone?"

"I'd rather see you to be certain you understand my offer."

"Offer?"

"Just get here and we'll talk." Call ended by the network.

161

CHAPTER NINETEEN

GOD DAMN him to hell. Should he ignore it? He'd said it was about Ian. *Damn.* Jim reached for the phone and dialed.

Ken's voice sounded happy. "Hey, are you on your way?"

"I was, but I just got this weird call from my father. He says he needs to talk to me about my brother."

"Ian?"

"Yeah. He says it won't take long, and I'm kind of scared to ignore it."

"Does he do this often?"

"He's never called me once in ten years."

"I guess you better go." He sounded disappointed, which gave Jim a thrill.

"Can I still come over after?"

"That would be great. I'll make us a snack here, and we can go to dinner this weekend."

Jesus, he loved the sound of all that. "Okay. See you later. I'll call when I'm on my way."

He hung up, smiled for a second, then let the knot in his stomach take over. What the hell did his father want?

Twenty minutes later, he pulled through the gate at Pelican Hill. When he gave his name to the gate guard, he waved him right through. That made him more nervous. By the time he pulled up in front of the huge Tudor, he could have puked. He turned off the ignition and sat with his hands on the wheel. *This is for Ian. You can walk out any time. This dude can't hurt you. Yeah, just keep saying that.*

The march to the door felt like two miles and two inches at the same time. He knocked. The dark-haired dude who answered was somebody he'd never seen before. "Uh, hi. I'm here to see Dr. Carney."

"You're Mr. Carney?"

"Yeah."

"Follow me, sir."

Jeez, this was the butler. *Come on, Dad.*

When they got to his father's office, the guy stepped aside and waved him in. "I'll get Dr. Carney."

"Okay." The room was déjà vu all over again. How many horrible memories could be traced directly to this room?

Your science grades are awful. How can you become a professional with this kind of performance?

Who ever heard of a boy from our family getting an A in shop?

What do you mean, you don't want to go to college?

Your mother has told me some shocking things, James. Where did these filthy magazines come from? I expect young boys to be curious, but this is perversion.

He's gone. You're never going to see that horrible boy again.

"James?"

For a second he stayed back in the memory, then glanced up at his father walking into the room. "Yeah. Sorry, I was just—thinking." About how much he hated being here.

"Please sit down."

He perched on the edge of the guest chair in front of the huge leather-and-mahogany desk while his father took the high-backed chair. "How is Ian?"

Jim frowned. "Why the hell would you care?"

"I'm not without compassion for his situation."

"You could have fooled me."

His father's lips tightened, then relaxed. "Regardless, that's not why I asked you here. Not exactly, anyway."

Jim sighed and let it be audible. "Okay, I'm listening."

"I understand you've been dating Constance Murch?"

What the fuck? "That's not exactly true, but what business is it of yours?"

"In what way, not true?"

"We've had a few business lunches. Only one date."

"I see. Perhaps you're aware that her father, Alex Murch, is a board member at the club and one of Orange County's wealthiest businessmen."

163

"Yes, I know. I met him. Aside from being a prejudiced asshole, he's a good guy."

For a second his father's brows drew tight, and then he laughed. "Interesting assessment. And what do you think of Constance?"

He shrugged. "Not sure why we're discussing this, but she's smart and capable. I like working for her."

"Would it interest you to know that she likes working with you too?" He smiled, cat and canary-wise.

"Not really. I'm aware that Constance likes me, if that's what you mean. So?"

"So, Constance's father is very protective of his daughter."

Jim held up a hand. "He's got nothing to worry about from me. I just want to do a good job. I have no designs on his daughter, so tell him to quit chewing his fingernails and butt out."

His father sat back in his chair and steepled his fingers in front of his mouth. "And what if it was advantageous to you to have *designs* on her, as you so euphemistically put it?"

"What the hell are we talking about and how does this have anything to do with Ian—or did you just say that to get me here?"

"What I'm saying is that Alex Murch is in favor of you dating his daughter. In fact, he'd like to see a more long-term, even permanent, relationship develop."

"What the fuck?"

His father sat forward, frowning. "Control your disgusting mouth, James."

Jim met him eye to eye. "Constance can get her own boyfriends. Her father doesn't have to pimp her out."

"Apparently not. She is very picky and has devoted her life to her work. She's reached thirty-five with no real marriage prospects on the horizon."

"Lots of women do."

"Yes, well, Constance likes you. Hard for me to understand, but I gather many of her previous suitors have been gold diggers and she likes that you aren't. Trust me, I assured Alex that you had zero interest in money." He snorted. "Anyway, Alex is prepared to be very grateful if you continue to date his daughter."

His eyebrows practically crawled into his eyes. "What do you mean?"

"For one thing, he'll endow the club with a much needed multimillion-dollar grant."

"Why needed?"

His face got icy. "That's not your concern, but he's also prepared to give your little company a lot of work and bring you into his business. He'll train you and, if things work out, even put you in a senior position that could have real chops when he retires." His father leaned forward, his handsome face looking like he smelled something bad. "It's a rare opportunity for someone like you."

"And why are you telling me this and not him?"

"I think he senses you might turn him down."

"Then he senses right. I like Constance. I admire her and wish her well, but I'm not for sale. I have my own life. Tell him you tried." He stood.

"Sit down, James."

"Why?"

"Because you haven't heard the price of your purchase yet."

Not good. He sat slowly.

His father leaned forward, eyes glittering. "I believe you know your brother has his heart set on attending architecture school at Berkeley."

No, please. Don't say this.

His father smiled, and Jim's heart hammered. *Don't say it. Don't.* "If you do this—if you make your business lunches with Constance Murch into actual dates and turn this into a long-term relationship, I'll send your brother to Berkeley with bells on. Full tuition, housing, spending money, a vehicle, recommendations for the best internships, the works."

"You bastard."

He pressed a hand to his chest. "I think it's a very generous offer."

"It's what you should do for him anyway. He's your son."

"I'm doubly generous. I'm letting you do it for him. Of course, he'll never know that. And you won't tell anyone else about this arrangement. No one."

The screaming inside his head got so loud, he couldn't hear himself. "People will think it's strange."

"Strange? She's an attractive woman, and Alex will shower you with so many rewards you won't have time to feel dirty." His father laughed.

JIM SAT in his truck on the side of the road outside the Pelican Hill gate and shook. *Want to talk to somebody.* No one. His father's voice rang in his head.

Can't do this. Can't do this. Can't.

Shit, the old man couldn't even know what his plan would do to Jim. He just thought he was arranging Jim's life for him, and he knew Jim would hate that. No way he could understand he was condemning Jim to misery and breaking his heart. Sweet Jesus, he'd be so happy if he knew.

He dropped his head on the steering wheel. *Ken. Oh God, Ken.*

Come on, he won't miss you. He'll move on in one day.

He picked up his phone and held it against his chest. *But I won't.*

A tapping on the truck's window brought his head up, and he stared into a flashlight. Behind it he could just make out the security guard from the gate. He rolled the window a couple of inches. "Yeah."

"No loitering in this vicinity. Would you please move on?"

The top of his head exploded. "Fuck you!" He smashed his fist against the window, the edge of the phone caught the glass just right and cracked it into a spiderweb of pieces, as the perfect pain seared up his arm, into his shoulder, and out though his brain. He cranked the key, stomped the gas, and pulled out as a Porsche wheeled around the corner. The Porsche skidded to the side as Jim floored it, and the old truck showed it was pissed too as it sailed down the road toward the ocean, leaving the sports car driver leaning on his horn. His hand hung at his side. *Oh shit, that hurts. Hurts. Good.*

I could go to Ken's. He'd fix it. I could tell him everything. Maybe he'd fix that too? His hand trembled. *Why would he do that? Take on the chairman and board member of the club he loves? Take on a doctor who could ruin his career? For a casual date with no future? Shit, why?*

He could practically hear the discomfort in Ken's voice, feel his embarrassment at having to tell Jim that no way was he wrecking his life for a quick lay.

Before he could crap out, he switched the phone to his left hand on the wheel and pushed the speed dial number. He heard the ringing.

Ken sounded happy. "Hi, baby, on your way to see me? I made some salads. I know, you hate anything healthy, but I promise to slather them with blue cheese."

"Can't. Can't come. I'm so sorry. Family matter."

"Oh hell. I'm really sad not to see you, but I sure know about family. Can we get together tomorrow night?"

"No. No. I'm going to be tied up. Oh God, tied up for a while, quite a while." Bile rose up his throat, and somehow his face got wet.

"Jim, are you okay?"

"Yeah. Just hurt my hand. But I'm fine. Thanks. Thanks for everything."

"Jim, wait—"

"Can't." He clicked off, pulled to the side of PCH, jumped out, and puked his guts all over the scrub grass beside the highway that led to Crystal Cove.

When his heaves turned dry, he dragged himself back into the truck. *Never felt this empty.*

Get used to it, asshole.

He drove slowly. The road looked like water. What had he said to Ken? He couldn't remember. And what the hell was he going to tell Ian? He arched over the wheel and tried to press his back hard against the seat. His chest hurt.

Finally, he pulled into his parking space. *Could sleep here. Pretend to Ian that I spent the night with Ken. No, he'd find out.*

Oh God, want to spend the night with Ken. What if I just forget the whole thing? Turn around and drive to Ken's?

And forget you could have given your brother the thing he wants most?

He crawled out of the truck, hand throbbing like an open wound, and walked slowly up the stairs to the apartment. With his key in the lock and the door half-open, he heard a giggle. Oh shit, he'd forgotten about Rico. He closed the door and headed back to the stairs.

"Jim? Where are you going?"

He stopped and turned toward Ian, who stood in the doorway with Anderson peering out from beside his feet. His brother looked puzzled but not pissed. Jim tried to smile. "Sorry. I forgot about your date. I'll be back later."

"Hell, no. We're just watching TV. Come on, it's your apartment."

He should go get drunk, but all he could think about was sleeping. "I'll just go to bed. Won't be in your way at all." He walked toward the door, trying to keep his hand from bouncing.

"What happened? Why aren't you on your date?"

"Uh, something came up for Ken." He shrugged. "Like I told you, he's got a lot going on." He stepped inside and saw Rico sitting on the old couch. Sure enough, the TV was on with a movie on pause. He even had all his clothes on. "Hey, Rico."

"Hi, Jim."

Ian closed the door behind him. "Jeez, I'm sorry." He grabbed Jim's arm, and Jim flinched. "What?" He got a look at Jim's hand that was slowly swelling to the size of a loaf of bread. "What the hell happened?"

"I, uh, got distracted and closed it in the door of the truck."

"Jesus, Jim. This looks bad."

"Looks worse than it feels."

"That's such a lie. Do you think it's broken?"

"No. I can move all my fingers. Hurts like hell, but they move." Having the phone in his hand probably saved him. Didn't do the truck window any good.

Ian gently held Jim's hand. "Rico, get some ice from the freezer. There are some plastic bags in the bottom drawer on the right." Rico hopped up and trotted into the kitchenette. Ian looked at Jim. "Come on, let's get you undressed, into bed, and some ice on this hand."

That sounded better than anything—if he couldn't be in bed with Ken. *God, don't think about that.*

A half hour later, he lay in bed, tucked in by his brother, the ice both hurting and feeling good. "Sorry I wrecked your date."

Ian sat on the edge of the bed and grinned. "You didn't wreck it. It's just getting started. Actually, we were kind of watching a movie but mostly working on this design Rico needs to finish for a client of his firm."

"You're giving him free advice, huh?" He smiled.

168

"It's fun for me."

He touched Ian's hair with his good hand. "You're going to be such a great architect."

He nodded. "Right. One way or the other." He stood. "Now get some sleep."

"Thanks, bro. Glad to have you in my life."

"Back atcha." He closed the door softly as he left.

Jim stared after Ian. Funny how the kid had become so important to him. But those were the facts, and he wasn't going to let more bad shit happen to Ian. He slipped out of bed, setting the ice on the floor, and padded to his laptop naked. He found the e-mail from Constance where she had given him directions. He hit Reply and typed with his left hand, *Look forward to seeing you Friday.*

His hand trembled over the keypad. He stabbed his finger down on Send, closed the cover of the laptop, and dropped his head onto it.

CHAPTER TWENTY

KEN SLAMMED the door on the Lexus and beeped the lock as he hurried toward the building. Jim had to be there by now. He'd wanted to arrive earlier, but he had to make a stop at the hospital. It was after nine, which meant Jim would have been working for hours—assuming he was even at the job site. God, he'd sounded so awful last night. Maybe something was wrong with his brother? Ken wanted to run over to his apartment, but, shit, they hadn't even had a first date exactly. He couldn't go intruding on a family emergency. Jim would have asked him for help if he wanted it—wouldn't he? *You're crap at this relationship thing, Tanaka.* But he didn't want to be. He'd tell Jim he wanted to help.

Inside the building he stopped and looked at his watch. Only ten minutes until his first appointment, but he'd cancel if Jim needed him. He hurried over to the lobby suite and pushed open the door. Three guys looked busy painting and installing baseboards, but no Jim. He looked at the nearest worker. "Excuse me, have you seen Jim Carney?"

The man shook his head and Ken backed out, slammed the door, and headed to the elevator, where he pumped the up button three times. "Come on."

Jumping out on eight, he followed the dusty footprints on the carpet to the suite they were renovating. If Jim wasn't there, maybe he should try his apartment. Hell, if Ian was sick, he was a doctor, for crap's sake.

Plastic hung in front of the door to the suite. He pushed it aside—and stopped.

The tableau spread in front of him could have been taken from the cover of a romance novel. Jim stood in the center of the room with Constance holding his hand in one of hers and her other palm against his forehead. But it wasn't just the posture. She looked at him with total possession. A few of the guys on ladders looked at them with smirks.

He wanted to sink into the woodwork. He wanted to kill Constance Murch.

Before he could do either, she looked up. "Oh thank God, Dr. Tanaka. Look at what Jim's done to himself. Please."

Jim glanced up. Their eyes met. Jim's dropped.

"Ken, look." Her voice sounded strained, like the deep concern of a lover.

Slowly he sleepwalked across the dusty suite, hammers ringing in the background. Held delicately in Constance's hand, Jim's paw glowed black-and-blue at twice its normal size. "What happened?"

Jim's voice sounded far away. "Car door."

He glanced up but couldn't keep the edge from his voice. "During your family emergency?"

"Uh, yes."

Constance relinquished his hand to Ken. "Did you have a family problem?"

Jim nodded. Ken felt around carefully on the hand. "Does this hurt?"

"Like hell."

"Can you move your middle finger?"

"Yeah." It wiggled slightly.

Ken let go, and his own hand clenched. He wanted to run, or he'd make more parts of Jim Carney black-and-blue. "You should have it x-rayed, but it's probably not broken."

Constance took his injured hand in hers again. "But hands are so delicate. I think we should get you to the lab right away and then to an orthopedist or even a hand specialist. After all, Dr. Tanaka specializes in hearts." She smiled. "Not hands."

Jim seemed to stare at where Constance held his hand. He looked up at Ken, then away quickly. He sighed and seemed to sink.

Ken nodded. "Good idea. Do that. Keep icing it. Bye." He turned and walked back toward the door.

Constance called, "But Ken, what did you want? I'm sorry I got you off track."

He paused but didn't look back. "Nothing important." He was already off track. The plastic smacked his face as he left the suite.

"WHAT DO you mean, you're going out with Constance?" Ian's big green eyes consumed his face.

Jim tied the other shoe. He felt so tired, he'd like to curl in a ball and sleep for days. What he didn't want to do was have this conversation. "No big. I'm just taking her to dinner and some event."

"But that's like a date."

"I guess."

"She's a woman."

"Yes."

"You said you're gay."

He leaned his elbows on his knees and stared at the rug. "I said I thought I might be gay. I was wrong."

"But you fucked a guy!" Anderson leaped off the bed when Ian pounded both fists on it.

"Yeah, and it was great, but like you said, you don't have to be gay to want to fuck Ken Tanaka."

"That's not what I said, but even if it was, what happened with Ken?"

"Nothing. I just realized that I'm blinded by the damned yaoi I loved as a kid and Ken's a major player. If I was seeing straight, I wouldn't be chasing his ass. I've loved women for twenty-six years, and there's no reason to change for a comic book."

That speech took everything he had. Done.

Ian opened his mouth, "But—"

Jim stood and held up a hand. "That's all, Ian. I'm done talking about it." His brother looked hurt, which made him want to cry, which made him mad. "I know it would have been nice if I could have been gay too, but it's not working out." He stomped out of his bedroom, out the apartment door, and into the truck before he melted down. Shit, he was mean to his brother. Worse, he lied to him. Big time. *Get used to it, asshole.* Ken Tanaka's disgusted face flashed in his mind.

Oh God, how can I do this?

You're doing something good. You're helping Ian. Just keep saying it.

He'd said he'd pick Constance up at her house. Yes, house. A full-blown, grown-up, single-family residence in Corona del Mar.

Pulling his POS truck in front of that California beach city cottage probably violated several city ordinances. He turned off the ignition and stared out the window. Coming here conjured all sorts of lurid thoughts of good night kisses and good night fucks. *Can't go there. Can't. What's your plan, Carney? Holding her hand for five years?*

The door opened with a screech, and he stepped out. His father hadn't said how he'd know if Jim complied with his demands, but there must be a covert spy system. There sure as fuck better be. He couldn't do this for nothing. *You're doing something good for Ian.*

When he got to the porch, the door opened and Constance stood there, looking pretty damned good in tight jeans and a leather jacket that probably cost his year's income. She grinned. "I heard the truck."

He nodded. "How could you miss it?"

"It's a valiant vehicle, but I'm happy to take mine if you'd like."

"Sure. That'd be great." He should feel embarrassed but mostly didn't feel anything.

"How's your hand?"

"Okay." He held it up. The paw had returned to its normal size but still featured a rainbow of colors. Seemed appropriate.

"I still think you might want to have it checked by a doctor. You don't have to be the big, tough guy with me, you know?" She smiled.

"No, I've had worse." To his hand, but not his heart. He tried to smile back.

"Want to have a drink before we go?"

"Okay." A drink sounded damned good.

He followed her into the house. Beautiful. Just the right amount of homey and classy. "I like your place."

"Thanks." She led the way into a smallish kitchen with a view into a lighted backyard. Corona del Mar was right by the water, but it was flat; you only got a view if you were perched on the one street overlooking the ocean. Most of the town was like an old-fashioned village in some other part of the country. He sat on a stool at her kitchen island.

"What would you like? I have wine, beer, scotch, and Dubonnet, which doesn't impress me as your drink." She laughed.

"Scotch, neat."

"Oh my, I've never seen you drink."

He stared down at his hands. "I'm sneaky."

She poured a couple of fingers of good scotch into a cut crystal glass and handed it to him, then took a glass of red wine for herself. He swirled the scotch. Just the smell made him woozy and woozy sounded very, very good. Slowly he took a sip.

"Meet with your approval?"

"Oh yeah." He slugged back the rest and let it burn like a son of a bitch all the way down. When it hit his stomach, first it cramped, then his heart started pounding, and then that sweet, warm floatiness took over.

She gave him a little look and didn't offer him another one, which was good if he wanted to carry on a conversation at dinner.

She set the glasses in the sink, hers still mostly full. "So where to?"

Fortunately, he'd thought about the fact that he asked her, so he better make a reservation. "Want to try that Mexican place in Crystal Cove?"

"Yes, I went there last week. It's really good."

"Well, damn, I wanted to take you someplace new."

"That's okay. My father loves new restaurants, so he hauls me on some of his excursions."

"I'd think he'd be popular with the ladies."

She smiled. "He is, but he likes taking me along on his dates."

"Putting the women in their place, I'd say. Telling them they'll never be as important as his daughter."

"What a nice way to interpret that. A lot of people would just assume he thought I was lonely."

Her honesty took his breath. How crappy was it that he had to lie to her too?

She grabbed her purse from the counter. "My car's in the back." She pulled out her phone. "I just need to send a quick text."

Being chauffeured to the restaurant in a new-model Mercedes sports car didn't make him feel any better. He managed to down a shot of Jack at the bar while they waited to be seated, then sipped another on the rocks with dinner.

"You okay, Jim? I've never seen you drink before."

"Funny. People ask me if I'm okay when I don't drink." He swallowed a burning mouthful.

"Oh?"

"Yeah, I tried ginger ale for a while, but it didn't agree with me." He cut another bite of pork chop and chewed with some mashed potatoes.

She smiled. "I think I understand why Dr. Tanaka yelled at you. You don't pay enough attention to your health. Too busy solving problems for the rest of us."

His stomach tightened. "Dr. Tanaka needs to butt out."

"He's just trying to look after your health, Jim."

The works "fuck off" burned on his lips, but she didn't deserve that. "He told me himself the heart thing is nothing to worry about. I get lots of exercise. He says that's good for me." Jesus, that almost made him cry.

"Has he given you dietary guidelines?"

"I don't want to talk about Ken Tanaka."

If she was startled, she hid it. "I understand. Tell me about what you like to do for fun."

That seemed like a safe subject. It turned out she adored football and knew quite a bit about it. After dissecting the potential of the Buckeyes versus the Ducks, he settled down and even enjoyed himself for a while.

"So would you like dessert?" He didn't want to think about the cost of all this, but Billy was giving him good pay for this job, so he could afford it. *Keep telling yourself that.*

She gave him a funny, playful smile. "Well, let me look at the dessert menu." After a glance around the big restaurant, she stared intently at the array of sweets. "What are you thinking of having?"

What he wanted was another shot of Jack, but her earlier comments talked him out of it. "Not sure. Want to split something? I was—"

"Good evening, you two."

He looked up to find Constance's father standing beside the table with a much younger, slinky brunette on his arm.

Constance laughed. "Surprise! Hi, Daddy."

Jim tried not to frown. "Uh, hi. This is quite a coincidence." *Like hell.*

Constance squeezed his arm. "It's not a coincidence. I texted Daddy where we'd be because he has a surprise for you."

"Oh?" He hated surprises.

"Want to sit down, Daddy?"

"No, it'll just take a minute. Good restaurant, by the way. Tiffany and I were sitting at a table in the bar."

Jim nodded to the prettyish girl who was mostly staring around the restaurant.

Constance smiled. "Yes, we liked it too."

Murch leaned against the edge of the table. "So what I wanted to say was, I'd like to get together with you and your business partner to discuss work you can do for Murch Development." He grinned. "Think that'd be possible?"

Just like his father had promised. He wanted to vomit. *Smile, dammit.* Both Murch and Constance stared at him with giant shit-eating grins like they'd just given him the winning lottery ticket. Yeah, they did. He forced his lips to curve up. "I think that can be arranged. He's away right now on his—uh, vacation, but he'll be back Monday."

"Good, good. We'll give him a day to settle in, so let's talk Tuesday and set a date."

"I'll tell him." *Jesus, be happy. This could make Billy's company.* "Thank you."

"I'm expecting this to be good for both of us, if what Constance tells me is true. Of course, she may be blinded by your good looks."

Constance wrapped her hands around Jim's arm. "My vision's 20/20 as you know, Daddy."

"Yep, not much gets past this girl."

"Are you bringing him to the thing?"

She glanced sideways. "Shh. I haven't asked him yet."

Oh shit.

"Have a great night, you two. Don't do anything I wouldn't do." He laughed.

"Daddy!" Constance laughed too, although she probably felt Jim flinch. Just like he'd said to his brother.

Once her father was out of sight, Constance turned to him. "Excited?"

"Yeah. It's great. Your dad's girlfriend doesn't talk much."

She frowned a little, then shrugged. "She's one of a string. I think he picks them so he'll never be tempted to marry one." She clapped her hands. "So, my invitation. This Friday there's a big black-tie fundraiser event at the club, and I wondered if you'd like to go?"

"Club? Like Pacific Crest?"

"Yes. Daddy's very involved with their fundraising."

A lot more than she knew. "I'm not much of a black-tie guy."

"You don't have to wear a tux if you don't want to. Hell, I don't care if you come in jeans."

He really did like her. "I can't dance."

"Me either. When would I have learned?" She grinned. "We can hang out at the bar, if you want."

He sighed all the way to his soul. "Okay."

"Thanks. It'll be fun to have the handsomest date at the party."

He snorted. "What was that you said about your 20/20 vision?"

"You're so cute. You really don't know how good-looking you are, do you?"

He glanced at her, then looked at his empty glass. She made him nervous.

As they drove back to her house, he got antsier. He liked the numbing effects of the scotch, but he was out of practice. The stuff made him feel weird. Or maybe it was just knowing Constance expected something from him he didn't want to—no, couldn't—give. How could he explain that his cock was not going to rise for her? Would it ever rise for anybody again—except Ken Tanaka?

In her garage, he crawled out of the passenger side. Now what? He walked toward the garage door.

"Would you like to come in?"

He stopped. "Uh, no. I can't. My brother." *You're a chickenshit coward to be blaming Ian.*

"Of course, I understand."

He paused, then turned and walked back to her, controlling his long, slow breath. He forced a smile. "Thanks. I had a good time. You're a really fun person."

She looked up at him. "Thank you. That means a lot."

Come on, Carney, you know what to do. He leaned down and pressed his lips against hers. Soft, pleasant. Her light floral perfume filled his nose. His stomach tightened and throat closed. *Gotta get out of here.* He pulled back so suddenly, she tripped forward a step. "Sorry. Late. Got to go. Thanks again."

He turned on his heel and walked to his truck as fast as he could without looking like he was running. When he got inside, he cranked the engine and the old beast sprang to life. It wanted to leave too. Oh God, Constance still stood in the garage watching him. He waved and pulled away from the curb.

Awful. This is awful. He couldn't do this to such a nice lady. *It's not fair.* He floored it and hoped the Newport Beach police were asleep at the wheel. By the time he got to Aliso Viejo, he knew it wouldn't work. He couldn't do this. There had to be another way.

He pulled into the parking place and practically jumped out of the car. Should he tell his father he wasn't doing it or just let him guess? Guessing was better.

Halfway across the parking lot, he got hit by a flying missile. "Jim, Jim, you won't believe what happened."

His heart stuttered. "What?"

"Dad's sending me to Berkeley. Full tuition, room and board, books, the whole thing. He even submitted my name for an internship to one of the coolest firms in northern California. Jesus, Jim, I don't know how this happened. It's unbelievable."

"Yeah. What did he say?" Jim felt heat pushing behind his eyes, and he looked away.

"I didn't talk to him. I got an e-mail from his personal assistant."

"Seems like the chickenshit should have talked to you."

Ian grabbed his arm. "Jim, are you listening? This is Berkeley! Jesus, I don't care if the message came by stork."

"Good. That's good." He walked toward the apartment, and Ian fell in beside him.

Ian kind of skipped. "I do wonder what made him change his mind."

"Yeah."

Ian stopped and smiled at his brother. "Maybe—maybe he doesn't hate me as much as he said."

Jim put his arm around Ian's shoulders and kept walking, but he wanted to sit on the apartment stairs and cry.

CHAPTER TWENTY-ONE

KEN LEANED forward in his office chair and stared at his phone. The one that didn't ring. It didn't ring even after he'd broken down and called Jim to ask how his hand was and to be sure his brother was okay. No answer. He'd left a message, which was a first for him. Still no answer. Not much reinforcement from the fucking universe on caring about somebody. *Shit.*

He turned back to the patient file on the computer.

The phone rang, and he practically turned over the chair grabbing it. "Jim?"

Dead air.

"Hello?"

"Kenji, who is this Jim?" His mother.

"He's a patient of mine, mother." He sighed very silently. "I'm glad you called me. I wanted to apologize for my behavior at dinner. I was impolite to you and your guests. I'm very sorry." Hell, what was he fighting for anyway?

"That's good, Kenji. I was sure you'd reconsider your rudeness."

"Yes."

"So you'll come to dinner tonight and make amends."

Why the hell not? He wasn't doing anything more important. "What time shall I be there?"

Five hours filled with patients and pain later, he dragged himself out of the car at his parents', staring at the blue sedan parked at the curb. The Okuwas's car. He wanted to pick up a rock and break the window—or better yet, climb in his Lexus and drive until he didn't recognize a person or a landmark. But no, he was Dr. Kenji Tanaka, second son of an honorable family, brother to a glorious ghost to whom he owed his life and future because his mother's tears could never be dried—but he had to keep trying. *Shit.*

He watched his feet move up the walkway. *Why are you doing this? Because Jim made me brave, and now Jim's gone.*

Inside the house, five pairs of eyes stared at him as he entered. He bowed slightly. "Good evening."

Mickey gave him a big smile. "Hey, bro, thought I'd never see you again. I'm really glad you're here."

That's nice to hear—I guess.

For three hours he made polite conversation while everyone else seemed to tiptoe around, trying not to piss him off. Finally the evening was over and he walked out with Mickey, the parents staying inside to give them space, apparently. Jesus, was he back in high school?

Mickey looked up at him. Cute, no doubt. Rakish grin, longish hair that stuck out in many directions adding to the wild-guy look, and that adorable ass. Why did it add up to nothing? No tough guy broken nose, no uncut blond hair, no crinkly green eyes that always looked wary.

Jesus H. Christ. When had he fallen in love with Jim Carney?

Cosmic joke. The player gets played. He'd finally cracked open his heart for a man he couldn't have.

Mickey added a little more sass to his smile. "So are we doing this or no? I'm interested. You're the holdout."

"I'm not sure I'm up for this happy-ever-after shit, Mickey, no matter what my mother wants." He sighed.

"Me either, man. Hell, I just want to have some fun, and if that means pretending to be a little more serious than we are, who does it hurt? Let's go someplace and fuck."

Ken stared. Had it come to this? He couldn't even fall in bed with some guy for the fun of it? He was that wrecked? "I've got to go to this charity event at my club Friday night. How about you come with me? It's black tie. We'll see where it leads."

"I'd settle for a fast poke behind those bushes, baby."

"Black tie or leave it."

Mickey laughed. "What time will you pick me up?"

JUST FOCUS on the circuit. The circuit. Don't think. Jim twisted the wires and connected the lighting. Around him, the sound of hammers drowned out conversation. Finally he couldn't do one more thing at the top of the frigging ladder, so he climbed down to move to another location.

He could sense Charlie's eyes on him. His back felt hot. *Ignore him.* He made a big production out of moving the ladder, then climbed up again and pulled out his cutters.

"Jim?"

Well, hell, not Charlie. Billy. He looked down and forced a smile. "Hi. You're not due back until Monday. How come you're not honeymooning?"

"The suite looks great."

He really smiled this time. "Yeah, it does, doesn't it? I gotta make sure Ian sees it before the tenant moves in. He did a great job."

"You've done a great job."

He ducked his head. "Thanks."

"Can I talk to you?"

Oh hell. Jim turned on the ladder step so he half faced forward. "Sure. Shoot."

"Come down."

Double hell. Slowly he climbed down the steps. At the bottom Billy pointed toward the door. Jim followed him out in lead boots. In the hall Billy walked him into the stairwell and closed the door. "I got a call from Constance Murch to set up the conversation with her father for next week."

"Yeah." Maybe Billy was just excited?

"She mentioned that you'd be seeing her father at the fundraiser you're attending—with her."

Jim swallowed.

"I thought we talked about this? I don't expect you or even want you to date Constance as a benefit to this company."

Jim stared at his shoes and shook his head. "That's not it."

"Then what is it?"

Jesus, his father said not to tell anyone. What would happen if he told Billy? Billy would try to make it better. Shaz would be worse. He'd go charging in with his freak flag flying. Meanwhile his brother would lose his ride to Berkeley. "I just like her."

"Yes, she's a nice woman. What does that have to do with anything?"

"I don't mind dating her."

"Crap, Jim, do you think she'd be thrilled to hear that ringing endorsement?"

"Maybe not, but there's no reason not to date her and if it does the company good too, what's the big deal?"

Billy leaned against the wall and crossed his arms. "If you don't know, then I guess I can't tell you."

Jim's heart pounded. *I can't help it!* The words screamed in his brain but wouldn't come out his mouth.

Billy sighed. "I'm going to tell Constance that it's probably best if we don't meet with her father." He pushed off from the wall. "You can do what you want." He opened the door to the hall and was gone.

Shit. What just happened? All he'd wanted was to make things better for Billy and Ian. To help the company. *Only you could make it come out the opposite, Carney.* The tight stairwell spun and his knees turned to water. Down he went on his ass. The first sob echoed in the small space. Another. He dropped his head in his arms and cried.

JIM STARED out the window as they approached the Pacific Crest Club in Constance's Mercedes. She'd offered to drive. Probably figured he'd drink too much. *Good guess.* He'd let everyone else run his life pretty well so far; why should tonight be any different?

She cleared her throat. "Did you know that Billy Ballew called me?"

What should he say? "He said he might."

"He doesn't want to meet with my father."

"Yeah. He thought more about it, and I guess he's afraid your dad will find out and think we tried to pull something on him."

"How would he know?" She slowed as the cars ahead stopped at the valet.

"For one thing, Billy's husband is pretty high profile. But that's not the issue, really. He doesn't want to lie." Right, Jim could do all the lying for the company.

"It's possible Daddy likes you so much, he won't care about Billy at all."

Jim's jaw tightened. *Right.* Murch liked Jim dating his daughter so much. "Maybe." But Billy wouldn't take the business anyway. How the hell would he explain that to Constance? Crap, was there a hole big enough to hold him and all his lies?

She stopped in front of the club, and the valet pulled open the door. He stared at his shiny shoes as he stepped out onto the pavement. Constance walked around the car, tucking her parking ticket in her little purse. He sighed and offered his arm.

She smiled up at him. "Thank you, sir."

"If I didn't tell you, you look real nice." That was true. Her deep blue evening gown set off her blonde hair and showed her killer figure. A figure he still hadn't checked out undressed.

"You too."

He shrugged.

"You got a haircut."

"Yeah. Once a year whether I need it or not."

"You feeling okay? How's your hand?"

He held it up. "Bruised but functional. I'm fine." He glanced up at the subdued façade of the Pacific Crest Club. Could you hate a structure? Really hate it? He was practicing.

Inside, the host greeted Constance effusively, and a number of other people said hello. She left her shawl that looked like it was made from some very pricey sheep with the coat-check girl, and they walked into the dining room. Fancy. The room had been arranged with large round tables decorated with tall flower arrangements in the center, with long, rectangular tables around the perimeter of the room. Glass bowls stood on those in front of big baskets for the drawings.

Constance nodded toward the display. "Let's check out the drawings and the silent auction, shall we?"

"Have they got a bar?"

She nodded to the far corner of the room. "Over there."

"Why don't you start looking at the stuff and I'll get us some drinks?"

"Okay. I'll have champagne."

He set off skirting between the tables to get to the bar, where he joined the end of the line. *Come on. Come on.*

"Well, well, look who's here. Mr. Blue-Collar Loverboy."

Jim didn't even look at the sneering voice. "Hello, Willings."

Willings stepped up beside him so Jim couldn't pretend he wasn't there. "Where's Ken? I wouldn't have expected him to let you out of his sight. Never know when he's going to brush off another guy and need you to protect him."

Jim clenched his fists and bit his tongue.

Willings nudged him, pushing his luck. "Really, where is he?"

Jim stared at the heels of the guy in front of him. "I haven't seen him."

"What?" Gene started to laugh. "Don't tell me he left you too? Perfect. There's no way he'd have spent much time with a Neanderthal like you anyway. I love it. He blew you off." He laughed.

"The only one I remember doing any blowing around here is you."

"Don't let him break your heart, Lover Boy."

"Don't suck any wooden cocks, Willings."

Willings's eyes widened, but he walked away. Jim's heart beat so hard he could pass out. The guy in front of him finished his drink order, and Jim stepped up. "Jack on the rocks and champagne." He held the edge of the bar tight. When the bartender set the highball glass in front of him, he grabbed it and tossed it back. The hot/cold flash seared down his esophagus and hit his empty stomach like a bonfire.

The bartender set the champagne beside the empty glass. "Another, sir?"

"Yeah, thanks." He tossed bills with enough for a tip on the bar and grabbed the fresh Jack and champagne. *Breathe.* He sipped his drink to try to make his heart stop pounding.

Balancing the two glasses, he started back across the dining room toward the raffle baskets. He skirted a table and turned left. Ken Tanaka stood a few feet in front of him with that pretty, pretty boy attached to his side like a barnacle. *No.* Like a step back in time, Jim's foot caught the chair leg, he flew forward, champagne and whiskey flying, and landed in Ken's arms.

"Got you."

Jim looked up into the beautiful black eyes. Weirdly, heat flashed in his head, and he blinked against the tears pressing behind the back of his eyes.

Constance hurried up. "Jim, are you all right?"

Ken looked at her, then back at Jim. He kind of shrugged. "I guess I don't have you, do I?" He set Jim away and back on his feet.

Jim's heart tried to run after Ken as he walked away with that boy beside him.

Constance brushed liquid from his sleeve as two busboys hurried over with rags to wipe up the disaster. "Did you hurt your hand?"

"No. Just busy making a fool of myself. Sorry I dropped your champagne."

"Good God, that doesn't matter. As long as you're okay."

Was he okay? Hell to the fucking no. "Let me go get another drink—for you." He looked in the direction Ken had gone. Maybe he'd never be okay again.

She grabbed his arm—still warm from Ken's hands. "I'll come with you this time just to keep you safe."

Safe. Right.

KEN WALKED straight toward the door of the club with Mickey practically running to keep up. "Hey, man, how come everywhere we go, that fucking hunk shows up?"

"Just lucky, I guess."

Mickey sidestepped a white-haired matron. "Where are we going?"

"To get some air."

Outside, he gulped breaths. A couple on their way into the club stared at him. He must look sick or desperate.

He stopped beside a tree and stared at the grass. Mickey stepped up beside him. "So how do you know that guy again?"

"He was a patient." The lie in those words rattled in his brain.

"That must be his rich bitch girlfriend, huh?"

"Yes, I suppose she is."

"Those tough blue-collar dudes get all the girls." He glanced to the side and grinned. "Even you."

"Fuck off."

He chuckled. "No skin off my ass. You can't have him, how about me?" Mickey looked around. "This is some fancy club, but wacked, man. These fossils will make you old."

185

"Hell, I feel old." And sad and tired.

Mickey laughed. "Come on, let's get the hell out of here. We can get a couple drinks, then go to my place and see what comes up. Wha'd'ya say?"

"Yeah."

CHAPTER TWENTY-TWO

KEN FOLLOWED Mickey through the apartment door. Mickey flipped on a light and tossed his tux jacket on a pile of clothing at the end of a long sectional couch that looked like it might have been shopped from the street corner. Sort of like Jim's. Mickey grinned back at Ken. "Make yourself at home. I'm pretty sure my roommates aren't here."

Ken stopped. Roommates? Christ, he forgot how young Mickey was. "Why don't we just go to my apartment?"

"Nah. We're here now." Mickey sidled over and helped Ken out of his tux coat. "What do you want to drink? I've got beer and—beer."

"Hey, I think I'll have beer."

Mickey started to throw Ken's jacket on the pile, but Ken grabbed it and hung it on the edge of a closet door that stood half open. Mickey chuckled and sashayed into the kitchen. A giant TV dominated the living space, with Mickey's guitar on a stand taking second place. Ken perched on the edge of the sectional. Now that he was here, he didn't want to be. He should just go home.

Mickey walked in with two beer bottles and handed one to Ken.

"Thanks. I'm actually feeling a little under the weather. I think I'll take off and get some sleep. Sorry the event wasn't better for you."

Mickey sat close next to Ken and looked down at his bottle. "Yeah, well, you can make it up to me."

Ken nodded. "Sure. Maybe we can go to dinner and a film next weekend."

Mickey slid even closer until his side pressed against Ken's. "I think we're past that, don't you?"

Ken frowned. "You don't like movies?"

Mickey looked up in to his eyes. "No. I think you should be making it up to me right now. Here. Tonight."

Ken sighed. "Did you hear me say I'm not feeling well? So that's not going to happen." He stood. "I'll call you and set up another date." *Sometime the next century.*

Mickey grinned.

Ken heard the footsteps behind him and turned. Walking out of the hall to the bedrooms came GG and Tommy.

Mickey put a hand to his cheek and gasped. "Oh my. I guess my roommates were here after all." He started to laugh.

JIM SLUGGED back his third Jack. Fourth? *Whatever.* He stood in a circle of people waiting for the drawings to start, with Constance to his right holding on to his arm and Alex Murch on his left with an elbow slung casually around Jim's neck. Had he ever felt this uncomfortable? Rich guys—club members—looked at him like the appointed heir or some crap. That's how Alex had treated him all through dinner.

More like the appointed whore. The appointed bull being led into the mating stall.

A waiter walked by with a tray of complimentary champagne, and he twisted and grabbed two glasses, dislodging both holds on him. "Sorry, I saw Constance was empty." He handed her the glass and kept the other for himself.

"Thank you." She smiled sweetly, and her father smiled bigger.

"Jim, I know you and Constance probably plan to leave us old folks behind as fast as possible after this shindig ends, so let's go talk a minute."

Did he have to? He followed Murch and Constance to a quieter corner of the big room, sipping the champagne the whole way. Murch turned. "Constance told me about your business partner."

He looked at Constance. "Excuse me?"

She nodded. "I told him about Billy Ballew being gay."

What the fuck? "He's not my partner. He's my boss. He owns the company."

Murch waved a hand. "Right. I misspoke, but that can be changed. Constance is impressed with you, Carney, and so am I. I could use a man like you in my business. Or, if you don't want to work for Constance's dad, there are a number of contractors I deal with that would be lucky to get you. I'm sure with a recommendation as weighty as Constance's or mine, they'd be delighted to take you on as a partner—"

The room spun. "Wait. I never said I wanted to leave Billy. He's a great boss. And I haven't got anything to bring to a partnership. I like what I do." How did his heart get in his mouth? His temples pounded.

"Good evening, James."

No, please God, no.

Murch looked over Jim's shoulder with a big smile, and Constance did the same. "Good evening, Dr. Carney. How good to see you again."

Jim's father took Constance's hand and kissed it. He'd always been able to get away with crap like that. "You look beautiful this evening, my dear." He looked up at Alex Murch. "Sorry I missed dinner, Alex. I had an emergency."

"Glad you could make it now, James."

Jim stared into the depths of his empty champagne glass. *Drowning. Can't breathe. Why is it so cold in here?*

Murch put a hand on Jim's shoulder. "I was just making your son an offer I hope he can't refuse. Seems to me he ought to be working at least as a partner. Constance believes in Jim, and I'd like to see him set up on a growth trajectory that allows him to use more of his skills."

"What a good idea." His father's voice shivered down Jim's back like an ice cube. "He's never lived up to his potential. It would be good to see him in a place where he can excel." His father sipped champagne. "Get him out from under the thumb of that fucking fag."

Jim's head snapped up. "That fucking fag, as you call him, could teach you a few things about being a man."

Murch patted his shoulder. "I understand that the guy's been your friend for a long time, Jim, and I admire loyalty. But I gotta go with your dad on this one. No queer's gonna go far in construction, and you've got a big future ahead of you."

Constance frowned. "I never asked you to try to take Jim away from his current company."

"But you want what's best for him, right?"

Jim held out a hand and stepped back. "Stop. Just stop." God, the water was at his nose and rising. "I never asked anybody to help me. I don't want your help."

Murch nodded. "I know. You're an independent guy like me. Your father told me how you'll do anything to help your brother be an architect."

Ian! Jim took another step back. Did Murch know his deal with his father? Did everyone know he was a hired rent boy?

Constance reached out toward him. "Jim, are you okay? You're white as snow. Sweetheart—"

"No. Can't—" His heart hammered, but it didn't seem to help. No blood reached his brain. Black dots swam in a sea of white light.

Falling. *Am I?* The floor hit his hip. *How?*

KEN STARED at GG and Tommy walking toward him. Three against one, and one of the three made mountains look small.

Mickey leaned against the edge of the couch, casual and self-assured. "We thought you'd enjoy a little ménage." He shrugged. "It's my kink, you see."

Think, dammit. "I don't do multiples."

"No worries, baby. You just have to lie there."

"Like I would have done if the drug had worked?"

"Exactly. You didn't drink your beer, so no drug tonight, but that's okay. I enjoy a little slap and tickle too."

"You're a sick little fuck." His eyes darted around the room.

"Awww. That's not what your mommy would say. If you weren't such a mama's boy, I never would have had a chance. You'd be with that big blue-collar white hunk and Mommy be damned. But not the doctor. Oh no. When his mother says jump, he says how high—in Japanese."

Jesus, his own condemnation. "Out of the mouths of assholes."

Mickey laughed. "I do love your sense of humor, doc. I hope it holds up." He flicked his fingers, and Tommy started toward Ken.

Instead of backing up, Ken stepped forward. No weapons by the walls. He needed something.

"JIM, OH my God. Jim. Somebody help!" Candace leaned over him, supporting his head with her arm.

How did he get here? Chest hurt. "Heart."

"Sweet Jesus. He's having a heart attack."

He whispered against her ear. "Ken. Call Ken, please. Please."

"Ken? Oh, Dr. Tanaka. Your doctor."

"Heart. Need Ken."

His father's face loomed in his fuzzy vision. "An ambulance is coming."

"No, no. Ken. Please."

From far, far away, Constance said, "He wants his cardiologist. I have his number. He's my tenant." Pause. He tried to keep consciousness. Constance's voice rang in his ears like a bell. "Ken, oh Ken, thank God—"

Jim sighed and let the blackness have its way.

THE PHONE buzzed in his pocket. *Thank God.* He grabbed for it and sidestepped Tommy as the huge dumbass made a grab for him. Ken clicked. "Help. Help—"

"Ken, oh Ken. Thank God."

"Constance. Help—"

"Jim's in trouble. We think it's a heart attack. He's asking for you. His father is going with him to the hospital in the ambulance. I'm following."

Every drop of blood drained from his head. "It's not a heart attack. It's mitral valve. Tell Carney mitral valve. It's important."

The three assholes had stopped and stared at him like he'd lost his mind. *Good.*

He screamed into the phone, "Tell Jim—I'll be there."

With one hand he swept forward and grabbed the guitar. With every particle of will, he slammed it into Tommy's head. The guitar cracked but didn't shatter as the big man went down.

Mickey and GG stared with open mouths. *Who's most dangerous?* Ken rammed the broken remains into GG's gut, then smashed him with a fist to the chin, which hurt like bloody hell. He spun on Mickey, who raised his hands and backed up. "Run, asshole, because when I'm through with you, you'll need your law degree to get yourself out of prison."

Ken ran for the door, made it to the parking lot, and raced the Lexus toward the hospital with his foot pressed to the floorboards. He hit a stoplight on Harbor Boulevard. "Come on. Come on." Traffic thinned in the opposite direction, and still the light didn't change. In a break between cars, he stomped the accelerator and sped through the intersection to a cacophony of honking from angry drivers. He cut to the right onto residential streets and set new neighborhood speed records, forgetting about stop signs completely. Finally he pulled up in front of the hospital, stopped, and jumped out. The guard rushed forward. Ken flashed his credentials. "Sorry. They just brought in my patient. Can you park it for me?"

"Sure, doc. No problem."

Ken ran into the lobby and raced down the hall to Emergency, waving at the volunteers at the reception desk. He stopped at the nurse's station. "I'm looking for Jim Carney. They just brought him in."

The older nurse cocked her head. "Dr. Carney?"

"No. His son is my patient."

She looked at the computer. "Yes, they're doing tests, and he's been scheduled for emergency surgery."

Shit. He nodded. "Thanks."

He trotted toward the emergency waiting room. When he rounded the corner into the smallish room, Constance sat by herself on the couch, leaning forward and holding her middle like she hurt. She really cared about Jim, which made Ken want to cry. Alex Murch paced at the back of the room. When he looked up at Ken, he frowned. Constance stared at him for a moment like she didn't see him; then she leaped to her feet, ran to him, and threw her arms around his neck. "Oh God, I'm so glad you're here." She stared up into his face. "Were you having some kind of problem when I called?"

"Long story but okay now. Did you tell Dr. Carney what I said?"

"I told him about the mitral valve, if that's what you mean?"

Murch walked up beside Constance. "What's going on?"

She held up a hand at her father and looked at Ken squarely. "I'm concerned. Jim doesn't get along with his father. I know Dr. Carney is supposed to be really good, but—"

Murch scowled. "You're not serious, Constance? Carney may not be my favorite pal, but he's an okay guy and I hear an excellent surgeon."

Ken nodded. "He won't do the surgery. It's not permitted on a family member."

Constance glanced at her father. "But he might be in the operating room, right?

He took Constance's hands. "I'll make sure Jim's safe. Don't worry."

He turned and ran out of the waiting room toward the operating rooms. As he approached, he saw the hospital's chief of surgery, Malcolm Nishimura, walking toward him. Ken slowed. "Mal, I'm looking for Jim Carney, Dr. Carney's son. He's my patient."

"Eloqua's doing an emergency surgery with Carney scrubbed in. I didn't realize it was his son." His frown said he didn't like it.

"I'd like to scrub for the surgery."

Mal frowned. "It's going to be a crowded in there. Is there an issue?"

"No. Just want to observe, if I can."

"Ask Eloqua."

"I'd rather ask you." Ken gazed at Mal. *Don't flinch.* Carney was talented but not well liked. He multiplied the arrogance of cardiovascular surgeons times ten. Fortunately Nishimura was a neurosurgeon, the only specialty with more inherent clout.

Mal hesitated, then nodded. "You got it. Grab scrubs in the locker and tell them I authorized your observation."

"Thanks, Mal. I owe you."

"OR Six."

It took five long minutes to find scrubs and suit up. Shit, he felt like *he* was having the heart attack. Outside the prep area, he looked in. Carney was talking to Eloqua. Ken pushed open the door, and Carney looked up. "What are you doing here?"

"Observing."

"Like hell."

"Authorized by Nishimura."

Carney narrowed his eyes. "My, you do stick together. Just stay out of my way."

Eloqua flashed his dark eyes at Carney. "Don't you mean my way, James?"

"Of course."

Ken looked at Eloqua, a big, kind man who he generally liked. "You're doing this minimally invasively?"

"Of course."

Carney sneered. "We need to get him back to his highly productive life as soon as possible, right?"

Ken looked at Eloqua but let his eyes shift to Carney. "And you're going to repair the valve, not replace it?" He held his breath. A valve replacement for a man so young would compromise his freedom and his life, but repair could be tricky.

Carney's eyes shifted.

"Repair it. You can do it."

"It's Dr. Eloqua's surgery."

Ken shifted his eyes to Eloqua. "Just save the valve. You can do it."

Carney sneered, "You're awfully interested for a doctor who should have told James how serious his heart problem was. You practically killed him."

Ken's sore hands clenched. What Carney said was too close to the truth.

Eloqua shook his head. "It's almost impossible to tell the severity of a mitral valve prolapse without surgery." He ducked his head a little since Carney was the senior surgeon. "As I know you're aware."

Ken stepped forward. "Also no disrespect, but Jim's had this problem since birth. You had sixteen years to diagnose it." Carney stared back, but his eyes shifted an inch. Ken nodded at Eloqua. "Just repair it, if it's possible."

Eloqua looked worried. Even Carney would have trouble with a tricky valve repair. Was Eloqua up to it? He gave a sharp nod. "I have a valve standing by, if needed."

He walked into the operating room. Ken followed and stopped. Jim lay silent and still, covered with a cloth, his face masked and an endotracheal tube protruding from his mouth. The hisses and beeps of the OR filled the icy cold room. *Want to climb on the table with him. Hold him forever.* But Jim wasn't his to hold. Instead he positioned himself at the back where he could see clearly but not get in the way.

The surgery began. Ken stared at the spot where Eloqua's scalpel incised the skin between Jim's ribs. He didn't want to watch but had to see. Had to be sure there was no slip. One slip of a surgeon's hand had altered his life by killing his brother. Another one would kill him. Red blood covered Eloqua's fingers as the skin and ribs were separated. Jim's life ebbing out. The hiss of the ventilator hypnotized as Eloqua's hands moved surely—impersonally. Had the hands of the surgeon who failed his brother been like that? There hadn't been anyone to speak for Ryoichi. He'd died because of someone who was supposed to care for him.

Eloqua paused and looked at Carney. The nurse reached for a jar of solution with the porcine valve floating. *No.* With a tissue valve, Jim would require surgery several more times in his life. A longer-life mechanical valve meant he'd have to take blood thinners. Repair would give Jim a largely normal life. "Repair it!"

Carney looked over, frowning. Eloqua said, "It's bad, Tanaka. Replacement is indicated."

"Repair it. Damn it, he's twenty-six."

"It's what's best for the patient."

Ken stepped toward Carney. "Please. He's your son." His voice shook, but he couldn't control it.

It was like the operating room staff took a breath. Obviously most didn't know that Carney had scrubbed in on a surgery on his son. The anesthesiologist looked up and frown lines appeared over his mask.

Ken's hands balled into fists so tight his nails cut into the gloves. He wanted to scream and grab the scalpel. Why hadn't he become a surgeon? *Save him. Save Jim.*

Carney looked toward Ken. "It's entirely Dr. Eloqua's decision. I have no say in this."

Eloqua visibly took a breath, nodded, and extended a hand. The OR nurse slapped vascular scissors into his grip, then turned and closed the container holding the heart valve. Ken's knees dissolved to fluid, and he stepped back so the wall could hold him up.

For two hours he stared, watched every move, kept Jim alive with the force of his will. Finally it was over and he staggered into the scrub room and collapsed on a bench. Carney and Eloqua walked in and Ken stood. "I know that was incredibly difficult. Thank you."

Eloqua nodded, then smiled.

For a second that sneer of Carney's popped into place; then it melted. "He'll be better off without the valve—at least for now."

"Yes."

"But he may need it downstream."

"I understand that."

He stared at Ken for several beats and then nodded, turned his back, and focused on cleaning up. Ken ripped off the scrubs and hurried into the hall. He had to be there for recovery.

CHAPTER TWENTY-THREE

JIM SUCKED in a breath. Damn, his throat hurt like fire. *Wait, where am I?* He opened an eye. Dim light filtered in, but it still hurt. Shut. He moved his head slightly. *Whoa. Weird.* Man, he felt like he'd had six shots of Jack. Woozy and strange. His body lay like a lump while he floated around somewhere.

Focus.

Vaguely, he felt pressure against his hip.

Slowly he blinked open his eyes. *Hospital. Beep. Beep.* He looked down without moving his head. Constance sat in a chair beside him with her head resting on his bed pressed against his hip, sound asleep. *Where did she come from? Why?*

Noise. Creaking. Staring past his nose, he looked to the other side of the bed. *Holy shit.* Ken sprawled in a chair, likewise asleep. How did he get here? *Hell, how did I get here?*

Room spinning. He closed his eyes. His brain conjured an image of him lying on the floor begging Constance to call Ken.

He heard movement. *Open my eyes or close?* He opened them.

Ken was beside him in a flash. "Jim. You're awake. Hi, guy. How are you feeling?"

Jim smiled. "Am I dreaming?"

Ken grinned. "I don't know. Are you?"

"Must be. Seeing visions."

Their eyes swam together. Jim drew a breath. "I—

"Jim, oh God. How do you feel?" Constance leaned over him and pressed a hand to his head.

He blinked. "Oh, not too bad. I can hardly feel anything. They must have me pumped full of drugs. I'm not even sure what happened."

"You collapsed at the fundraiser and were brought here in an ambulance."

197

She looked at Ken, who nodded. "They repaired your mitral valve."

Jim laughed, and it came out as a giggle. *Drugged for sure.* "The floppy one?"

"That's the one." Ken smiled, but looked down at his hands.

Constance nodded. "Ken was in the operating room with you for the whole surgery."

Wait, what? "What do you mean?"

"He attended the entire operation. To be sure everything was handled correctly."

Ken frowned a little. "It wasn't necessary, really. The surgeon did a great job. But you were my patient, so—" He shrugged.

Right. Patient. Jim sighed.

Ken looked up at Constance, then toward the door. "I should be going and leave you two alone. I'll let the nurse know you're awake and responding well."

Alone. So Ken had come to check his vital signs. Jim closed his eyes. Maybe being awake wasn't so great after all. He heard Ken moving toward the door as he fell back to sleep.

LIGHTS. BEEPING. *Right, hospital.* Jim opened his eyes.

"Hey, bro, you awake?"

Jim looked to the side. "Hi, Ian. Where am I, how am I, and what day is it?"

"You're at OC General, the resident says you're doing well, and it's Saturday afternoon. Why the hell didn't you tell me your heart was so bad?"

Jim shrugged. "I didn't exactly know."

"Oh really? Dr. Tanaka says you did."

Jim sighed.

"Knock, knock." Constance peered around the half-open door. "Can I come in?" She looked toward Ian. "Oh, sorry. I can come back later. I just brought you some sports magazines." She walked in and dropped them on the table beside his bed, then smiled. "You must be Ian. I'm Constance Murch."

Ian smiled back, but it looked tight. "Glad to meet you. Jim really likes working for you."

She glanced at Jim, then back at Ian. "I like working with him, too." She started toward the door.

Jim shook his head. "Don't go. I'm having trouble connecting with what happened."

She dragged a chair over beside Ian. "We were at the fundraiser. You were drinking a lot, which I've since learned you shouldn't have been." She frowned. "You were defending your employer to your father and suddenly fell to the floor grabbing your chest. I thought you'd had a heart attack. But fortunately I got a hold of Dr. Tanaka, who told me it was a mitral valve problem."

"You got a hold of him?"

"Yes, I had his number since he's my tenant."

"Why did you call him?"

"You told me to."

"Oh."

Constance frowned, and Ian stared at his hands.

"Hey, buddy, can I come in?" Billy walked into the room, filling the small space with his big frame.

Jim smiled. "Hi, Billy. I see they'll let just anybody in here."

Billy leaned over and gave him a pretend punch on the arm.

Holy shit. "I hope this doesn't mess up the company insurance."

"No. Tanaka says it won't be covered since it's a pre-existing thing, but your father's not going to charge you."

"My father?"

Constance nodded. "Yes, he was there for your surgery. He couldn't do it himself. Not allowed. But I guess he supervised—along with Ken."

Ken. Jim took a breath.

Billy smiled. "And the company will pay the hospital, so no worries.'

"You don't have to do that."

Billy nodded. "Yeah, I do, since company principals need to be covered by the policy."

Jim nodded before it sank in. "What?"

"I mean, as my partner, you need to have the company pay for your healthcare."

"Partner? Billy, I don't understand—"

Constance put a hand on his arm. "He means that he's offering you a partnership in the company, Jim. Which I think is wise before somebody else snatches you up."

Billy nodded. "Shaz and I planned the whole thing while we were gone, but then I was afraid you wanted a different kind of future. Maybe you don't want to work for a gay contractor?"

Constance gave Billy her most direct stare. "My father believes that a gay contractor won't make it in the industry. I'd like to see you and Jim prove him wrong."

Billy returned her gaze. "I would too."

"You've earned my business, and I plan to see you have a lot of it."

Billy glanced at Jim. "What do you say?"

Oh God, how could the fucking universe give him so many of the wrong gifts? "I—I don't think I can."

Billy's sweet face clouded. "Oh, okay. I understand."

"No, wait, it's just that—Constance, I really like working with you."

Billy nodded. "Sure, Constance and her father can do so many more things for you. I don't blame you at all."

"No, I mean—"

Constance frowned. "Jim, I—"

"Are you supposed to have this many visitors?" Ken Tanaka walked in the door, and Jim's improved heart valve skipped six beats.

Constance looked up. "Should we go?"

Ken smiled. *Suns and moons.* "No, just kidding. The nurses are going to get Jim on his feet, and he'll be ready to go home tomorrow. I just wanted to check in." His eyes connected with everyone but Jim. Finally he looked over, but he stared at Jim's chest. "So how are you feeling?"

"Okay."

He nodded. "Good, good."

Phoniest thing he'd ever heard. Ken must be dying to get out of there.

Constance looked between Ken and Jim. "Billy just asked Jim to be his business partner."

"Oh, yes, wonderful. He deserves it." More phoniness. "So I'll tell the nurses to hold off a little while on getting Jim up. Just don't tire him too much with all the good news, okay? The resident will be releasing you. Good to see everyone." He turned and started out the door. A dull gray cloud settled on Jim's chest. So this was the future. Maybe he'd just drift off again.

"Just a damned moment."

Jim's eyes flew open to see Constance standing with her hands on her hips, staring toward Ken. "Where the hell do you think you're going?"

Ken frowned. "To speak to the nurse."

"And after that?"

"Home. I've been up since yesterday morning."

"Before you go anywhere, we have to clear a few things up." She circled, looking at all the men in the room, then pointed at Ken. "I think you have the impression that Jim is devoted to me and can't live without me. Is that true?"

Ken shrugged. "Something like that." He stared at the floor, which was not fascinating, as Jim could testify.

Constance let out an exasperated huff. "It's a lie created by my father who, bless him, is a meddling fool who also happens to be damned insulting. Jim doesn't love me." She turned to Jim, a crease carved between her eyebrows. "Why did you do it? I thought we were friends."

Jim struggled to sit up before Ian pressed the button on the bed to raise it. "I hope we are. It's just that I never knew, uh, who I was, really, and I genuinely like you a lot."

"But you're gay, right?"

Ken's head snapped up and Ian yelled, "Yes!" Then he blushed. "Sorry. He's had a tough time admitting it."

Constance skewered him with her stare. "So you're admitting it now?"

Jim inhaled and nodded. "I didn't mean to deceive you. I was figuring out my own shit and was just about ready to come clean when my father—" He glanced at Ian. "—when my father got involved and—" What the fuck could he say?

Ian looked horrified. "How did Father get involved?" Some dawn broke all over his face. "Shit, is that how I got the full ride to Berkeley?"

Constance glanced back and forth between them. "What do you mean?"

"I was dying to go to Berkeley for architecture school. My father wasn't going to send me after he threw me out—and suddenly changed his mind. Now I know why. And the weird thing is, I decided not to go to Berkeley. I'm applying for a scholarship to Cal Poly. I don't want to take anything from my father. Hell, he's an asshole homophobe. And I want to stay close to Rico."

Holy shit. Jim shook his head. What had he done?

Constance crossed her arms. "I guess these chauvinist pigs were at least paying a high price for me. Why the fuck would your father care who you date?"

He sighed. "It has something to do with a contribution your father said he'd make to the Pacific Crest Club."

"Those conniving sons of bitches."

Ken took a step closer, frowning. "I heard a rumor that Jim's father got the club involved in a bad investment. He's probably trying to make up for it."

Constance spit out the words. "Using me as collateral."

"It seems so."

She narrowed her eyes at Jim. "And you went along with it."

He hung his head. "I'm really sorry. It was stupid and unfair, but I thought if I was going to spend my life with a woman, I wouldn't mind it being you."

Her mouth opened—and then she laughed. "That is the most bizarre and backhanded compliment I ever got, but I think I'll cherish it." She sat on the edge of the bed and took Jim's hand that wasn't connected to the IV. "So why don't you want to be partners with Billy?"

"I do, but I don't think I've done anything to deserve it."

"You brought Billy my business."

Jim glanced up, startled.

She shook her head. "You don't think I'd give a man my business just because I wanted to sleep with him, do you?"

Jim smiled. One inch of sugar over solid steel. "No, ma'am."

"I'm going to say this out of true experience. Stop letting your father define you."

Jim frowned. "I barely see my father."

"Right, but he calls you a loser and you try to act like one. No one I know is less a loser than you. But you've even let your father tell you who you can and can't love. You know who you love. You clearly defined that when you were semiconscious on the floor back at the party."

"I did?"

"Yes. You said, 'Call Ken. My heart.'"

Ken looked back and forth between them. "He meant he was having a heart attack."

"No." She stood. "He meant what he said." She spun on Ken and extended a finger. "And you, Dr. Tanaka. I have only one thing to say. You broke his heart. You fix it."

Constance put both hands on her hips. "I think it's pretty sad when two gay men owe their love life to a woman." She stood on Jim's other side. "I really like you. I wish you weren't gay. But since you are, for God's sake, do it right." She kissed his cheek. "And get well fast. We have a lot of work to do." On that life-changing exit line, she swept out of the room.

Billy started to laugh, and Ian joined in. "Man, Jim, for a gay man, you sure attract great women." He looked at Ian. "I think that's our cue to leave. I'll bring you some papers to sign by the end of the week."

Ken put a hand on Jim's arm. "Bring them to my condo, please. I'm taking Jim home with me for recovery."

Jim practically broke his neck, it turned so fast. "What?"

Billy held up a hand. "Yeah, bye, you two. I'll see you later in the week."

Jim half nodded but never stopped looking into Ken's dark eyes. When the door closed, he let himself frown. "Why would you want to take care of me? I can take care of myself."

Ken glowered back. "Yeah, I can tell that. That's why you're here, right? This attack was a lifestyle problem. If you'd done what I told you, you probably wouldn't have had to have the surgery—at least not on an emergency basis."

Jim's voice rose, but he couldn't help it. "I got news for you, doc. Don't tell me I'll die if I don't reduce my stress, because that just fucking stresses me out. And don't tell me to be calm when not having you makes me want to kill something." He gasped. *Did I just say that?*

Silence. Ken stared at Jim. "So how about we take care of each other?"

"How could the likes of me take care of the likes of you?" But still his heart beat fast.

Ken sat back and wrapped two hands around his knee, the dark eyes looking deep and distant. "You make me brave, Jim. You showed me that all the tradition and status in the world aren't worth shit without love. You showed me it's worth fighting for." He rubbed the knuckles of his right hand.

A tight lump clogged Jim's throat, but he got the words out. "I've spent ten years running from who I am."

"You spent ten years becoming who you are."

Jim leaned his head back. "So you want to take care of me, huh? Force me to eat green stuff and drink carrot juice."

Ken grinned. "Yep. And I have lots of other good things you can eat."

Jim snorted.

Ken's face sobered. "I think we should move Ian and that feline in too."

"That sounds permanent." And pretty damned great.

"Hey, let's see if we can't form a partnership between a perfect Japanese son and a model heterosexual electrician. It'll be one for the gay record books."

Jim ran a hand across Ken's smooth wrist. "My heart."

"You said that, huh?"

"I guess I must have."

"Maybe that's what I was really longing for when I went to med school. To become the heart of someone who I loved."

Jim's breath hushed out in a long, slow sigh. "And you love me?"

Ken grinned. "Well, I'd admit it except you've had way too much excitement for a man just out of surgery."

"Bet I could handle a kiss." Jim's eyelids drooped.

He felt soft lips against his own and Ken's silky voice whispered, "We're going to take care of your heart together. It's my job. And we're going to send your brother to architecture school. But you have to get well and strong fast—because, darling, you have to meet my mother."

CHAPTER TWENTY-FOUR

KEN SMILED and tried to look relaxed as he turned onto his parents' street. No use freaking out Jim any more than he already was. Whatever was going on outside that car window must be fascinating, because Jim sat glued to it. Only his fingers moved, folding and unfolding the fabric of his sport coat, a new addition to his wardrobe just for this occasion. Ken slid his hand over Jim's. "Relax. Nothing she can say or do will change our being together. We're an item." He laughed and squeezed.

He nodded but didn't turn. "I know."

Ken pulled in front of the house and Jim got out his side, straightening his collar. He'd worn a tie, for crap's sake. But man, he looked handsome. Jim had dragged Ken to Bloomingdale's after he'd recovered enough to be out, where he'd tried on every jacket that would fit his broad shoulders and narrow waist without too much tailoring. Ken just enjoyed the show.

On the porch, Ken knocked. He glanced at Jim to see if he thought that was strange, but Jim seemed too nervous to notice. His father answered.

"Good evening, Father. May I present my friend, Jim Carney."

His father extended his hand, and Jim shook it. "Pleased to meet you, sir."

Jim stepped inside and, as Ken had warned him, removed his shoes. Ken did the same. His father gave Ken a quick glance and then led the way into the living room.

Jesus, his knees were shaking. He'd called his mother and warned her that he was bringing someone who mattered to him, and he expected everyone to be on their best behavior. He'd been a little more subtle than that, but not much. She hadn't resisted much since Ken had threatened to throw Mickey Okuwa in jail and had only backed off when he and his friends were arrested after being accused by two other guys. She might have been chastened, but still, bringing a white, blue-collar guy home wasn't something he'd ever expected to do.

His mother sat in her queenly chair, straight backed and unsmiling. *Well, shit. Oh well, here goes.* "Mother, may I present my dear friend, Jim Carney."

Her eyes traveled up Jim's tall, hard-muscled, work-strengthened body. She nodded.

And then it happened. Jim bowed low at the waist. "Hajimemashite. Ome ni kakarete kouei desu. Douzo yoroshiku onegaishimasu." Ken's mouth opened, then closed. Jim had just told his mother that he was honored to meet her in unaccented Japanese.

Her eyes widened, then narrowed. "Nihongo ga dekimasu ka?" *Do you speak Japanese?*

He replied, "Only a little."

"Please be seated, Mr. Carney."

He sat across from her. "May I offer you something to drink?"

"Tea would be excellent."

She smiled and asked the serving person to bring tea. Ken released a little breath. If she hired a caterer for the evening, she was trying to impress.

"May I ask what you do for a living, Mr. Carney?"

Jim smiled. "I'm a partner in a construction company, ma'am."

Ken almost laughed. Getting Jim to admit he deserved the job had been child's play beside persuading him to use the title, and now it slid off his tongue like butter.

Ken's father nodded. "Excellent established position."

His mother smiled. "But of course, Mr. Carney is a grown man. How do you feel about children, Mr. Carney?"

Dear God, she'd never stop.

"I'm very fond of them, ma'am. In fact, my younger brother lives with me. I take care of him."

Ian would love to hear he'd become a minor again. Ken bit his cheek to hold it together.

"Isn't that excellent? A man who believes in family. And your father?"

"He's a cardiovascular surgeon, Mrs. Tanaka. One of the best in the world."

If her eyes had been bright before, now they lit up like a fireworks display. "Did you hear that?" She spun on Ken. "Kenji, why have you never brought Mr. Carney home to meet us before?"

Ken just smiled. Three impossibly amazing hours later, they walked into their condo to find Ian and Anderson sound asleep on the very nice sofa. They covered them both and went to bed. When they were tucked in, Ken turned to Jim. "You're amazing. Nobody could have done a more thorough job of charming my mother. She'll have you ejaculating into a tube and interviewing surrogates in a week."

Jim laughed. "I liked her. She's kind of like Constance. Sugar over steel. But in your mom's case, not too much sugar."

"Where in the hell did you learn Japanese?"

Jim grinned and crawled out of bed. Ken frowned. "Wait. I didn't mean to chase you away. We haven't had near enough time in a bed yet."

Jim's voice came from the other bedroom, where they'd stashed a lot of Jim's stuff in preparation for the two of them looking for a house. "Hang on." He walked back in stark naked with his cock half-erect and his green eyes peeking out over the top of a magazine. He scrambled back under the covers. That tough face had to be blushing.

Ken cocked his head. "What is it?"

"My yaoi hero."

Ken looked at the still-vivid drawings of the beautiful blond guy fucking the pretty Asian. "You think I look like him?"

"You're more beautiful."

"Thank you."

"But please notice, the books are all written in Japanese. Hiro used to read them to me and taught me some Japanese at the same time. I brushed up when I knew I'd be meeting your mom." He laughed. "I guess those novels did me a lot of good after all."

After acting out every scene in the novel from blow jobs to rimming, Ken whispered, "Before you fall asleep, I have a surprise for you."

"Ummm. Better than the ones I just had?"

"Not better, but different." Ken crawled out of bed and got his laptop. Jim barely stirred. Two orgasms would do that. "Open an eye for a minute."

Jim sat up and leaned against the headboard. "I'm all yours."

Ken kissed his cheek. "I'm glad. Look."

He clicked on the page he'd found in a Japanese news magazine. It showed a photo of a lovely, graceful young man standing beside a tall Caucasian who had an arm around him protectively. It seemed the young Asian man had just received an award in science, and he was celebrating with his husband, whom he had married in the United States. His name was Hiro Takahashi.

Jim touched the screen. "Hiro."

"Yes. I searched until I found him."

"Look how he's smiling."

"Yes."

Jim wiped his eyes on the edge of the sheet. "How can I thank you for doing this? It's the most amazing gift."

"I wanted you to have your Hiro."

Jim turned and touched Ken's cheek. "You're my hero. He was my first real friend. He taught me a lot, from the good and from the bad stuff we shared together. I guess he knocked at a door in me that it took ten years and you to open." He stared at the pretty, smiling face on the computer screen, then up into the grin of the man he loved. His yaoi man. "Isn't it amazing that we could both end up so happy?"

Coming Soon

Prince of the Playhouse

A Love in Laguna Novel

By Tara Lain

Success for fashion designer Rupert "Ru" Maitland is in grasp. Since he got beat up as a kid for designing Barbie clothes, Ru's known that living well is the best revenge, and he means to succeed at it. When the Laguna Theater hires him to do costumes for a special performance by movie star Gray Aston, Ru understands that Hollywood will be calling, but one look at the gorgeous film icon and Ru's priorities start to change. Ru wants Gray and Gray wants Ru, but the actor can't find the back of his closet, it's so deep. He's sacrificed a lot for his stardom, and no matter how PC the film industry might be, only comedians can be gay and keep their audience. Gray takes Ru to Hollywood and old visions of fashion glory start to manifest—while Ru watches the man he loves get engaged to a woman and start planning a wedding. Two lives. Two dreams. But only one can come true if they're going to be together. Who's going to be Prince of the Playhouse?

Coming Soon to
http://www.dreamspinnerpress.com

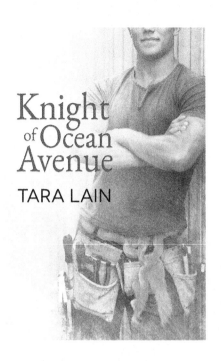

Knight
of Ocean
Avenue

TARA LAIN

How can you be twenty-five and not know you're gay? Billy Ballew runs from that question. A high school dropout, barely able to read until he taught himself, Billy's life is driven by his need to help support his parents as a construction worker, put his sisters through college, coach his Little League team, and not think about being a three-time loser in the engagement department. Being terrified of taking tests keeps Billy from getting the contractor's license he so desires, and fear of his mother's judgment blinds Billy to what could make him truly happy.

Then, in preparation for his sister's big wedding, Billy meets Shaz— Chase Phillips—a rising-star celebrity stylist who defines the word gay. To Shaz, Billy embodies everything he's ever wanted—stalwart, honest, brave—but even if Billy turns out to be gay, he could never endure the censure he'd get for being with a queen like Shaz. How can two men with so little in common find a way to be together? Can the Stylist of the Year end up with the Knight of Ocean Avenue?

http://www.dreamspinnerpress.com

TARA LAIN writes the Beautiful Boys of Romance in LGBT romance novels that star her unique, charismatic heroes. Her bestselling novels have garnered awards for Best Series, Best Contemporary Romance, Best Erotic Romance, Best Ménage, Best LGBT Romance, and Best Gay Characters, and Tara has been named Best Writer of the Year in the LRC Awards. Readers often call her books "sweet," even with all that hawt sex, because Tara believes in love and her books deliver on happy-ever-after. In her other job, Tara owns an advertising and public relations firm. Her love of creating book titles comes from years of manifesting ad headlines for everything from analytical instruments to semiconductors. She does workshops on both author promotion and writing craft. She lives with her soulmate husband and her soulmate dog (who's a little jealous of all those cat pictures Tara posts on FB) in Laguna Niguel, California, near the seaside towns where she sets a lot of her books. Passionate about diversity, justice, and new experiences, Tara says that on her tombstone it will say "Yes!"

E-mail: tara@taralain.com
Website: http://www.taralain.com
Blog: http://www.taralain.com/blog
Goodreads:
http://www.goodreads.com/author/show/4541791.Tara_Lain
Pinterest: http://pinterest.com/taralain/
Twitter: http://twitter.com/taralain
Facebook: https://www.facebook.com/taralain
Barnes & Noble: http://www.barnesandnoble.com/s/Tara-Lain?keyword=Tara+Lain&store=book
ARe:
http://www.allromanceebooks.com/storeSearch.html?searchBy=author&qString=Tara+Lain

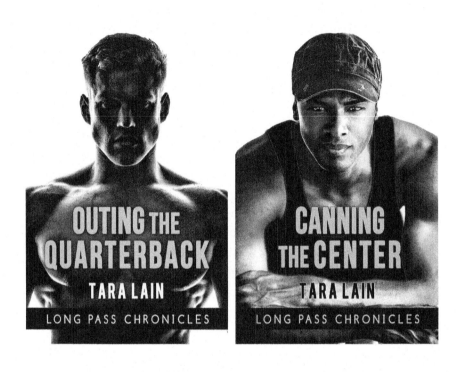

Visit Tara's page at
http://www.dreamspinnerpress.com
for blurbs and more info!

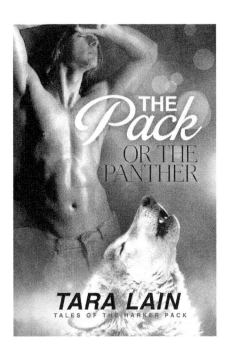

Cole Harker, son of an alpha werewolf, is bigger and more powerful than most wolves, tongue-tied in groups, and gay. For twenty-four years, he's lived to please his family and pack—even letting them promise him in marriage to female werewolf Analiese to secure a pack alliance and help save them from a powerful gangster who wants their land. Then Cole meets Analiese's half-brother, panther shifter Paris Marketo, and for the first time, Cole wants something for himself.

When Analiese runs off to marry a human, Cole finally has a chance with Paris, but the solitary cat rejects him, the pack, and everything it represents. Then Cole discovers the gangster wants Paris too and won't rest until he has him. What started as a land dispute turns into World War Wolf! But the bigger fight is the battle between cats and dogs.

http://www.dreamspinnerpress.com

Socialite Lindsey Vanessen wants someone to love who will love him back—an impossibility for a gay, half-human, half-werewolf. Too aggressive for humans, too gay for wolves, and needing to protect the pack from human discovery, Lindsey tries to content himself with life as a successful businessman. But when someone starts kidnapping members of wealthy families, Lindsey meets tough cop Seth Zakowsy—the hunky embodiment of everything Lindsey wants but can't have.

Seth has never been attracted to flamboyant men. What would the guys in the department think of Lindsey? But intrigue turns to lust when he discovers Lindsey's biting, snarling passion more than matches his dominant side. It might mean a chance at love for a cop in black leather and a wolf in Gucci loafers.

http://www.dreamspinnerpress.com

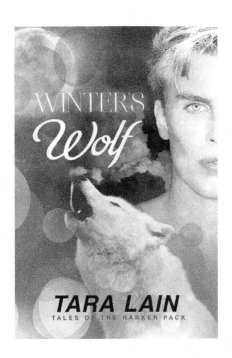

Winter Thane was raised on the two cardinal rules of werewolf existence: don't reveal yourself to humans under penalty of death, and there's no such thing as a gay werewolf. It's no surprise when his father drags him from his wild life in remote Canada back to Connecticut to meet his old pack in hopes it will persuade Winter to abandon his love of sex with human males. Of course Dad's hopes are dashed when they come face-to-face with the gay werewolves in the Harker pack.

Winter takes one look at FBI agent Matt Partridge and decides bird is his favorite food. Partridge is embroiled in an investigation into drug dealing and the death of a fellow agent. He can't let himself get distracted by the young, platinum-haired beast, but then Winter proves invaluable in the search for clues, a move that winds them both up in chains and facing imminent death. Winter quickly learns his father's motives are questionable, the pack alphas are a bunch of pussies, humans aren't quite what they seem, and nothing in the forests of Connecticut is pure except love.

http://www.dreamspinnerpress.com

FOR MORE OF THE BEST GAY ROMANCE

DREAMSPINNER PRESS
dreamspinnerpress.com

CPSIA information can be obtained at www.ICGtesting.com
Printed in the USA
BVOW06s2156030815

411677BV00005B/26/P